a...
Macmil...

"YOU'VE STOLEN MY DOG!" SAID THE FIRST MAN. "I SHALL TELL THE POLICE!"

"STOLEN THE THING!" EXCLAIMED THE OTHER. "I DON'T BELIEVE YOU EVER HAD A DOG!"

(See page 49)

William

RICHMAL CROMPTON

Illustrated by Thomas Henry

MACMILLAN CHILDREN'S BOOKS

ISBNs: paperback 0 333 37394 4
hardback 0 333 37388 X

First published in this edition 1984 by
MACMILLAN CHILDREN'S BOOKS
A division of Macmillan Publishers Limited
London and Basingstoke
Associated companies throughout the world

Reprinted 1987

Phototypeset by Wyvern Typesetting Ltd, Bristol
Printed in Hong Kong

Contents

An invitation from William

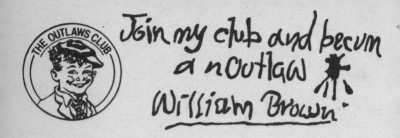

Join my club and becum a nOutlaw
William Brown

You can join the Outlaws Club!
You will receive
✻ a special Outlaws wallet containing
your own Outlaws badge
the Club Rules
and
a letter from William giving you the secret password

To join the Club send a letter with your name and address written in block capitals telling us you want to join the Outlaws, and a postal order for 45p, to

The Outlaws Club
577 Kingston Road
Raynes Park
LONDON SW20 8SA

You must live in the United Kingdom or the Republic of Ireland in order to join.

Chapter 1

The Mystery of Oaklands

It was due partly to a spell of wet weather and partly to a sudden passion for detective novels on the part of Hector and Robert, who were Ginger's and William's elder brothers respectively. If Hector and Robert hadn't been seized with a sudden passion for detective novels, the houses of the Merridews and the Browns wouldn't have been filled with them from top to bottom, and if there hadn't been a spell of wet weather William and Ginger wouldn't have read them. On the first fine day after the wet spell, William and the three other Outlaws met and walked slowly down the road together.

"I bet ole Potty would be glad if he knew what a lot of readin' I've been doin'," said William virtuously. "He said in my report I oughter read more. Well, I've jolly well been readin' all these wet days. He jolly well oughter be pleased if he knew."

"What've you been readin'?" said Ginger.

" 'The Mystery of the Blue Square'——" began William importantly.

"I read that, too," interrupted Ginger, "so you needn't be so swanky. An' what's more I read it before you 'cause it was Hector's an' Hector lent it Robert an' I read it before he lent it Robert."

"Oh, well," said William, "that's a good deal better for me than you, then, 'cause with you readin' it first you've probably forgot it an' with me readin' it after you I prob'ly remember it much better than what you do."

"I jolly well bet you don't. Who killed him?"

"The man livin' nex' door."

"What with?"

"A poisoned pen-nib."

"Well, I bet I remember lots you don't. What else did you read?"

" 'The Myst'ry of the Green Light.' "

"So'd I."

"Well, I read that one first 'cause Robert bought it an' lent it to Hector an' I read it before he lent it Hector."

"Well, then, I mus' remember it better than you accordin' to you with readin' it after you."

"Oh, shut up. . . . All right, we both remember them the same. What else did you read?"

" 'The Mystery of the Lonely House.' "

"So'd I. An' 'The Myst'ry of the Haunted Wood.' "

"So'd I. An' 'The Myst'ry of the Seventh Staircase.' "

"So'd I."

"Readin' all those books makes me wonder whether anyone ever dies natural."

"They don't," said William mysteriously. "Robert says so. At least he says there's hundreds an' thousands of murders what no one finds out. You see, you c'n only find out a person's died nacheral by cuttin' 'em up an' they've not got time to cut everyone up what dies. They've simply not got the time. They do it like what they do with our desks at school. They jus' open one sometimes to see if it's all right. They've not got time to open 'em all every day. An' same as every time they do open a desk they find it untidy, jus' in the same way whenever they do cut anyone dead up they find he's been poisoned. Practically always. Robert says so. He says that the amount of people who poison people who aren't cut up and don't get found out mus' be enormous. Jus' think of it. People pois'nin' people all over the place an' no one findin' out. If I was a policeman I'd cut everyone dead up. But they aren't any use, policemen aren't. Why, in all those books I've read there hasn't been a single policeman that was any good at all. They simply don't know what to do when anyone murders anyone. Why, you remember in 'The Mystery of the Yellow Windows,' the policemen were s'posed to have searched the room for clues an' they di'n't notice the cigarette end what the murd'rer had left in the fender and what had the address of the people what made it on it an' what was a sort they made special for him. Well, that shows you what the policemen *are*, dun't it? I mean, they look very swanky in their hats an' buttons an' all that, but when it comes to a murder or cuttin' dead people up or findin' out murd'rers, they aren't any good at all. Why, in all those myst'ry tales we've read, it's not been the police that found the murd'rers at all. It's been ordinary people same as you an' me jus' usin' common sense an' pickin' up cigarette ends an' such-like. . . . Tell you what it is," he said, warming to his theme, "policemen have gotter be stupid 'cause of their clothes. I mean, all the policemen's clothes are made so big that they've gotter be very big men to fit 'em an' big men are always stupid 'cause of their strength all goin' to their bodies 'stead of their brains. That stands to reason, dun't it?"

"Course it does," agreed Ginger, and added slowly, "seems sort of funny they don't see it."

"They don't see it 'cause they're stupid," said William, "an' they're stupid 'cause they're so big and they

hafter be big 'cause of the uniforms. So there you *are*,"
ended William on a note of finality.

Henry and Douglas, who had listened to this conversation with deep interest, agreed that William's logic
was unanswerable.

They were just passing two small houses called Oaklands and Beechgrove, that stood together on the
outskirts of the village. A man was working in the garden
of each—an old man in the garden of Oaklands, and a
young man in the garden of Beechgrove. The old man
had only lately come to the village. The Outlaws did not
know his name but had christened him Scraggy. The
Outlaws never troubled to learn the family names of
newcomers to the village. Like the savages they resembled in so many other ways, they preferred to call them
by a name descriptive of their appearance or character.
The owner of Oaklands had earned his name by a neck
that was longer than perfect proportions warranted and
of a corrugated character. He had a grey beard and wore
dark spectacles. They stood at the gate and watched him
at work. The Outlaws never made the pretence affected
by the super-civilised, of indifference to their
neighbours' affairs. On the other hand, the Outlaws
took an absorbing interest in their neighbours' affairs
and had no compunction about showing it. It would have
been evident to anyone more sensitive than were the
Outlaws that the owner of Oaklands objected to them as
interested spectators of his horticultural labours. He
frequently raised his head and scowled at them. It took,
however, as he soon discovered, more than a scowl to
dislodge the Outlaws from any position they had taken
up. So, finally, he raised himself from his stooping
position, glared at them and said:

"What do you want?"

"Nothin'," said William pleasantly.

"What are you standin' there for?"

"Watchin' you," said William, still pleasantly.

"Well, go away."

"A' right," said William still pleasantly but without moving.

"Go *away*," said the old gentleman irritably. "Did you hear me? Go *away!*"

Reluctantly and slowly the Outlaws moved off to the gate of Beechgrove and hung over that. The owner of Beechgrove objected to their hanging over his gate (one hinge was already broken) as much as did his neighbour, but he wasted less time in roundabout methods. He filled his syringe with water from a bucket that stood near him and levelled it at them with a curt "Clear off!" Hastily the Outlaws cleared off.

"Might have killed us," said William indignantly. "You could drown anyone like that. Stands to reason. Givin' 'em a great mouthful of water so's they can't get their breath. Then when you can't get your breath you die. Stands to reason. No one can go on livin' without breathin'. Then he'd 've got hung for murder an' jolly well serve him right."

"I bet he wouldn't've got hung for murder," said Ginger gloomily, "what with the police bein' so stupid they'd prob'ly think we died natural unless some ord-'n'ry man came along same as they did in all those books an' got hold of a clue. Found our mouths full of water an' his syringe buried in the garden or somethin' like that."

"D'you remember in 'The Myst'ry of the Lighted Room,' " said William excitedly, "when the man found that the top of the murd'rer's umbrella unscrewed into a dagger an' that was what he murdered folks with. I think that was jolly clever. I'd never have thought of that. I wouldn't before I read that book, I mean. I would now, of course. I'd always look to see if a person's umbrella unscrewed into a dagger first thing now if I thought they'd murdered someone. Then I'd look to see if they'd got poison at the end of their tie-pin same as the man in 'The Myst'ry of the Empty House.' I think that was a jolly clever thing to think of. If I wanted to kill anyone now I know lots of clever ways of doin' it after reading all those books. I bet I could do it so's the police wouldn't find out too, now, after reading all those books. And I bet if I found anyone murdered I'd pretty soon find out who did it. It's always the one you wouldn't 've thought did it and of course the police don't know that. It seems sort of silly to me not to make the police read all these myst'ry books. They'd soon find out murd'rers then. D'you remember in 'The Black Mask' how he'd got a flower with a pois'nous scent and he jus' asked people to smell it and they died straight off lookin' as if they'd died natural so that no one thought of cuttin' 'em up to see if there was any poison inside of 'em. Till that man came along what found out all about it. I think that was jolly clever."

"Let's be detectives when we grow up," suggested Douglas.

"No," said William. "It's more fun bein' the man that comes along an' finds out all about it when the detectives have stopped tryin'. I'm goin' to be one of that sort. I'm goin' to go on readin' myst'ry tales all the time from now till I'm grown up an' then I bet there won't be any way of killin' folks that I won't know all about so I'll be able to catch all the murd'rers there are an' I bet I'll be famous an' they'll put up a stachoo to me when I'm dead."

"I bet they won't," said Ginger, irritated by William's egotism. "You'll prob'ly get murdered yourself before you've found out anythin' at all an' then Douglas an' Henry an' me'll find out who did it an' get famous."

"Oh, *will* I?" said William stung by this prophecy. "Well, I jolly well *won't* be an' if I am you can kin'ly leave me alone an' not come fussin' tryin' to find out who did it. If I'm murdered so's I can't find out who did it I jolly well don't want anyone else to. An' anyway I won't *let* anyone murder *me*. I'd always carry round a bottle of the stuff you drink that stops poisons pois'nin' you called Anecdote or somethin' like that an' whenever anyone tried to poison me I'd drink a bit. And I'd always carry a pistol in my pocket so if anyone ever tried to shoot me I'd shoot him first."

"You're *jolly* clever, aren't you?" said Ginger sarcastically.

"Yes," said William simply, "I am. I mayn't be clever at Latin an' G'om'try an' things like that—though I bet I'm not as bad as what they try to make out on my reports—but I *am* clever at findin' out murd'rers."

"All right. Kindly tell us one murd'rer you've ever found out," challenged Ginger.

"Kin'ly tell me," retorted William heatedly, "when I've ever had a chance to find out a murderer. If I came across anyone murdered I'd find out who did it pretty quick. I've read so many myst'ry books that I know all the ways there are of killin' folks and I know just what the sort that do it are like."

"Oh, *shut* up!" said Ginger.

They had reached the old barn where they always held their meetings and games.

"Let's play at something," said Douglas.

"Let's play a sort of myst'ry game," said William. "Let Henry be murdered an' Ginger the one that really did it an' Douglas the one everyone thinks did it an' I'll be the man that comes along and finds that it was Ginger that did it and not Douglas."

But the Outlaws refused thus to offer themselves as

food to William's self-glorification. They each agreed, however, to play the game on condition that William should be the murdered man and he the one who disclosed the murderer, so finally the idea was given up and they played Red Indians till bed-time.

*   *   *

There followed a long spell of fine weather. Robert's and Hector's passion for adventure tales died. The books were given away and no further ones bought. The Outlaws' interest in it, too, would have waned had it not been for the owner of Beechgrove. Every day they passed the two houses. Every day they hung over the gate of Oaklands watching the tenant of Oaklands at his labours till he ordered them off. Then they passed on to Beechgrove. It is probable that the owner of Beechgrove had had wide experience of boys of their age and disposition. The minute they appeared at his gate he made savagely threatening gestures with either syringe or spade and they fled incontinently down the road. These episodes kept alive William's interest in criminology.

"I bet you anything," he said, "that that bucket he puts his squirt into is full of poison. Bet you anything he killed hundreds of folks that way. Squirting them with poison out of a bucket like that. He looks *jus'* the sort that would squirt poison at people. I bet he's got poison on his spade, too. D'you remember the man in 'The Mystery of the Odd Glove' what had poison in his garden forks? To me he looks just that sort of man. If we hadn't run away quick we'd 've been dead now. An' the police would've come along and found us dead an' took for granted we'd died natural 'cause of being so stupid. Jolly good thing we c'n *run*. Bet you we shouldn't be alive now if we couldn't."

"But why should he want to kill us, William?" said Henry the practical.

"Why not?" said William. "A murderer's gotter be murderin' someone or else he isn't a murderer, is he? You get sort of fond of it same as you do of anythin' else. Football or cricket or draughts or collectin' stamps. When you've murdered one person you want to go on an' murder another. You keep thinkin' out better ways of murd'rin' people an' then nacherally you want to try 'em on someone. I bet he'd jus' thought out that way of squirtin' poison at someone an' wanted to try it on us jus' to see if it acted all right. Of course he *may've* got a real reason. He *may've* found out that one of us is goin' to come into a lot of money what we don't know anythin' about yet an' he may be the next heir though none of us know him 'cause of everyone thinkin' his father was drowned in a shipwreck. It was like that in 'The Mystery of the Greenhouse.' It might be like that with him. He's tryin' to kill us so as to get the money himself."

"Yes," said Henry, "but none of us have any relations that we think was drowned in a shipwreck."

"Oh, do shut up arguing about everything I say," said William wearily. "You've got no sense at all. D'you think our parents would bother to tell us about every single relation they ever had and what happened to 'em?"

"I'll ask mine to-night," said Henry, "whether they've got any relation they think was drowned in a shipwreck."

"They'll prob'ly say they haven't 'cause they'll have forgotten him but I bet you anythin' one of 'em has. Why's he tryin' to kill us if they haven't?"

The question seemed so unanswerable that the Outlaws did not attempt to answer it.

But for a time there was so little to feed their suspicion

that it might have died away altogether had they not happened to go past the two cottages one day a week or so later and found the garden of Oaklands empty, the blinds of the house drawn and a general air of desolation over the whole. They hung over the gate for some time, but it is of course no fun hanging over the gate of a garden when there is no one in the garden to send you away. So after a time they walked on down the road.

They had long since ceased to dally over the gate of Beechgrove.

"Wonder where he's gone," said Ginger meditatively.

"He's killed him, of course," said William. "Squirted him with poison or jabbed at him with a poisoned spade same as he'd 've done at us if we hadn't run off so quick. Poor old Scraggy." William heaved a compassionate sigh for the victim. "He couldn't run off quick so he got him."

"But why should he want to kill Scraggy?" said Henry. "I thought it was us he wanted to kill 'cause of the money that was comin' to us from the relation what people thought was drowned in a shipwreck."

"You talk," said William irritably, " 's if there was only one reason for anyone wantin' to kill anyone. 'F you'd read all those books what Ginger 'n' me've read you'd know that there's dozens an' *dozens* of reasons for people killin' people. I bet this ole man Scraggy had a hoard of money hid in his house. He was a miser, an' the other man found out he was a miser with hearin' him countin' his money through the wall. The noise of it kept him awake at night prob'ly so's he couldn't sleep, an' he made a hole in the wall so's he could watch him to see what he was doin' an' he saw him countin' out sovereigns. An' then he made his plot. He's been practisin' with poisons all this while prob'ly pretendin' to be gard'nin'. He tried to practise on us an' I bet if he'd 've been able to hit us we'd be dead 'n' buried by now."

"What d'you think he's done with the body?" said Ginger hoarsely.

"Oh, there's lots of ways of gettin' rid of bodies," said William carelessly. "That never worries anyone—gettin' rid of bodies. Buryin's the easiest . . . Yes, I think most of 'em bury 'em. Yes, I think that's what they do. Bury 'em. . . . *Course!*" with a sudden burst of inspiration, "that's what he's been doin'—pretending to be int'rested in gard'nin' all this while jus' so's to be able to bury him without people suspectin' anythin'. You see, if he sudd'nly dug a hole to bury him people would suspect somethin' an' they'd dig up the bit he'd dug to see what he'd buried there, but if he'd been diggin' up his garden for weeks an' weeks no one could find where he'd dug the hole to bury him 'cause it would all look fresh dug up an' so no one would suspect anythin'. I bet he's one of the very clever ones. Well, I mean, that's clever, isn't it? I bet we wouldn't 've thought of that—I bet that if we'd murdered anyone we'd never think of doin' that—diggin' over our gardens for weeks beforehand to make it all look fresh dug over. No, I bet if we murdered anyone we'd simply dig a hole an' bury 'em an' then someone clever 'd come along an' find someone disappeared an' a bit of our garden dug up jus' about the size of a man an' he'd dig it up again an' find 'em an' then we'd get hung. No, he's one of the *very* clever ones. I bet he's one of the sort that have poison in a ring an' jus' when they're goin' to be caught they raise it to their lips an' fall lifeless to the ground. Sooner than be hung, you know. I'd sooner do that than be hung myself. I bet that's the sort I'd be if I was one."

"Wonder what he'd say," said Douglas thoughtfully, "if you asked him where ole Scraggy was."

"Let's go'n' ask him an' see," said William, promptly turning on his heel.

William had been walking away from the scene of the crime more and more reluctantly. After all, when an opportunity offered itself of entering his chosen career it seemed foolish to neglect it.

"That's how I'll start," said William, assuming his stern frown of leadership. "I'll ask him quite innocent where Scraggy is an' I'll watch how he looks an' what he says. That's what they often do. Only the very cleverest ones can help lookin' guilty. D'you remember in 'The Myst'ry of the Sundial' the man couldn't help keep lookin' at his rose bed where he'd buried him? Couldn't help lookin' at it. Kept on lookin' at it. Sort of scared of it. An' they noticed that an' that was what made 'em suspicious."

"William," said Douglas, "I don't think you ought to go back an' ask him that, you know. It seems sort of dangerous to me. S'pose he got savage an' squirted poison at us. It seems sort of silly to me to go back talkin' to him now we *know* he's a murderer."

"No, I think it'll be all right," said William earnestly. "I *think* it'll be all right. I don't think they often do two murders so near together. They'd be frightened to. You can kill one person without anyone suspectin'—except someone very clever—but if you start killin' everyone what comes along nacherally people get sort of suspicious. I mean when nearly everyone someone meets dies they nacherally get suspicious an' start cuttin' 'em up to see if they really died nacheral. That's how most murderers get found out. They get sort of reckless. They say, 'Well, that one went off all right. Let's try another.' But I don't think this one's one of the reckless ones. I think he's too careful to be one of the reckless ones."

They had reached the gate of Beechgrove. William

approached it cautiously. Douglas still more cautiously
hung behind. William was relieved to see that the man
had neither syringe nor spade ready to hand. He was
engaged in the innocent occupation of tying up roses
with raffia. Emboldened by this, William leaned precariously over the gate.

"Come back, William," whispered Douglas. "He
might have a pistol."

The man looked up. Having no implement to hand,
and being at a critical point in his operation, he merely
growled at them ferociously.

" 'Scuse me," said William with elaborate politeness.
" 'Scuse me interruptin' you, but would you kin'ly tell
me where ole Sc——where the gentleman who lives next
door is?"

"Mr Barton?" snapped the man. "He's gone away
for a holiday, and be off with you or I'll——"

William hurled valour to the winds and fled discreetly.

At the end of the road he collected his panting
followers.

"Thought I'd better pretend to be scared of him," he
explained casually, "to put him off the scent. It's always
best to pretend to be scared of 'em to put 'em off the
scent."

"D'you think p'raps he has gone away for a holiday
really, William, after all?" said Henry tentatively.

"Course not!" said William with deep scorn, "course
not. That's what he'd say nacherally. He's lucky, of
course, that no one lives with old Scraggy an' so no one
can have suspicion. That's what they always say. They
always say they've gone away for a holiday. Then they
stay on for a bit so as not to be suspicious, then go
abroad, so's not to get caught."

"He di'n't *look* any richer, William," said Henry,
doubtfully, "he hadn't bought a new suit or got new

curtains or had his gate mended or anything."

"No," admitted William, "but sometimes they kill the man an' then can't find the money. D'you remember, Ginger, in 'The Myst'ry of the One-Eyed Man,' how he did that? He *knew* he was a miser an' had a lot of money hid away in his house, so he killed him shootin' through the little hole he'd made to watch him countin' his money, an' then he cun't find the money. Looked for it everywhere but cun't find it. So he had to hang about lookin' for it, an' that was how they got hold of him 'cause of him hangin' about lookin' for the money 'stead of goin' off abroad where they couldn't catch him. I bet that that's what he's doin'. I bet that he's killed ole Scraggy for his money an' now can't find it same as the man in 'The Myst'ry of the One-Eyed Man.' He's buried ole Scraggy in his garden an' now he's hangin' about tryin' to find his money." He stopped dead in the middle of the road. "I say, let's go back again an' see what he's doin' now."

The Outlaws, ever ready for a little more excitement, agreed. Very, very cautiously they crept back down the road till they reached the two cottages again. They happened to arrive there at the moment when the tenant of Beechgrove was issuing from his neighbour's doorway, having watered his plants and fed his cat as he had promised to do in his neighbour's absence.

Unaware of the eight eyes watching him through the hedge he paused for a minute in his own garden and thoughtfully contemplated his rose bed. His roses weren't doing at all well. It was very disappointing. He must get some sort of insecticide to-morrow. He went slowly indoors. The Outlaws emerged from the ditch.

"*There!*" gasped William. "*There!*" Well, if that isn't proof. Abs'lute proof. Di'n't you see him? All of you? Comin' out of his house where he'd been lookin' for the money. Frownin' cause he cun't find it. An' simply cun't keep his eyes off his rose bed. D'you notice that. Simply *cun't*. Jus' like the man in 'The Myst'ry of the Sundial.' That's where he's buried him. An' he can't find the money. Well, that's *proof*, i'n't it?"

"I think we oughter go to the police," said Douglas, "now that we *know*."

"No, I'm goin' to do it same as they do in books," said William firmly. "They never go to the police in books. They find out all about it first an' then they jus' send for the police to take 'em to prison."

"Well, we've found out all about it," said Ginger.

"We've not found out *enough*," said William earnestly. "Not enough to send him to prison. If we hand him to the police now he'd just get out of it somehow. We've gotter get so much proof that he *can't* get out of it before we send for the police."

"How we goin' to get any more than what we've got?" said Ginger. "Dig up his rose bed for the dead body or somethin' like that?"

"N—no," said William slowly. "I don' think we'd better do that. We've gotter be cautious. I mean I haven't got a pistol yet nor a bottle of that anecdote stuff an' I haven't any money to buy any till nex' Saturday an' I bet I shan't have then what with all the money they take off me for breakin' things. I don' quite know how much pistols an' bottles of anecdote costs but I bet they cost more than they'll give me when they find the mincing machine's broke though I bet you anything it would have broke anyway an' they were quite tiny bits of wood I put through an' it must 've been a rotten mincing machine to get broke with them . . . what was I talking about?" he ended abruptly.

"You were sayin' you wun't go diggin' up the body," said Ginger.

"Oh yes," said William. "Well, I wun't. We cun't do it without makin' a noise an' he'd jus' come out an' kill us an' bury us in his garden in the night an' no one would ever know what had happened to us. They'd prob'ly think we'd run away to sea an' not bother any more about us. It would be silly to let him murder us like that before we'd got him hung."

"What shall we do, then?" said Ginger anxiously; "he might find the money any time an' go off abroad before we've got him."

"We'll have to think out a plan," said William, thrusting his hands into his pockets with a scowl indicative of deep thought. "D'you remember in 'The Myst'ry of the One-Eyed Man' he dressed up like the man the man had murdered an' went to the man an' got someone to hide with pieces of paper an' pencils an' write down all the man who'd murdered the man said an' he was so scared thinkin' he saw the man he'd murdered that he carried on somethin' terrible tellin' all about the murder an' the men that were hid with pieces of paper an' pencils wrote down all he said an' that counts in lor. I mean, if you can get a murd'rer to tell about his murder an' get men hid with pieces of paper an' pencils to write down what he says, it counts. He gets hung."

"Yes, but who could dress up as ole Scraggy?" said Douglas dubiously.

"I could," said William. "I bet you anythin' I could. I've got a white beard an' a bald head wig at home. Or, rather, Robert's got 'em, but I could borrow them off him without him knowin'. An' you could be hid with pieces of paper an' pencils to take it down."

They looked doubtfully at William. Even with a white beard and a bald head wig it seemed difficult to imagine anyone more unlike Old Scraggy in appearance than

William. Still—they were accustomed to follow William blindly.

"All right," said Ginger, "we'd better go home an' look for pencils and paper. I never know what happens to all the pencils in our house. I'm always bringin' them home from school and then someone always bags them."

"We'd better start that part of it to-morrow," said William. "It's nearly tea-time and——"

"Quick," said Douglas, "he's seen us an' he's gettin' his squirt."

Like lightning the amateur detectives streaked down the road.

*   *   *

The next afternoon they met together in the old barn to discuss their plans. William had brought his white beard and bald-headed wig, together with an old pair of trousers of Robert's, which he had cut down to make long trousers for himself, an overcoat and muffler and a pair of dark spectacles. The trousers were still so long that he had to fasten them round his neck with string.

The Outlaws inspected him carefully.

"I think you look *jus'* like him, William," said Ginger loyally.

"Well," said Douglas, a little less enthusiastically, "you look as if you might be tryin' to look like him, but—but you've gotter *young* sort of face for one thing an' your own hair shows under the wig, an' your trousers look sort of funny where you've cut 'em off."

"They're jolly good trousers," said William indignantly, as he pushed his hair out of sight under the wig. "Robert paid a lot for 'em when he had 'em new. An', anyway, I've got a bowler hat same as men wear an' they can't see my neck isn't scraggy 'cause of my muffler. I think it was jolly clever of me to think of that."

"I think you look quite all right," said Henry. " 'Specially if you go out to him when it's getting dark when he can't see you prop'ly."

"Well, anyway," said Ginger impatiently, "let's start doin' somethin'. We shall look silly if he finds the money an' gets off abroad while we're standin' talkin' here."

Guarding William carefully on either side, the little company set off across the fields. Certainly William looked a curious enough figure to attract attention anywhere, though he himself was evidently unaware of this and imagined his resemblance to the tenant of Oaklands to be complete.

"You needn't try to hide me from people on the road," he said testily; "if they see me they'll only think it's ole Scraggy back from his holiday. Come to that, I think it would be a good thing to go into the village an' talk to a few of them pretendin' to be ole Scraggy so as to get a bit of practice in bein' him."

They managed, however, to dissuade him from this. They had had experience of William on occasions when his enthusiasm ran away with him.

"You don't want *him* to get word of it," said Ginger; "he'd know someone was after him then an' jus' slip off abroad before anyone could stop him. That's what they do when they know the man's nearly got 'em. D'you remember in that one—I've forgotten its name—with a green face on the back—he did that. He knew they were after him an' so he slipped off down to the ship to go abroad an' they only jus' managed to stop him in the nick of time jus' as he was goin' on to the ship that was goin' abroad by pretendin' to send him a message from a confederation——"

"A what?" said Henry.

"A confederation," said Ginger impatiently. "A

"YOU NEEDN'T TRY TO HIDE ME FROM PEOPLE ON THE ROAD,"
WILLIAM SAID TESTILY. "IF THEY SEE ME, THEY'LL ONLY THINK
IT'S OLE SCRAGGY."

confederation means another crim'nal. Well, they sent him a message from a confederation to say that he'd found the money an' put 'em off the track. An' he believed it an' came back an' they were all detectives in disguise an' they got him."

"Yes, I remember," said William, "that was a fine one. Wasn't that the one where they saw a green skeleton walkin' down the attic stairs?"

"No," said Ginger, "it wasn't that one at all. That was the one with the picture of a big splash of blood on the back."

"I remember that one," said William. "That was a jolly clever picture. If ever I write a book I'm goin' to have a picture of a big splash of blood on the back like that. It'd make anyone want to read it. Anyone 'd buy a book that had a picture of a big splash of blood on the back 'cause they'd know it would be a nice excitin' one. I can't think why more books don't have excitin' backs like that. It's 'str'ordin'ry to me to see books like what one sees with girls' faces an' such-like on the backs. Who'd want to read a book with a girl's face on the back? Anyone sens'ble would sooner read about a murder than a girl any day."

They had reached the point where a lane ran by the side of Farmer Jenks' field. The Outlaws, as habitual trespassers on his property, were cordially detested by Farmer Jenks.

"We'd better go by the lane," said William regretfully, for his proud spirit hated to surrender to a foe. "I'm not quite sure how I c'n run in these trousers of Robert's. They may be all right for runnin' in or they mayn't. They feel sort of big an' as if they'd come off rather easy so we'd better go by the lane 'cause we'd better be a bit careful till we've caught him. D'you remember last time Farmer Jenks ran after us he said he was goin' to tell the police about us, so p'raps we'd better be careful for a bit."

They went slowly down the lane to where the two cottages, Oaklands and Beechgrove, stood together by the road side. The other Outlaws cast sidelong glances at William. Their doubts as to his appearance were growing stronger. His trousers were cut unevenly, his beard was obviously meant to adorn a larger face than William's and his wig was askew. Moreover, what of his face could be seen was, if not beautiful, uncompromisingly youthful. Only William himself had no doubts at all of the success of his disguise.

"Won't he get a shock when he sees me," he said with a chuckle that dislodged the insecure ear hook of his beard. "When he sees, as he thinks, his vict'm come back to life to avenge his foul murder. It said it that way in the 'Myst'ry of the One-Eyed Man,' " he admitted modestly as he hooked his beard over his ear again. "I di'n' think of it myself. I think it was a jolly clever way to say it. All those myst'ry tales are written by speshully clever writers. Not the ornery sort of writers that write books with girls' faces on the backs an' such-like. I may start writin' myst'ry books too after I've finished catchin' murd'rers. An' if I do, I'm goin' to have pictures of splashes of blood on the backs of all my books jus' to make sure of everyone buyin' 'em. I bet I'll be one of the richest men in the world by the time I've finished."

"Yes," said Ginger, "but what 're we goin' to do now? We've got to his house."

Brought down to earth, William looked about him.

Both gardens were empty, though the tenant of Beechgrove could be seen in a further greenhouse.

"Let's get round to the other side of his house," said William, "so's *he* can't see us. 'S no good spoilin' it all by lettin' him see us too soon. Tell you what, I'd better wait till he's workin' in his garden an' come walkin' out of the door of ole Scraggy's house. He prob'ly murdered him in his house so that'd be quite all right. Come walkin' out of the door of his house. An' then he'll be so scared he'll start tellin' all about the murder. You all got your pieces of paper an' pencils?"

"Mine hasn't a point," admitted Douglas gloomily. "It had one when I started but it got broke in my pocket."

"Well, find the point an' write with that," suggested William.

Douglas took the larger objects out of his pocket and then began to burrow among the residuum of shaving chips, marbles, nut shells, spent matches, boiled sweets, pieces of string, and bits of putty. His search was unavailing. Moreover, so many boiled sweets adhered to the piece of paper he had brought that writing on it would have been impossible.

"I'll learn it off by heart as he says it," he said, giving up the attempt. "That'd be best. If he doesn't talk too quick, of course."

"All right," said William. "Yes, that'd do all right. You learn it off by heart as he says it."

Ginger produced a fountain pen of uncertain habits and the crumpled back of an envelope. William looked at them with the air of a general holding a review.

"If I know anythin' about that pen of yours," he said sternly, "it'll stop writin' jus' when he's got to tellin' about the murder."

" 'T oughtn't to," said Ginger, inspecting it earnestly, "it's full of ink. At least," he corrected himself as his eye fell upon his ink-soaked fingers and handkerchief, "at least it was when I started."

"Yes, but it dun't seem to know what ink's *for*, that's

what's wrong with your pen," said William, still very sternly; "dun't seem to know anythin' about *writin'*. Seems to think that ink's jus' for splashin' about. That's what's wrong with it in *my* opinion," he ended with heavy sarcasm.

"It's a jolly good pen," said Ginger indignantly, "a *jolly* good pen."

"Yes, it's a jolly good pen for splashin' ink about," said William. "I never said it wasn't a jolly good pen for splashin' ink about. If anyone ever asked me to advise them a good pen for splashin' ink about I'd advise yours. I'd say no one could have a better pen for splashin' ink about than yours. But writin's a different matter an'——"

"Oh, shut up talkin' so much," said Ginger. "I don't see how you think you can catch murd'rers an' such-like if you never stop talkin' from mornin' to night."

"I *do* stop talkin'," said William indignantly. "I'm only doin' absolutely *necess'ry* talkin' now. How d'you think anyone can arrange about catchin' murd'rers an' such-like without talkin'? 'F you know of any deaf and dumb man what's become a famous detective kin'ly tell me his name."

Ginger, thus challenged, sent his mind back over the vast amount of lurid literature on which it had lately fed in search of a famous deaf and dumb detective, and William seized the opportunity to continue.

"An' I don' think you c'n get a whole murder on the back of a little env'lope either. You oughter 've brought somethin' bigger for a murder. Not that I s'pose it'll matter much 'cause if you had a whole book full of paper your pen 'd splash ink over it stead of writin' murders."

Henry, however, retrieved the honour of the company. With an air of conscious virtue he brought out a little note-book, and a small neat pencil with a sheath over its point. William was touched and softened. He gazed at Henry admiringly.

"That's jolly good," he said. "*That'll* be all right, then. I mean, with one thing like that it won't matter the others not havin' proper things. One'll be enough. It'd prob'ly only be muddlin' havin' three people takin' it all down, anyway. I vote that jus' Henry takes it down an' the rest of you jus' listen an' tell him how to spell the words he doesn't know."

"I bet I c'n spell as well as *them*," said Henry indignantly, and with perfect truth.

"Well, we'd better be gettin' on with the plan," said William briskly. "We've gotter find some way of gettin' into his house an' then I've gotter walk out of his door when *he's* workin' in the garden. An' you be hid behind the door to take down what he says when he's all scared stiff at seein' me. He's sure to let out all about the murder same as the man did in 'The Mystery of the One-Eyed Man.' "

"How're we goin' to get into his house?" said Ginger.

William had entered the little back garden gate and the others had followed. Fortunately the lane was empty and so their operations were undisturbed and unchallenged. Had anyone come down the lane, William's strange appearance would certainly have attracted comment and investigation.

"I bet if I climbed up that pipe an' over that little roof I could get into that little window. I bet it isn't locked."

He was quite right. It wasn't locked. After a precarious ascent, during which both beard and wig (with bowler hat attached) were dislodged and rolled down to his watching assistants, he managed to make his way up to the little window, open it and tumble through. Then, after tying the string of his trousers (which his efforts had broken) round his neck again, and brushing off some of the dust from his person, he went downstairs to unlock the back door. Cautiously the Outlaws crept into the little kitchen and handed William his properties. He readjusted his wig and beard and hat with a jaunty air. He was feeling exhilarated and stimulated by the adventure.

"Well, we've nearly got him *now*," he said, "he hasn't got much chance now. . . . Go'n' see if he's in the garden, Ginger."

Ginger peeped very cautiously out of the window.

"Yes, he's jus' goin' into his garden," he said excitedly, "he's lookin' at his rose bed again. . . . Look."

The Outlaws peeped from behind the blind. The tenant of Beechgrove was standing in his garden, leaning on his spade and gazing sorrowfully at his roses. They still looked sickly. Perhaps he'd over dosed them with liquid manure. . . . He didn't quite know what to do about it.

"Look at him," said William excitedly. "*Jus'* like the man in 'The Myst'ry of the Sundial.' Can't keep his eyes off the place where he buried him. Keeps goin' out to look at it. Gotter sort of *fascination* for him jus' like what the place had for the man in 'The Myst'ry of the Sundial.' Look at him lookin' at it. Jus' standin' *lookin'* at it. Sort of mournful. That's his guilty conscious. Some of 'em *do* repent. It comes over them how wicked they are. It did over the man in 'The Myst'ry of the Blue Cat.' But of course it's not so excitin' when they do. . . ."

The tenant of Beechgrove turned away from the rose bed and the Outlaws moved hastily from the window.

"Well," said Henry taking out his note-book and pencil with an air of importance. "You goin' out to him now?"

"In a minute," said William, picking up his beard

which had fallen off again. "Now we're here, we may as well have a look round." He gazed about the neat and spotless little room. "Look!" he said, "that shows you how clever he is. He must 've been lookin' here every day for the money but he leaves it lookin' jus' as if no one had been in it. He's one of the *very* clever ones. I said so right from the beginning. . . . I say, now we're here, I vote we have a try at findin' the money ourselves. Come on."

The Outlaws instituted a thorough search of the downstairs room. In one of the cupboards they found a tin of biscuits and for a few minutes they forgot the money. It was William who first remembered the stern purpose of the expedition. He was reminded of it by the sudden descent of his beard caused by the energetic movements of his mouth.

"Well," he said, swallowing half a biscuit unmasticated, "what 've we come here for?"

"*Dates!*" said Douglas excitedly. "Look! Dates. A box of dates in the corner of that cupboard."

"We've come here to catch murd'rers," said William sternly, "not to eat dates." He replaced his wig, which had slipped over one ear, replaced his bowler hat, and assumed his air of leadership.

"Look 'n' see if you can see him in his garden again," he said to Ginger.

Ginger peeped from behind the blind.

"*Crikey!*" he gasped, "*he's* comin' along."

The Outlaws hastened to the window. It was true. The incredible spectacle was there before their very eyes. Old Scraggy himself was walking up the road carrying a bag.

Anyone but William would have owned himself beaten and retreated. Not so William. When William formed a theory all the facts of the situation had to fit into it or William would know the reason why.

"Well, I *never*," gasped William. "Someone else dressin' up like him to give him a fright. I bet it's someone from Scotland Yard. I bet it's someone from Scotland Yard who's read 'The Myst'ry of the One-Eyed Man' same as I have an' thought it was a good trick same as I did. It *is* a good trick, too. Fancy both of us thinkin' of it. Nacherally I'm not the only one to get suspicious with him sudd'nly disappearin' like that an' *him* standin' all day watchin' the place he buried him when he isn't goin' to his house lookin' for the money. . . ."

The figure was drawing nearer.

"He—he's got up jolly well," said Ginger doubtfully.

"Yes," admitted William. "Of course they've gotter lot of things for that sort of thing at Scotland Yard. Yes," he went on as the figure drew still nearer. "Yes, he *is* got up jolly well. He's done somethin' to his neck to make it look scraggy same as the real ones did. Yes, he's done his neck very well indeed. But of course they've got people at Scotland Yard what have nothin' else to do but make people look like other people. It's quite easy when you've had a bit of practice. I don' think he looks *much* more like him than me. It's his neck he's managed better, that's all. . . . Course, he may've had a neck like that to start with. That's prob'ly it. That's prob'ly why they chose him out to do it 'cause he had a neck like that to start with. . . . Look, he's goin' to speak to him. Now—listen."

Henry took out his note-book again, importantly.

"He's not got anyone to take down what he says," he said, "so I'd better do that."

They opened the door very slightly and peeped out.

The old man paused at the gate of Beechgrove and said:

"Afternoon, Mr. Smith."

The tenant of Beechgrove looked up from his rose bed and said:

"Afternoon, Mr. Barton . . . you back from your holiday?"

"*Well!*" said William. "*Well!* Jus' listen to that. He's cleverer even than I thought he was. He *knows* it's a trick an' he's not goin' to be took in by it. You see? He's pretendin' he thinks it's the real Scraggy jus' to put 'em off the scent though he knows that poor ole Scraggy's dead an' buried in his rose bed. Let's listen what he'll say now. . . ."

They listened, but there was nothing more to hear as the tenant of Oaklands was coming up to the front door.

It occurred to the Outlaws suddenly and for the first time that their position was open to a certain amount of misconstruction.

"Upstairs, quick!" gasped William as the old man opened the garden gate.

The Outlaws followed their leader up the narrow stairs and into a little bedroom at the top. William held the door ajar and placed his ear against it for some moments in silence. Then he spoke in a hoarse and sibilant whisper:

"I c'n hear him messin' about downstairs. I tell you what. I b'lieve he's another thief after the money, dressed up like ole Scraggy to avoid suspicion. That's what I think. I think he's another thief after the money. There was a man like that in 'The Myst'ry of the Creaking Stair.' There was a man who——".

"Look, William," whispered Ginger, "come and look out of the window at what he's doin' in his garden. He's squirtin' stuff on to his rose bed again."

The Outlaws clustered about the window.

"Poison," explained William. "Jus' to make quite sure he's dead. He——"

At that moment the Outlaws were startled by the sound of the door being suddenly pulled to and the key turned in the lock. Then came the sound of steps descending the stairs. William tried the door. It was locked. They were prisoners.

"*Well*," he said. "They know we're on their track an' they're tryin' to get rid of us. Yes, that's what it is. He isn't a Scotland Yard man tryin' to find out the murd'rer. I was on the wrong track there. They gen'rally get on the wrong track first even in books. He's a confederation. That's what he is. An' he's dressed up like the man they killed so's to be able to come into the house lookin' for the money without arousin' suspicions. There was a man like that in one of the myst'ry books. I've forgotten which one but there was a man like that in it an'——"

"Well, what're we goin' to *do?*" asked Douglas nervously.

"It's jus' what happened to the detective in one of the myst'ry books," said William. "He got locked in the room by the murd'rer but he'd got a pistol an' when the murd'rer unlocked the door an' came in to kill him he got out his pistol before the murd'rer got out his an' he walked the murd'rer downstairs an' out to the police station. I said all along I oughter have a pistol. If I'd got a pistol now I'd be all right. It's not having a pistol that's the trouble. I——"

He stopped. They could hear voices coming up the stairs . . . a deep, bass voice and a high, squeaky one that they recognised as belonging to the master of the house.

"Heard voices," the squeaky voice was saying, "heard voices . . . house supposed to be empty . . . been away for holiday . . . went upstairs and just caught sight of them in room . . . several men there—large, powerful-

"NOW," THE POLICEMAN DEMANDED STERNLY, "WHAT'S ALL THIS 'ERE?"

"THIEVES," SPLUTTERED OLD SCRAGGY; "THIEVES, THAT'S WHAT THEY ARE!"

WILLIAM, GINGER AND DOUGLAS STARED BLANKLY. HENRY
TOOK HIS NOTE-BOOK OUT WITH AN AIR OF IMPORTANCE.

looking men . . . slammed door on 'em, locking 'em in . . . then went out for you. Lucky to find you just at corner. . . ."

The bass voice answered rather dubiously:

"Four of 'em, you say? An' powerful-lookin' men . . . well, I'd p'raps better go back to the station first an'——"

"One was a fairly elderly man," said the squeaky voice. "I noticed a beard—noticed a beard distinctly . . . the others all young and powerful-looking. . . ."

"Well," said the bass still more dubiously. "I dunno but what I'd better—— Wait a sec. . . ."

He evidently withdrew the key from the keyhole and applied his eye to it. Then he unlocked the door and flung it open. The Outlaws stood there before the gaze of old Scraggy and the village policeman. The policeman said: "Well, I'm——" and forgetting the dignity of his office burst into a guffaw of laughter. Then he quickly remembered the dignity of his office and changed the guffaw to a cough.

"Now look 'ere," he said sternly, "look 'ere, look 'ere, look 'ere. What's all this? What's all this 'ere?"

He took the ears of Ginger and William in one enormous hand, the ears of Douglas and Henry in the other and led them downstairs to the garden. There he surveyed them in the full light of day, and at the sight of William another guffaw burst from him which he turned again in a masterly fashion into a cough.

"Now," he demanded sternly again, "what's all this 'ere?"

"Thieves," sputtered old Scraggy, "thieves, that's what they are."

The policeman took his note-book from his pocket. Henry, not to be at a disadvantage, took his out too.

"D'you wish to prosecute?" said the policeman in his most official manner.

The householder hesitated. He could imagine this minion of the law repeating his report of four powerful-looking men—one elderly. He looked just the sort of man to do that. . . .

"No," he said irritably. "No, no, no. The whole affair's most exasperating. Box their ears and let them go."

The policeman replaced his note-book in his pocket. Henry replaced his.

" 'Tain't none of my business, boxin' ears," said the policeman. "I'd see 'em boxed with pleasure but it ain't none of my business doin' it. . . ."

William at last found his voice. "He's not him at all," he said, pointing dramatically at the old man; "they've murdered him an' he's a thief tryin' to get his money. He's dressed up like him but he's not him. They've murdered him an'——"

The outburst seemed to draw the policeman's attention to him more closely. He looked at him, then at Ginger, then at Henry, then at Douglas.

Then a gleam came into his eye and he took out his note-book again.

"Look 'ere," he said, "aren't you the four nippers what Farmer Jenks said——"

But the Outlaws were merely four dots on the horizon.

Chapter 2

The New Game

"What shall we do to-day?" said Ginger. There was in his voice a certain touching confidence in fate as a never-failing provider of thrills.

They looked at William. William was generally fate's instrument in the providing of thrills.

"I think," said William with a rather self-conscious nonchalance as if pretending—only pretending, of course—to be unaware of the originality of his suggestion, "I think we'll try greyhound racin' for a change."

"Greyhound racin'?" repeated the Outlaws in surprise.

They had expected William to say pirates or Red Indians or perhaps smugglers, but greyhound racing was so novel, so unexpected, so daring and up-to-date, that they could only repeat the words and stare at William helplessly.

"Yes," said William, still with his exaggerated nonchalance, "I—I heard Robert an' some other people talkin' about it last night. It seemed—sort of simple. It seemed jus' the sort of thing we could do."

It was Douglas who voiced the first objection.

"But—we haven't got any greyhounds."

"We've got Jumble," said William with spirit.

Jumble was William's dog, though some people thought that dog was too definite a term for Jumble.

Ginger laid his finger at once upon the weak spot in William's argument.

"Jumble isn't a greyhound," he said.

William looked at him coldly.

"No one's ever found out exactly what sort of a dog Jumble is," he said distantly, "an' I bet he's as likely to be a greyhound as anythin'."

The Outlaws forbore to touch further upon the delicate subject. William was apt to resent as an outrage upon his personal honour any reflections upon Jumble's pedigree.

They turned hastily to another aspect of the matter.

"There can't be *racin'* with only one dog," objected Henry.

"We can easily find another dog," said William carelessly. "This country's simply overrun with dogs. I heard my father say so yesterday. One had jus' bit him."

"An' how d'you make 'em race?" demanded Ginger. "Seems to me they'd only start playin' or fightin'. Dogs don't race nacherally."

"They have a mechanical hare for them," said William kindly and with a superior air of knowledge, "that makes 'em race."

"Well, we haven't got a mechanical hare," said Ginger, as if that settled the matter.

"No," retorted William as if it didn't, "but I've got a clockwork mouse an' that's jus' the same."

They were nonplussed for the minute and then, as usually happened, they became infected with William's optimism.

"Well," said Ginger, "it oughter be all right. It'll be *fun* anyway."

Preparations for the race began at once and it seemed likely to grow into quite an elaborate affair.

"Let's have refreshments," said William, "an' bettin' an' all."

"Bettin's wrong," objected Henry piously.

"Only when it's horses," said William hastily; "it's all right when it's greyhounds."

"Besides," said Ginger, as if exculpating them still further in the matter, "Jumble's not *exactly* a greyhound either so it's prob'ly *quite* all right."

The first difficulty was to find a race track. They finally decided on an open space in the wood near William's home.

"We'll let 'em out at this tree," said William with a business-like air, "an' let 'em run to that tree. That'll be the winnin' post an' Ginger 'll stand there with a note-book puttin' down which comes first."

"S'pose they catch the mouse before they get to this tree," objected Ginger.

"The hare?" said William coldly. "They never do that, I don't think. Anyway," optimistically, "we won't let 'em do that. And Henry will see to the bettin'."

"I don't know how to," said Henry. "I've never done it. How do you do it?"

Henry's helplessness and lack of initiative seemed to irritate William.

"It's quite easy," he said. "You—you sort of stand with a note-book an' say 'bet you a penny Jumble wins' or 'bet you a penny that the other one wins' to everyone, and if they take it on put down their names in the note-book."

"An' if Jumble wins the ones that said he wouldn't give me a penny?"

"Yes."

"An' if he doesn't I give 'em a penny?"

"I s'pose so."

"Where do I get it from?"

"You get it from the pennies that the people who don't win the bets give you."

Henry considered this for some minutes in silence, then said:

"Let Douglas do that part an' I do somethin' else."

"All right," said William coldly. "It's *ever* so easy, Douglas."

"An' who'll come to the race?" demanded Ginger.

"Anyone," said William, "but they'll have to pay money to come in."

"No one'll come if they have to pay money to come," said Ginger with simple conviction.

William could not help admitting the truth of this.

"Then we'll jus' invite the people we like an' not let any of the others come," said William.

"Not Hubert Lane nor any of the rest of them," said Ginger.

The Outlaws carried that by acclamation. Between the Outlaws and the Hubert Laneites had existed, since any of them remembered, a deadly feud, which sometimes merely smouldered and sometimes burst into open warfare.

"Crumbs, no!" said William. "None of *them*." A smile of satisfaction broke over his face. "But we'll let 'em know we're having it. They'll be *mad* at not bein' able to come."

Preparations continued during the next few days. To tell the truth the Outlaws concentrated most of their attention upon the refreshments. They did many small services at home—consisting mostly of sawing wood—on a strictly cash basis. They sold sundry of their less precious possessions to their friends. They affected suddenly perfect manners when in the neighbourhood of elderly and prosperous relatives. The net result was one and elevenpence farthing (the farthing had been found by Henry in his coal shed). The Outlaws were delighted by it. With it they provided a magnificent feast—eight bottles of liquorice water, two bottles of ginger ale and an array of the cheapest and most indigestible cakes that the Outlaws after a long and patient search (which drove several confectioners to the verge of madness) could find.

The next thing to do was to find a second greyhound to race with Jumble. William still seemed inclined to think that Jumble alone would do. He liked to think of cheering Jumble as victor past the winning post and with a second competitor there was always the chance that Jumble might not arrive as victor at the winning post, but he admitted the logic of the argument that with only one greyhound it could not strictly be called a "race."

With Ginger he roamed the fields and roads in search of stray dogs and found none. It was amazing, as he frequently remarked, where all the stray dogs had got to just now. Why, ordinary days they were all over the place. They must be all hiding away somewhere. Extraordinary, he said, how animals seemed sometimes almost human in the way they do things just to spite you.

The day of the race arrived and still no rival to Jumble had been found. William had laboriously written out a notice:

"grahound racing got up by mister william brown ennywon may bring dogs to run aganst jumble the grate racing grahound belonging to mister william brown."

He had meant to pin it on to his side gate, but the other Outlaws, though admiring it as a literary production, pointed out that its public appearance would only give an opportunity to the Hubert Laneites to turn up at the race. Suppose Hubert himself arrived with his mother's Pom? It was a horrible idea. William promptly destroyed his notice and went out again to look for a stray dog. He came upon a young pig that seemed to have wandered from its native haunts, gazed at it doubtfully, decided that by no stretch of imagination could it be referred to as a greyhound nor by any human means could it be made to resemble a greyhound and returned to the Outlaws again empty-handed. However, he was in an optimistic mood.

"We'll prob'ly find something on the way," he said.

They had decided to have the refreshments in a small clearing a very short distance from the racecourse, and thither they bore the provisions—packed precariously in school sachets—about half an hour before the race was timed to begin.

Jumble accompanied them, leaping exuberantly and running on in front, little dreaming that he was a greyhound and about to take part in a race. Had he known it, his deportment would have been sadly altered. Jumble disliked on principle all the varied rôles that his master thrust upon him. The only time he had ever bitten William was once when he was impersonating a viking in a play written by William. He found the stage directions confusing and ran amok.

Ginger had his little note-book for writing down the winner's name and a piece of string to tie to the winning post. Douglas carried his betting note-book and looked rather gloomy. The more he thought over the system of greyhound betting as expounded by William the more gloomy he became.

"S'pose they all bet right an' want pennies an' none of 'em bet wrong an' give me pennies," he said, "what happens then?"

But the others, feeling that he was trying to make out

his part in the proceedings to be unduly important, only said: "Oh, shut up."

William had the clockwork mouse in his pocket. He was frowning abstractedly, his thoughts still taken up with Jumble's—as yet—undiscovered rival.

"We may find one lost in the wood jus' where we're goin' to have the race," he said.

"Look!" said Ginger suddenly. They were passing the back gate of a house. It was open. On it was inscribed "Beware of the Dog," and just inside it was a kennel and chained to the kennel was a very friendly-looking fox-terrier, who wagged his tail propitiatingly when he saw that the Outlaws had stopped to look at him.

"I know him," said Ginger importantly, "I'm a friend of his. I've often gone in to play with him there, when there was no one about."

There was silence. The Outlaws stood gazing at the dog and then at each other, while the great idea took shape. Ginger at last broke the silence and voiced it.

"I votes we jus'—jus' borrow him for the race. I think they're all out. We can have him back again before they come back."

Without waiting for their answer Ginger went up to the dog and unchained it. It joined the party with jubilation, leaping down the road with them and fraternising exultantly with its fellow greyhound.

* * *

They had finished all their preparations. The feast was spread out in the space reserved for "refreshments." The Outlaws had determined to charge their patrons a penny per head and then let them fight for what they could get.

The patrons were now beginning to arrive. Douglas with his little note-book was doing brisk business.

He had reduced the ceremonial of betting to its simplest possible form. He had written on one page of his little note-book "For Jumble," and on the opposite page "Against Jumble." The news spread like wildfire among the patrons of the race.

"I say, if you go up to Douglas an' say, 'I bet you a penny Jumble doesn't win,' they'll give you a penny if he doesn't."

The patrons all did this. It was not that they did not admire Jumble, but a stranger at first sight often commands more respect than someone we have known all our lives, and there was something vaguely sporting-looking about the fox-terrier.

"I 'spect he's a *real* racin' dog they've got in," murmured one of the patrons with awe.

William caught the competitors and tied them to the starting tree, and then, looking very important, blew a blast on his whistle.

Henry cleared the track.

William wound up his clockwork mouse.

"One to be ready—two to be steady," shouted William, "and three——"

He blew another blast on his whistle.

He released his clockwork mouse.

Henry unleashed the greyhounds.

The clockwork mouse went forward two inches, then came to a slight irregularity in the ground and stopped. The greyhounds danced off playfully into the wood in the opposite direction, ignoring track and patrons and mechanical hare alike. The patrons began to grumble. This wasn't what they'd come to see.

"We'll have another try," said William in his most official manner.

They had another try.

The two greyhounds were recalled to the starting tree,

WILLIAM BLEW A BLAST ON HIS WHISTLE. HE RELEASED HIS
CLOCKWORK MOUSE. IT WENT FORWARD TWO INCHES AND
STOPPED.

were shown the clockwork mouse and told once more
what was demanded of them. Both of them wagged their
tails in cheerful understanding and compliance.

Again Henry cleared the track. Again William wound
up his clockwork mouse and blew his whistle.

But something had gone wrong with the clockwork
mouse and it now refused to function at all. The fox-

THE DOGS DANCED OFF PLAYFULLY INTO THE WOOD IN THE
OPPOSITE DIRECTION. THE PATRONS BEGAN TO GRUMBLE. THIS
WASN'T WHAT THEY'D COME TO SEE!

terrier leapt upon it, seized it by its tail, flung it into the air, fell upon it again, chewed it up and then scampered off in the opposite direction after his new friend.

"What do they do at the real races when they carry on like this?" demanded Ginger in a frenzied aside to William.

"I don't know," said William irritably. "They *don't* carry on like this. It's these dogs' fault. They don't seem to know what racin' *means*."

"It was your idea," said Ginger bitterly.

The patrons were crowding round Douglas, insisting that Jumble had lost whatever race there was, and demanding their pennies. Certainly it was not Jumble who had caught the mechanical hare.

A hunted look was coming over Douglas's face.

"I can't *help* it," he was saying. "I haven't *got* any. Well, it's your own faults. You shouldn't have all betted on the same dog. If half of you'd betted on one and half on the other then I'd have had money to give half of you from the other half. I don't care. It's not my fault. I can't help it, I tell you. I haven't *got* any."

"You *promised* us a penny if he won," growled the patrons.

"Well, he *di'n't* win. Neither of them won."

"He *did* win. He got hold of the mouse, anyway, an' that's winnin'."

"We want our pennies."

"You *promised* us pennies."

They grew more and more turbulent till finally Douglas, like so many others of his profession before and since, took to his heels pursued by an indignant crowd.

William stood looking down at the ruins of his mechanical hare. The greyhounds still sported joyously about in and out of the trees.

"Well," said William disgustedly, "it's all been a rotten sort of show, hasn't it?"

"It was all your idea," Ginger reminded him once more.

"It was a jolly *good* idea," said William indignantly. "Fancy blamin' *me* because these two dogs haven't any *sense!* Where's Douglas?"

"He's running away," explained Henry morosely. "They're all after him for their pennies." He turned to William. "*That's* all your fault, too. I don't believe you know anythin' about bettin'."

"It's *them* what don't know anythin' about bettin'," said William defending himself spiritedly. "Fancy them all bettin' on the same dog. Stands to *reason* there's no money for 'em if they all bet on the same dog. Well, anyway, let's go'n' eat up the food."

They went slowly through the trees to the place where they had left the refreshments. It was empty of refreshments. Every cake, every bottle had disappeared. In their place was a piece of paper bearing the words:

"Thank you very much from us all for a good tea.
                                        "HUBERT LANE."

"Hope it poisons 'em," said Henry viciously.

But William's blood was up. It was a relief to be able to concentrate his bitterness upon a concrete enemy.

"Come on," he said tersely, "let's catch 'em up. Prob'ly they're still somewhere in the wood."

But they weren't. William, Ginger and Henry, lusting for the Hubert Laneites' blood, scoured the wood from end to end and even searched all the roads leading to Hubert Lane's house. There was no trace of the Hubert Laneites, but from an upper window in Hubert Lane's house they were rewarded by the sight of Hubert Lane making triumphant jeering grimaces at them and licking his lips suggestively. They pretended not to see him and returned morosely to the racecourse.

"Fancy *that* happ'nin' on the top of everythin' else," said William, "jus' as if it wasn't enough the whole race goin' wrong like that."

It seemed to the Outlaws that sometimes Fate lacked artistic restraint in her effects.

There were no traces of the greyhounds on the racecourse, but Douglas was there. He had managed to elude his pursuers and was breathless and indignant.

"No wonder you wanted *me* to do the bettin' part," he said bitterly. "I don't *wonder* you all shoved it off on to me. I'm jus' about wore out with it all. I can't think what people *see* in bettin'."

When he heard of the latest catastrophe his gloom changed to consternation.

"*Gosh!*" he said, aghast. "Jus' to *think* of it. Me wearin' myself out sawin' wood an' earnin' money for *him*—for that Hubert Lane."

"Let's go home, anyway," said William. "I've had enough of it all."

"If only he'd done a bit of *sawin'* for it, but gettin' it all for nothin' like that, stealin' it. . . ."

"There's that dog," said Ginger, suddenly, "that dog we borrowed. We'd better be takin' him back."

At that moment Jumble and a fox-terrier came leaping through the trees.

William seized the fox-terrier and inserted a grimy handkerchief through his collar.

Douglas looked at him with distaste.

"Can't think what they wanted—all bettin' on him!" he said.

"Come on," said William impatiently. They went out of the wood and down the road to the house from which they had taken the dog. Ginger kept looking at the dog thoughtfully. They crept in by the back gate, which was still open, and fastened the dog to the chain. Then they came out and hurried down the road. Ginger was still very thoughtful.

"Where are we goin' now?" said Douglas.

"Back to the wood," said William. "I've left the bits of the mouse there. I bet I could mend it all right. An' I bet if we trained Jumble a bit he'd be able to race after it all right. It was only that he didn't quite *understand*——"

William's optimism was boundless.

"William," said Ginger very slowly and thoughtfully, "I don't think that was the right dog."

"What was the right dog?" said William impatiently.

"The dog we took back wasn't the same dog as the dog we took."

"It *looked* jus' the same," said William.

"It didn't look *quite* the same," said Ginger. "I mean, it was the same *make* of dog all right—a fox-terrier—but it wasn't *exactly* the same dog. I'm almost sure it wasn't. You see," he explained simply, "I'm one of its friends. I *know* it."

William was aghast.

"*Crumbs!*" he said helplessly. "Well, it'll have to stay there now. If it's not the right one *I* can't help it. The man it belongs to 'll have to find the right one. I've jus' about had enough of to-day."

They reached the racecourse once more. Jumble darted off again among the trees and William collected the bits of clockwork mouse and began to try to put them together again.

"You'll never do it," said Ginger gloomily. "There's sixpence gone. *An'* all the money we spent on the refreshments. *An'* all the money we might 've got through the bettin' if Jumble had any sense. *Greyhound Racin'!*" he exploded sarcastically, "he ought to 've been a monkey on a barrel-organ for all the sense he's got. Fancy a dog not havin' enough sense to race with another dog and run after a mouse. I'd be ashamed of havin' a dog that hadn't enough sense for that.

William, stung to the quick by this attack on his pet, rose to his defence indignantly.

"Oh, you would, would you? Well, let *me* tell *you* that Jumble couldn't race 'cause he's got *too* much sense for it. That's what it is. He's too *intell'gent* to make a racin' dog. That's what it is. Too intell'gent. Racin' dogs are all stupid. They've gotter be so stupid that they think a clockwork hare's a *real* hare and run after it. Well, Jumble's too *intell'gent* for that. He *knew* it wasn't a real one and that was why he wouldn't race after it 'cause he's too *intell'gent*." He appealed to Douglas for support. "Don't you think so, Douglas?" he said. But Douglas refused to be drawn from his own particular grievance.

"I don't *wonder* lots of people are against bettin'," he said. "It seems to me all wrong. I shall always be against it myself now."

At that minute a diversion was caused by Jumble who reappeared through the trees frisking about with another fox-terrier.

"*That's* the real one," exclaimed Ginger.

It greeted Ginger ecstatically and the others with jubilant friendliness. It was certainly the real one. All of them recognised it.

"We've got to take it back," said Ginger righteously. "We borrowed it an' we've got to take it back. We can't leave it loose all over the wood."

"All right," agreed William dispiritedly. "Come on."

He secured this fox-terrier too with his handkerchief and, accompanied by Jumble, they set off again for the fox-terrier's home. At the back gate of the fox-terrier's home, however, they stopped dead. The gate was still open, but the yard was no longer empty of humans. There were two men in it. Both were angry. Both were pointing with indignant gestures at the fox-terrier which the Outlaws had lately brought there and which was still chained to the kennel, watching proceedings with interest. One man was evidently its master and was accusing the other of stealing it. The other was indignantly denying the accusation and bringing a counter-charge of theft against his visitor.

"You've stolen it. Of course you've stolen it. Why do I find it chained up like this in your back-yard if you haven't stolen it. I shall tell the police."

"*Stolen* the thing! I've never seen it before. I tell you when I went out this afternoon my own dog was chained up there. What I want to know is how comes it that *my* dog's gone and this wretched cur's in its place."

"Wretched cur, indeed! You thought enough of it to steal it."

"I never stole it. My own dog——"

"I don't believe you ever had a dog."

"Liar!"

"What do you call me?"

"Liar!"

"Dog thief!"

"Dog thief!"

"I'll call up the police this instant."

"Do, and I'll give you in charge."

"Yes, and I demand my dog of you. What have you done with it? Stolen a valuable pedigree dog and put a miserable mongrel in its place."

"Liar!"

"Thief!"

"Thief yourself."

"Liar yourself."

"I'll call——"

"I demand——"

At that minute they turned and saw the Outlaws standing, a helpless, fascinated group. William was still holding the original fox-terrier by his collar.

"*There's* my dog!" yelled the terrier's owner.

The terrier leapt upon him in ecstatic recognition. He was a dog with a very large heart.

The spell that had till now held the Outlaws paralysed ceased to hold them and they fled precipitately down the road.

They were pursued by angry shouts from the two men. From the shouts the Outlaws gathered that they had recognised William and were going to tell his father.

"Crumbs!" panted William as they stopped at the end of the road to draw breath. "Crumbs! What a *day!*"

*   *   *

"Well," said William's father the next morning, "I really don't want to hear any more about it. I'm sick of hearing about that dog. I don't know why on earth you go about the countryside borrowing dogs. You've got one of your own, haven't you?"

"Yes, but you can't have races with only one dog," protested William earnestly.

"But why have races? The trouble with you, my boy, is that you're suffering from a superabundance of spirits and leisure time. There are a few logs in the wood shed. You can saw them all up into small pieces to-day. It will occupy your time and reduce your superfluous vitality."

"*Me!*" gasped William pale with dismay. "*Me! Alone!*"

"You may get your friends to help you," said his father pleasantly, "even so it will, I think, take you most of the day."

William joined his friends and communicated the news.

"*Jus'* when we were goin' to go *fishin'*," he said despondently.

After yesterday's fiasco the Outlaws had decided upon fishing as a safe and pleasant pastime that couldn't go wrong.

"What makes me so *mad*," said Ginger, "is the thought of that ole Hubert Lane an' the others eatin' up all those things we bought an' that we sawed an' *sawed* for an' now we've gotter saw again—*course* we'll come an' help, William—an'—an' I wouldn't mind so much if we could make *him* do a bit of the sawin'——"

A thoughtful expression had come over William's face.

"Let's go down by his house," he said, "an' see if we can meet him."

By one of the strokes of good luck that occasionally befell the Outlaws they did meet him. They met him in the lane leading to his house. At first sight he took them for a punitive expedition and his face paled with apprehension. But nothing could have exceeded the friendliness with which William accosted him.

"Hello, Hubert. How are you?"

Hubert, still looking a little apprehensive, said that he was very well.

The Outlaws began to walk down the lane with him.

"I say, that was a jolly good trick you played on us yesterday," said William. "As a matter of fact," he continued shamelessly, "we were jolly glad to see those things gone. We'd just been wonderin' what we were goin' to do with them. They were jus' a few ole bad ones left over from our tea. We'd eaten all the nice ones and we'd had all the ginger ale we could drink and we were jus' wondering what to do with those few ole bad cakes an' ginger ale left over, when we found you'd taken 'em. I can tell you we were jolly glad. We di'n' want to leave 'em about in the wood cause' of makin' the place untidy an' we di'n' want to take 'em home 'cause of none of us likin' 'em. So we were *jolly* glad, I can tell you, to find 'em gone."

Hubert's mouth had dropped open with dismay and disappointment. Hubert was very credulous.

"Oh!" was all he said.

"Yes. What 're you goin' to do to-day, Hubert?" went on William pleasantly.

"I don't know," said Hubert cautiously.

"We're goin' to have a *lovely* time," said William enthusiastically. "We've gotter go out this mornin', but this afternoon we're goin' to have a *lovely* time."

"What 're you goin' to do?" inquired Hubert with interest.

"Saw up wood," said William with a world of pleasurable anticipation in his voice. "We've been tryin' to get some logs to saw up into small pieces for *ever* so long an' now at last we've got some. They're in our wood shed. We'd rather saw wood than anythin' else, wouldn't we?" he appealed to the Outlaws.

The Outlaws said that they would.

"We'd rather do it than play Red Indians or—or *anythin'*," went on William. "We're jolly well lookin' forward to this afternoon when we're goin' to saw those logs. We've gotter be out all this mornin' but we shall be thinkin' all the time of those lovely logs an' the lovely time we're goin' to have sawin' 'em up this afternoon. Here's your house, isn't it, Hubert? You goin' in? Good-bye, Hubert."

The Outlaws turned and walked back down the lane.

"I bet it'll be all right," said William. "They'll want to do another trick on us 'cause of thinkin' that yesterday's didn't come off. Let's wait about quarter of an hour an' then I'll go'n' look."

In about a quarter of an hour William crept back to the garden and peeped in at the wood shed window. Hubert and his friends were there sawing up the logs.

William rejoined the Outlaws. " 'S all right," he called out joyously. "We can go fishin' all day."

Chapter 3

William's Double Life

It happened that William, unusually enough, was thrown upon his own resources. It was the holidays and all the other Outlaws were away from home. Douglas had gone to stay with an aunt at the seaside. He had been bored at the prospect and the visit was not turning out any more enjoyable than he had thought it would. His only consolation was that his aunt was finding it even more trying than he. Ginger had gone with his family to stay at a boarding house. Already the oldest resident of the boarding house had taken such a dislike to Ginger's rendering of "Let's Go Round to Alice's House," that he had issued an ultimatum to the effect that either Ginger or he must depart at once and for ever. He had left it to the boarding house proprietress to choose between them and she had done so. She had chosen the oldest resident. Ginger's parents were already packing. . . .

Henry was taking part in a camping holiday with some cousins of the same age and disposition as himself. The young schoolmaster who had organised the expedition had meant to camp in the same place for the whole fortnight, but as events turned out, they had moved on after each night. They had not moved on of their own accord. They had left a train of infuriated farmers behind them in their passage across England. The young schoolmaster had returned home with a nervous breakdown and had already had two successors.

And so William was thrown upon his own resources.

Though much relieved that his own family was not taking a holiday (for William hated to be torn from his familiar pursuits and the familiar fields and ditches of his native village) he was for the first two days rather at a loss as to what to do without the other Outlaws. And then he had an inspiration. An aquarium. He'd make an aquarium. He'd already made a zoo and a circus, he'd already organised greyhound racing (all without any striking success), but he'd never yet made an aquarium. He'd make an aquarium with two hundred inhabitants in a large pail (William's mind, like the minds of all great organisers, leapt ahead, arranging even the smallest detail). He'd start at once. . . .

The first thing to do, of course, was to find a pail. He was prepared to go to any lengths to obtain one and had just conceived the bold design of carrying off the washing pail from under the cook's vigilant and hostile eyes, when to his amazement she offered it him.

"That pail's just beginning to leak, Master William," she said carelessly, "if you'd like it for any of your contraptions you can have it."

William accepted it coldly. It was disappointing to have screwed up his courage for a daring *coup* and then to find that the *coup* was unnecessary. Moreover, William preferred the cook as an enemy than a friend. Life was very dull to William when he and the cook were being polite to each other. However, he found a little comfort in making a bold daylight raid upon a workman's hod when actually in action in the workman's hand in order to obtain some mortar to mend the leak in the pail. The workman, welcoming the little diversion almost as much as did William, threw down the hod and pursued him unavailingly to the end of the road, showering threats and abuse in his wake, then returned, cheered and invigorated, to his work.

The pail was mended, filled with water and put into the shed to await its two hundred inhabitants.

And here William's troubles began. For the fish denizens of the neighbourhood were coy. They refused to enter the net that William held in the stream with such patience and jerked up at intervals with such sudden cunning. They ignored his worms obtained with great labour and at the expense of some of the choicest garden plants. They scorned his bent pins. In the course of two mornings' hard work, he caught only an old tin, a curtain hook and a bottle in his net and on his bent pin a bootlace and the remnants of a grimy shirt discarded by some passing tramp. William was not the boy lightly to abandon any idea he had once taken up, but it was just as despair was descending upon him that he remembered the pond in the garden of The Laburnums. The Laburnums was a largish house at the further end of the village and in its garden just beyond the orchard was a pond—a pond teeming with potential inhabitants of William's aquarium. William and the other Outlaws had discovered it about a year ago, but the owner had then been an irate colonel who had caught the Outlaws fishing in his pond and robbing his orchard and had inflicted such condign punishment that even those bold spirits had not wooed that particular adventure again. But it occurred now to William that he had seen a "To Let" notice at the gate of The Laburnums and he set off at once—net, glass jar with string handle, worm, bent pin, stick and all—to reconnoitre. His impression turned out to be correct. There was a "To Let" notice at the gate of The Laburnums. He did not enter boldly at the front gate because in his acquaintance of empty houses (and it was a wide one) there was generally a caretaker in possession, and caretakers, though content generally to doze their lives away in the kitchen, were, nevertheless, of a savage disposition when roused, and, like the wild buffaloes of Africa, attacked on sight.

So he walked down the road till he found the place in the hedge where a year ago a serviceable hole had been made by the frequent passage of the Outlaws' solid bodies. Time had healed the breach to a certain extent, but there was still room just to admit William with his accoutrements. Having scraped through the hole with only a few casualties (the loss of his worm, a hole in his net and a forest of scratches on his hands) William cautiously made his way to the orchard. It took him longer than it need have done to cross the orchard. The amount of apples William could consume during a leisurely stroll across an average-sized orchard would have astounded anyone of normal digestive capacities. At length, however, gorged and happy, he made his way to the pond. And the pond exceeded his wildest expectations. It teemed with inhabitants and inhabitants of an engagingly friendly and trusting disposition. They jostled each other for entrance to his net and those who fell through the hole seemed to struggle to get back again. They impaled themselves willingly upon his bent pin. They even placed themselves confidently in his bare hand. He fished there for over an hour. At last, carefully carrying his glass jar by its string handle and glowing with the pride of the successful hunter, he sauntered slowly back through the orchard. The apples delayed him again for some time, and when even William had reached his limit (a limit to be spoken of with bated breath) he stuffed his pockets and wandered homeward, mentally composing (slightly exaggerated) accounts of the affair to tell the other Outlaws on their return.

Then followed a blissful week for William. He went to The Laburnums with his jar every morning. He first spent an hour or so in the orchard. After that he staggered to the pond in a state of happy repletion, filled his jar from the teeming population of the pond, then, with appetite restored, returned to the orchard.

He felt that it was too good to last, and it was. At the end of a week he saw a large removing van entering the front gate. He made the most of that day. He ate so many apples that he went home in a state closely bordering on intoxication.

The next day, more from force of habit than anything else, he went to the house as usual with his jar, his fishing-rod, and what a week's hard wear had left of his net. He went without any definite plans. It was no longer that most exciting of playgrounds—an "empty house." It was now inhabited, owned and presumably guarded. He would be liable now at any minute to a descent from a ferocious inhabitant. He watched the house from the front gate for some time. Maids were cleaning windows, shaking out dusters, pulling up curtains. An elderly woman with pince-nez and very elaborately-dressed hair was evidently the mistress of the house and she seemed to be in sole possession. That relieved William, who generally found women easier to deal with than men. The bustle within the house, too, reassured him. While they were cleaning windows and shaking out dusters and putting up curtains, they could not be making descents upon the pond and orchard. He might surely take this last day in his paradise.

He found it even more enjoyable than any of the others. He had decided that it must be his last day there, and yet the next morning he set off as usual with his jar and rod and net. He did this partly because the risk now attached to the proceeding enhanced it in his eyes, and partly because he'd only got 100 of his 200 fishes. He felt that 100 fishes in that pond still belonged to him and in fetching them he was only claiming his rightful property.

It was a beautiful morning. The sun shone brightly on the pond and orchard. The apples seemed riper and more delicious than ever before, the inhabitants of the pond more guileless and trusting. After his customary fruitful journey through the orchard he sat as usual happily fishing by the side of the pond.

Then—it happened. It happened without the slightest warning. He heard no sound of her approach. Suddenly a hand was laid on his shoulder from behind and looking up with a start his eyes met the eyes of the woman with the pince-nez and elaborately-dressed hair. All about him were the signs of his guilt. His jar containing his morning's "bag" stood on one side of him together with a little pile of apples gathered for refreshment in the intervals of fishing. On the other side of him lay a little heap of cores representing refreshment already taken. His pockets bulged with apples. His mouth was full of apple. He held a half-eaten apple in one hand and his rod in the other.

"You *naughty* little ruffian," exploded his captor. "How *dare* you trespass in my grounds and steal my fruit?"

William swallowed half an apple unmasticated and by means of a gentle wriggle experimented with the grip on his shoulder. He was an expert in grips. The gentlest of wriggles could tell him whether a grip was the sort of grip he could escape from or whether it wasn't. This one wasn't. It was, William generously allowed in his mind, an unusually good grip for a woman. So he abandoned himself to his fate, and contented himself with glaring at

his captor with unblinking ferocity. He certainly wasn't a
prepossessing sight. His face was streaked with mud. His
collar (sodden and muddy) was awry. He had used his tie
to repair his fishing rod. His legs were caked with mud up
to the knees. His suit was so thickly covered with mud
that its pattern was almost undiscernible. His captor's
closer inspection evidently did nothing to modify the
unfavourable opinion she had formed of him.

"What's your name?" she said sharply.

"William Brown," said William.

He knew by experience that people always found out
his name sooner or later and that to refuse to give it
made ultimate proceedings more unpleasant.

"Very well," said his captor meaningly, "I shall call
to see your father about it. Go away out of my garden at
once."

With great dignity William gathered up his jar of
fishes, his net, stuffed the pile of apples into his pockets
(his pockets held a good number of apples as William
had made a convenient hole through which they could
descend to the lining), kicked his pile of cores into the
pond, put on his bedraggled cap, raised it as politely as
he could considering his many burdens, stooped down to
pick up a fish that the effort of raising his cap had
displaced from his jar, and with a courteous "Good
mornin' '" walked very slowly and with an indescribable
swagger across the orchard to the lawn, across the lawn
to the front drive, and down to the front gate. He wasn't
going to give away his hole to her. At the front gate he
turned, raised his cap to her again, dropped his net and
another fish, picked them up without any undue haste
and strolled out into the road.

As he walked homewards he couldn't help thinking
that he'd carried off the situation with something of an
air. But that feeling of gratification was of short dura-

tion. She had said that she was going to tell his father, and he was pretty sure that a woman who could grip like that would be as good as her word. It meant, besides any other incidental unpleasantness, that an end would be put to his fishing activities and that, as likely as not, his aquarium would be thrown away. He still retained bitter memories of the wholesale destruction of a laboriously-acquired collection of insects that he had kept secretly in the spare room wardrobe until it was found and destroyed.

In a vague desire to propitiate authority he made an elaborate toilet for lunch—changing his socks and shoes, completely removing several layers of mud from his knees, brushing his suit, washing his face and hands, and severely punishing his hair. His mother greeted his appearance with a cry of horror: "William, what a *sight* you are! What have you been doing?"

He murmured "Fishin' " rather distantly and sat down to his soup.

"Why didn't you wash and tidy your hair before you came in to lunch?" continued his mother sternly.

"I did," said William simply, and not only received apparently unmoved his elder brother's snort of derision, but also pretended not to notice his further challenge of the gesture of a cat perfunctorily washing its face with its paw. This was no moment for reprisals. Robert could wait. At any minute the woman with the hair and the pince-nez might come to report his morning's activities, and the less he embroiled himself with Authority in the meantime the better.

"You won't forget where you're going out to tea this afternoon, William, will you?" said his mother.

"No," said William, sinking into yet deeper gloom.

He was going out to tea with the Vicar. Occasionally the Vicar, who disliked children intensely, but suffered from an over-active conscience, invited his more youthful parishioners to tea. He was a precise and tidy man and liked peace and quiet, and he hardly slept at all the night before such a party took place, but he felt that was part of his priestly duty and went through with it in the spirit of the early Christian martyrs. His youthful guests generally enjoyed their visits, partly because his wife made a peculiarly delicious brand of treacle cake, and partly because the Vicar was entirely at a loss how to deal with the very young, and, given the right blending of guests, the affair could be trusted to develop into a very enjoyable riot. The only drawback of it in William's eyes was the long and painful process of cleansing and tidying to which he was subjected before he was declared fit to present himself at the Vicarage. On this occasion, despite William's own heroic efforts before lunch, the process lasted an hour, and it was after three when —clean and shining in his best suit, a gleaming Eton collar, a perfectly tied tie, neatly gartered stockings and radiant boots with tags tucked down inside—he was allowed to set off down the road towards the Vicarage. He walked slowly. As all the other Outlaws were away from home, it wasn't likely to be a very exciting affair, but at any rate there would be the treacle cake—and the Vicar. The Vicar could always be counted upon for entertainment.

He was vaguely aware of a figure approaching him from the opposite direction, but beyond noting almost subconsciously that it was adult and feminine, he took no interest in it. He was surprised to find that it stopped in front of him. He looked up with a start. It was the woman with the pince-nez and the hair.

"Well," she said grimly, "I'm on my way to see your father." Then she stopped and faltered, "You—you *are* William Brown, aren't you?" she said uncertainly.

William saw at once what had happened. He was so clean and tidy as to be almost unrecognisable as the hero of the morning's escapade. As she scanned his features still more closely he saw her uncertainty changing again to certainty. William's features were, after all, unmistakable.

"You *are*, aren't you?" she said.

And then William had an inspiration—or rather an *INSPIRATION*—or rather an INSPIRATION—the sort of INSPIRATION that comes to most of us only once in a lifetime, but that visited William more frequently.

Fixing her with a virtuous and mournful gaze, he said: "No, I'm not William Brown. I'm his twin brother."

Her severity vanished.

"I see," she said. "I could see a *strong* resemblance, but yet I was sure that there was some difference, though I couldn't have said what it was. He was very dirty and untidy, of course."

"Yes," agreed William sadly, "I expect he was."

"You're very alike in features though, aren't you?" she went on with interest. "It must be difficult for people to tell you apart."

"Yes," agreed William, warming to his theme, "lots of people can't tell us apart. His nose is just a bit longer. That's one way of telling us."

"Yes," she agreed still with great interest, "I believe it is, now you mention it. And his ears stick out more."

"Do they?" said William coldly.

"I'm just on my way to call on your parents to complain of your brother," went on the lady, her interest turning to severity. "I found him this morning trespassing in my garden, stealing my apples and catching fishes in my pond. Do you know about it?"

William wondered for a minute whether to know

about it, and finally decided that it would be more effective to know about it than not to. His mournful and virtuous expression deepened.

"Yes," he said, "he told me about it. I was jus' comin' to—to see you about it."

"Why?" said the lady.

"I was comin' to ask you to let him off jus' for this once," said William more mournfully, more virtuously, than ever. "I was goin' to ask you not to go an' see my father an' mother about him this time."

It was quite evident that the lady was touched by his appeal.

"You don't want your dear parents troubled by it, I suppose?" she said.

"Yes," said William, "that's it. I don't want my dear parents troubled by it."

She pondered deeply.

"I see," she said. "Well, your consideration for your parents does you credit—er—what is your name?"

"Algernon," said William without a second's hesitation.

The name came in fact almost of its own accord. The Vicar at his last tea party had tried to instil some order into a party that was rapidly degenerating into pandemonium by reading aloud a moral story from which as a child he had derived much profit and enjoyment. Though not received quite in the spirit he would have wished, it had certainly succeeded in riveting his guest's attention. The hero—a child with a singularly beautiful disposition—had been called Algernon. For weeks afterwards "Algernon" had been the favourite epithet of abuse among the youngest set of the village.

"Algernon," she repeated. "A very pretty name, my dear." She was evidently disposed to be friendly to

Algernon. "Much prettier than William, don't you think?"

"Yes," said William with an expression of sheep-like guilelessness.

Then her gaze descended to an excrescence in William's pocket. It was an apple—the last remaining one of his morning's haul that he'd put in his pocket for refreshment on the way to the Vicarage. Suspicion replaced the lady's friendliness.

"What's that?" she said sharply, pointing to it. William was not for a second at a loss. He drew it out of his pocket and held it out to her.

"I was bringing it back to you," he said. "I got him to give it me. It was the only one he had left when he told me about it an' I pled with him——"

"You what?"

"Pled," said William rather impatiently. "Don't you know what pleadin' is? Beggin' a person. Askin' 'em. Well, I pled with him to give it me to bring back to you an' to tell you he was sorry an' to ask you not to—to —to come—come troublin' my dear parents about it."

No words could describe the earnestness of William's voice, the almost imbecile innocence of his regard. The lady's suspicions were entirely lulled. She was more deeply touched than ever.

"I'd like *you* to keep that apple, Algernon," she said generously, "but you must promise not to give it to your brother. Will you promise?"

William slipped back the apple into his pocket and duly promised. He promised with quite a clean conscience. He certainly hadn't any intention of giving the apple to Robert. The lady was still looking at him in a friendly fashion.

"I'm afraid that William must be rather a trouble to you, my dear boy," she said.

"Yes, he is," said William sadly.

"And I'm sure you do your best to improve him."

"Yes," sighed William, "I'm always at it."

"Don't despair, my dear boy," she said, "I expect your example will have its effect in the end. You told him how wrong he'd been this morning, I suppose?"

"Oh yes," said William hastily. "I told him that all right, I pled with him about it."

"You must speak to him again about it. You must tell him how *wrong* trespassing is. Tell him that a person who hasn't a clear idea of *meum* and *tuum* comes to no good in the end. And those apples and fishes are *mine*. I paid for them. Surely he knows that stealing's wrong?"

"I'm always telling him," said William with a sigh, "pleadin' with him an' such-like."

"And can't you persuade him to be clean and tidy as you are?" she went on. "He looked *disgraceful*. I've never seen such a dirty, untidy boy."

"I'm always pleadin' with him about that too," said William earnestly. "I'm always askin' him why he can't be clean and tidy like what I am."

"Dear boy," said the lady, laying a hand affection-ately on his head, "I feel that you and I are going to be great friends. My name is Miss Murgatroyd. Together we must try and improve poor William."

"Yes, an'—an' you—er—won't go troublin' my dear parents?" said William anxiously.

"No, my boy, set your mind at rest. I hope they realise what a dear little protector they have in you."

William, not knowing what else to do, cleared his throat and rolled his eyes. Then to his relief she said, "Well, I must get on now as I have some other calls to pay. Good-bye, Algernon."

"Good-bye," said William.

The interview had been enjoyable but rather difficult.

For one thing it had been a strain to retain his virtuous and mournful expression throughout it. His face, in fact, ached from his virtuous and mournful expression.

The visit to the Vicarage was dull except that the Vicar said to one of his guests who ejaculated "Crumbs!" "Don't use that vulgar expression, my boy. If you wish to express surprise, say simply 'How you do surprise me!' or, if you wish to use stronger language, say 'Dear me!' "—and that somehow or other—no one quite knew how—a quiet spelling game organised by the Vicar became a far from quiet game of Red Indians organised by William, and finally grew so unmanageable that the Vicar retired in despair to his study to calm his mind by reading *The Church Times*, and his wife only restored order by distributing pieces of her treacle cake wholesale, and then packing the guests off home. They rollicked homeward down the lanes ejaculating at intervals "How you do surprise me!" or "Dear me!"—while the Vicar was saying to his wife, "They are very trying, my dear, but I do think that they gain something of refinement and culture from their little visits here."

William, on reaching home, went straight to the shed where his aquarium was kept and counted its inhabitants. It still had only 120. There were 80 more to be got. He must pay another visit to Miss Murgatroyd's pond. In any case, it would be rather dull to leave the situation as it was.

The next morning he set off as usual to The Laburnums carrying his fishing paraphernalia. He spent a very happy morning in the orchard and by the pond. He exercised greater caution than before, frequently turning round to make sure that his enemy was not again approaching from the rear. So cautious was he that he saw his enemy approaching as soon as she entered the orchard, and hastily gathered up his paraphernalia and took to his heels without wasting time on any unnecessary courtesies. She did not pursue him, but her words reached him clearly as he fled across the orchard to his hole.

"I shall *certainly* tell your parents this time, William. I only let you off yesterday for your brother's sake. I shall not let you off again."

William ran down the road without stopping to reply and went straight to the shed where he kept his aquarium, to put in his day's bag and count the whole. He hadn't got as many to-day as he thought he had. Only 20. He must have dropped some in his headlong flight. He'd still 60 to get. He must get those to-morrow. He *must* get those to-morrow. William had a bump of determination that would put most ordinary bumps of determination to shame. He'd decided to have 200 fishes in his aquarium, and it was going to take more than a woman with spectacles and a lot of hair to stop him. He felt quite confident of success. There was still Algernon. The resources of Algernon had surely not yet been exhausted. . . .

After lunch, during which William behaved with an exemplariness that aroused his mother's deepest apprehensions, he went up to perform a drastic toilet in secret. His mother was lying down when he crept downstairs in that state of radiant cleanliness and neatness that served as his disguise. His mother would never have believed that William, alone and unaided, could have wrought such a transformation. Even his ears were clean. He wore his best suit. The tabs of his shining boots were tucked in. His knees were pink from scrubbing.

He walked mincingly up to the front door of The Laburnums and rang the bell. He fixed the housemaid who opened the door with a stern and defiant stare.

"Can I speak to Miss Murgatroyd, please?" he said.

The housemaid, who was a stranger to the village, treated him with more politeness than housemaids were in the habit of treating him, and merely said, "What's your name?"

"W—Algernon Brown," said William.

"Walgernon, did you say?" said the housemaid surprised.

"No," said William irritably, "Algernon."

He was shown into a drawing-room where Miss Murgatroyd received him affably.

"It's Algernon, isn't it?" she said.

"Yes," said William, and added with quite convincing anxiety, "He didn't come this mornin', did he?"

Miss Murgatroyd sighed.

"I'm afraid he did, Algernon," she said.

"I pled with him not to," said William sorrowfully. "I cun't stay with him to stop him comin' 'cause— 'cause an uncle took me up to London. But before I went up I *pled* with him not to come. I told him all you said about trespassin' an'—an'——"

"*Meum* and *tuum?*" supplied Miss Murgatroyd.

"Yes," said William vaguely. "An' I asked him how'd he like people comin' into *his* garden an' stealin' *his* apples and fishes. If *he'd* got a garden, I meant."

"And what did he say to that?"

"He said," said William unblinkingly, "he wun't mind at all. He said he'd *like* people to have a few of his apples an' fishes if he'd got any." He simply couldn't resist saying that.

"But that's very wrong, Algernon," said Miss Murgatroyd earnestly.

William rolled up his eyes.

"Yes. I told him so," he said.

"Did he tell you that I was going to tell his parents?"

William cleared his throat and with a superhuman

effort deepened his expression of virtue till it bordered again on the imbecile.

"Yes," he said, "that's why I came. I came to ask you not to tell them just this once an' I'll do what I can to stop him comin' to-morrow. My—my mother's got a bit of a headache an' so I thought it might worry her hearin' about William takin' your apples an' fishes, but if you'll let him off this once more, I—I'll try 'n' stop him comin' to-morrow. I'll plead with him."

"But don't you think," said Miss Murgatroyd earnestly, "that it would do William *good* to be punished?"

"No," said William with considerable emphasis, "I don't think so. I *reely* don't think so. I think it does him far more good to be pled with."

"Well, I can tell you," said Miss Murgatroyd with great severity, "if I'd got him here now I'd box his ears most soundly. Will you have a piece of cake, Algernon dear?"

He signified that he would and she opened a corner cupboard, brought out a rich currant cake and cut him a generous slice. He ate it, making a violent effort to display that restraint and daintiness that he felt would have characterised the obnoxious Algernon. She watched him fondly.

"You certainly are *very* like your twin," she said at last, but she spoke without any suspicion. "Which did you say has the longer nose?"

William had forgotten, but he said "Me," with such an air of conviction that Miss Murgatroyd believed him and said, "Yes, I see that you have, now you mention it."

"So—so you won't tell 'em about William?" he said when he had finished.

Miss Murgatroyd considered.

"DON'T YOU THINK," SAID MISS MURGATROYD, "THAT IT
WOULD DO WILLIAM GOOD TO BE PUNISHED?"
"NO!" SAID WILLIAM, WITH CONSIDERABLE EMPHASIS.

"Well," she said at last, "just because your consideration for your parents touches me, Algernon, I
won't this once. But you may tell William from me that
the very next time I find him trespassing and stealing on
my property I'll come *straight* and tell his father. Will
you tell him that from me?"

"Yes," said William anxiously, "I'll tell him that from you."

He rose to take his leave. He felt that there was considerable danger in these interviews and that the sooner they were brought to an end the better.

"And what place in London did your uncle take you to, Algernon?" said Miss Murgatroyd.

"The Tower," said William at random.

"And did you like the beefeaters?"

"It was the Tower I said we went to," said William, "not the Zoo."

Then he went home. His mother greeted him with pleased surprise.

"So you've got ready to go to the garden party with me, dear," she said; "how *very* good of you."

William had forgotten that he was going out to a garden party with her, but he hastily assumed his virtuous expression (he was getting really quite adept at assuming his virtuous expression) and, seeing no escape, prepared to set off.

The garden party was as dull as grown-up garden parties usually are, except that the hostess had a son about William's age who took William to show him the shrubbery. William invented several interesting games to play in the shrubbery and they had quite an enjoyable time there, only emerging on receiving imperative messages from their mothers to come out of it at once. William rejoined his mother, but before she could voice her disapproval of his now dishevelled appearance her harassed frown changed to a smile of social greeting. Her hostess was bringing a new-comer to the neighbourhood to introduce to her. The new-comer was Miss Murgatroyd. She greeted Mrs. Brown and then looked uncertainly at William. He wasn't quite dirty enough to be William. On the other hand he wasn't quite clean enough to be Algernon.

"This is—er——?" she began.

"William," said Mrs. Brown.

William met her gaze with an utterly expressionless countenance.

"Your other little boy isn't here, then?" went on Miss Murgatroyd.

"No," said Mrs. Brown, rather surprised to hear the 17-year-old Robert referred to as a "little boy," but assuming that the phrase was meant to be facetious.

"He and I are great friends," went on Miss Murgatroyd coyly; "give him my love, will you?" She glanced coldly at William. "I'm sure you wish that this one would copy him in behaviour and tidiness."

"Yes," said Mrs. Brown with a sigh, "I do, indeed."

Then with a final stern and meaning glance at William, who met it with his blankest stare, she went on in the wake of her hostess to be introduced to someone else.

Mrs. Brown gazed after her in bewilderment.

"How funny," she said. "Robert's never mentioned meeting her. I must ask him."

William had heaved a sigh of relief. It had seemed almost incredible that this meeting should have passed off without betraying his double life, but it had. He knew, however, that it could not be sustained much longer. Miss Murgatroyd would be certain to learn sooner or later of the non-existence of Algernon. The time was short. He must finish his aquarium to-morrow and then let events take their course. He'd only got sixty fishes to catch now.

The next morning he tried to elude his enemy by arriving at an earlier hour than usual. He thought that he had been successful till he was setting off homewards. Then he saw his enemy watching him grimly from an upper window and he knew that all was over. Algernon would be of no avail now. In any case he was getting sick of Algernon. He felt that he'd rather let events take their course than submit himself again to the torturing and degrading process of cleansing and tidying that Algernon's character demanded. And he'd got his fishes. He felt a glow of pride and triumph. He'd got his two hundred fishes. He didn't want ever to go to her silly pond again. And he was sick of her apples. They didn't taste half as nice as they'd tasted at first. He didn't care if he never saw her apples again. Anyway, Ginger was coming home to-day. He was looking forward to showing Ginger his aquarium.

"What are you going to do this afternoon, dear?" said his mother at lunch.

"I'm going to tea to Ginger's," said William.

"Well, you mustn't go till I've seen you're tidy," said Mrs. Brown. "You look dreadful now. Whatever *have* you been doing this morning?"

It was some time before she passed William's appearance as fit for his visit to Ginger's home. Though Ginger's mother saw William daily in his normal state Mrs. Brown had a pathetic trust that, if she sent him inordinately cleaned and tidied for all formal visits, Ginger's mother would come to believe that he really was like that. He set off jauntily enough, but at the bend in the road collided with Miss Murgatroyd. He looked round for escape but saw none. So he assumed a blend of his virtuous and defiant expressions and awaited events.

"William came again this morning, Algernon," said Miss Murgatroyd, "and I'm on my way now to speak to your parents about him. Nothing you say will make any difference to me. I have finally made up my mind. You must come with me, Algernon, and I will tell them how you have tried to spare their feelings."

So because there didn't seem to be anything else to do, William went with her.

Mrs. Brown was in the drawing-room. She received William's return so soon after setting out with something of bewilderment and the visit of this strange neighbour with even more surprise.

"I've come," began Miss Murgatroyd without wasting time on preliminaries, "to complain of your son William." William assumed his blankest expression and avoided his mother's eyes. "He has persistently and deliberately trespassed in my grounds, robbed my orchard and fished in my pond. This dear child of yours," she went on laying her hand affectionately on William's head, "has done all in his power to protect him and to spare your feelings." William, looking blanker still, studiously avoided his mother's astounded gaze. "He begged me not to complain of him to you. He has tried to induce William to stop trespassing in my grounds. He has pleaded with him—pleaded, not pled, Algernon. You are fortunate indeed in having a dear little son like Algernon."

Mrs. Brown's amazement was turning to apprehension.

"Er—just one minute," she said faintly. Then to her relief she saw her husband's figure pass the window. "There's my husband. I'll go——" she went hastily from the room to warn her husband that the visitor suffered from delusions and must presumably be humoured.

William, left alone with the visitor, looked desperately about him. The window was the only possible means of escape.

"I—I think I see William in the garden," he said hoarsely. "I'll go an'——"

He plunged through the window and disappeared.

"THIS DEAR CHILD," SAID MISS MURGATROYD, "HAS DONE
ALL IN HIS POWER TO SPARE YOUR FEELINGS."

MRS. BROWN BLINKED NERVOUSLY. THIS STRANGE NEIGHBOUR
WAS, SHE THOUGHT, SOMEWHAT UNHINGED!

His first thought was to carry the aquarium with its two hundred inhabitants out of the reach of paternal vengeance. Ginger had come to meet him and was waiting at the front gate, so together they carried the precious pail to their stronghold, the old barn. Ginger's excitement and admiration knew no bounds.

"It's the finest one I've ever seen," he said, and added wistfully, "I bet you had some fun getting it."

"Oh yes," said William meaningly, "I had some fun all right," and added, "what sort 'f a holiday 've you had?"

"Rotten," said Ginger mournfully. "Everyone cross. *Everyone*. Didn't come across a single person all the time that wasn't cross."

At this point Douglas joined them. Douglas, too, had just returned from his holiday.

His raptures over William's aquarium were as ardent and genuine as Ginger's. But after about ten minutes, he suddenly remembered something and said to William:

"When I passed your house there was your father and mother and another woman all out in the road looking for you."

"Did they look mad?" said William with interest.

"Yes, they did, rather," said Douglas.

"Well, it doesn't matter much," said William resignedly, "I've got the fishes away all right, anyway. They can't throw them away now. That's the only thing that really matters. An' I'll give 'em time to get over it a bit before I go home."

"How did you get 'em all, William?" said Ginger and Douglas as they hung spell-bound over the pail.

William settled down comfortably by his beloved aquarium and chuckled.

"I'll tell you about it," he said.

Chapter 4

William and the Waxwork Prince

It was William who first heard that a fair was to be held just outside the village, and arranged with the other Outlaws to visit it after school.

"'S goin' to be a jolly fine one," said William, proposing the plan. "There's goin' to be waxworks and all sorts of things."

The Outlaws' spirits rose. Life had been somewhat monotonous of late, and the prospect of a fair enlivened it considerably. The Outlaws loved fairs. They loved to wander from stall to stall, sampling brandy snaps and lemonade and toffee and even whelks. They loved to have a shot at Aunt Sally and Houpla and to ride on the glaring, blaring roundabouts. They liked the big roundabout in the middle best because it made a noise that was little short of diabolical. But these were all more or less familiar joys. Waxworks were a new joy. The Outlaws had never seen waxworks before. The fairs that had visited the village previously had had fat women, and indiarubber men, and dwarfs and giants, and Pictures of Two Hundred Forms of Tortures (the Outlaws had much enjoyed that), and Siamese twins in plenty, but not one had had waxworks. The only drawback to this fair was that it was coming to the village for one night and that it was not the night of the weekly half-holiday at the school which the Outlaws (reluctantly) attended.

"Any *decent* school," said William bitterly, "would give a half-holiday the day a fair's coming."

" 'Stead of which," said Ginger with gloom, "I bet someone keeps us in jus' 'cause they know we want to go to it."

"Well, so long as it isn't ole Markie——" said Henry, and left the sentence unfinished.

There was no need to finish it. Ole Markie was Mr. Markson, the headmaster, and he never "kept in" for less than an hour. His system of "keeping in" was simplicity itself. He sent for the victim to his own form room after school, set him a page of Latin verbs to learn, and then left him and went home to tea. But he made sure that the victim did not go home, by instructing Cramps, the caretaker, to make frequent journeys from his basement lair to the class room to glance through the glass panel in the door and make sure that the victim was intent upon his page of Latin verbs till the hour was up. Markie had never been known to return to the victim himself. He sometimes sent for him to hear the Latin verbs in the morning, but more often he forgot.

Hence Henry's "So long as it isn't ole Markie——"

For Markie's keepings in were always a full hour, and Cramps, the caretaker, was a very conscientious man.

"Just our luck if it is," said Douglas. But none of them, of course, really thought that Fate would allow such a tragedy as that actually to happen. Their pessimism was merely in the nature of a pose and they went on eagerly to discuss the coming fair.

"We'll go straight off the minute school's over," said William. "We won't go home to tea. We'll get off soon as the bell rings. Bet you I'm out first. Then we'll run to the fair ground an' stay there till bed time. Or p'raps jus' a little after bed-time. I bet I'm first in to see the waxworks."

"There's a woman with a beard," said Henry eagerly.

"I've seen one of them," said William scornfully; "they jolly well aren't worth a whole penny. But I bet waxworks 'll be worth a penny."

And all would have been well had it not been for the Hubert Laneites. The origin of the feud between William and his followers and Hubert Lane and his followers was lost in the mists of antiquity, but was none the less ardent on that account. There may have been no actual origin of the feud, even in the mists of antiquity, for Hubert Lane was fat and greedy and spiteful and cowardly, and William and his followers needed no excuse for their hostility to him. In open warfare the Outlaws were easily the better, but Hubert and his followers seldom risked open warfare. Together with his fatness and greediness and spitefulness and cowardice, Hubert had a good share of craftiness, and not infrequently this quality enabled him to score off the Outlaws.

The Outlaws gathered that the Hubert Laneites, too, were intending to visit the fair, but that did not trouble the Outlaws. The precious moments of the fair evening could not be wasted on hostilities that might well be deferred to enliven duller hours.

As William said, "They're all so fat that they won't get there till it's nearly time to go home and they're frightened of the big roundabout—an' the pull-out toffee makes them sick so they won't bother *us* much."

*   *   *

The day of the fair was fine. The Outlaws felt that fate was on their side. A wet fair day is of course enjoyable but not so enjoyable as a fine fair day.

Somehow or other the Outlaws got through the lessons before "rec." They did not shine in them but they got through them. Douglas, in giving up the answer to a sum, absently wrote that a woodcutter cutting down three trees a day would cut down twenty-three wax-works in a week; and Ginger, being asked the meaning of "circa," absently replied "roundabout," which, however, was so nearly right that he escaped reproof. And so things went quite well till "rec." But at "rec." the tragedy happened.

Hubert Lane was passing the open door of William's form room and, meeting William's eye, he contorted his pale, fat face into a grimace of ridicule and defiance that William found intolerable. Hubert did this in the comfortable knowledge that the headmaster, who was walking just behind him, would not see his grimace, but would probably be a witness to whatever reprisals William might think fit to take. The result exceeded his wildest hopes. William, infuriated by his enemy's impudence, seized the weapon nearest to hand, which happened to be his school satchel, and hurled it. It missed Hubert, but caught the headmaster very neatly on the face, completely enveloping it for a second or two before it fell to the ground.

There was a horrible silence, during which William's prayers that the end of the world might now take place remained unanswered. Then Ole Markie shot out a furious hand in William's direction and roared: "Did you throw that?"

William, thinking that he might as well go down with colours flying, assumed a debonair expression as he said gaily, "Yes, sir."

Ole Markie gazed at him wistfully for a few minutes, but he happened to be suffering from a rather severe attack of arthritis in his right arm, so he only roared,

"Stay in an hour after school," and passed on his majestic way growling.

The horror of the Outlaws was indescribable. Without William, their leader, the visit to the fair would lack all savour. There seemed to be nothing to do, however, but to bow to fate, and so the three remaining Outlaws set off disconsolately for the fair after tea, while William, still debonair, took his seat in the headmaster's room before a page of Latin verbs.

"Doesn't seem much fun without William," said Ginger dejectedly, as they trudged along the country road.

"We can buy him something," said Henry.

"What good's *that?*" said Ginger, annoyed by the inadequacy of this proposal. " 'S not the things you *buy* at the fair, it's the *fair* that's the fun."

"We can tell him all about it," said Henry, still trying to put a good face on the matter.

"Oh, shut up," said Ginger in disgust.

Ginger had an uncomfortable feeling that, were his and William's positions reversed, William would have managed somehow to free him. He felt that, as William's trusted lieutenant, the responsibility of releasing William from durance vile devolved upon him. And yet he couldn't think of any way of doing it.

They entered the fair ground. It was as if somehow William's absence had affected even the fair. There didn't seem to be any "go" in it at all. They wandered round in silence for a few minutes and Henry tried to enliven the proceedings by buying a pennyworth of pull-out toffee, but somehow it didn't seem to taste as it had tasted when William was with them.

"Shall we go on the roundabout?" said Douglas without much enthusiasm.

Ginger looked at the roundabout. It was a very

satisfying roundabout—all noise and glare and colour, but somehow it didn't satisfy Ginger. When he looked at it he didn't see the gilt and silver and the coloured life-sized negroes with tambourines and the looking-glass panels. He saw William sitting in old Markie's room before a page of Latin verbs.

"Oh, no," he said dispiritedly, "we'll try it later."

"Well, let's go'n' look at this waxwork show," said Douglas in a voice which was unconvincingly bright and cheerful.

They wandered round to the waxwork tent. But it was as unsatisfying as everything else. It wasn't even open yet. A man stood on a platform outside the closed door of the tent announcing vociferously that the show would be open in half an hour's time. The closed door whetted the Outlaws' curiosity.

"I bet that if we go round to the back and look under the tent we could see it all," said Henry, his spirits rising.

So they went round to the back, lay down on the grass, and cautiously raised the flap of the tent. And Henry had been right. They could see it all beautifully. The inside of the tent was fortunately empty of human beings, so they could feast their eyes on the dazzling array of historical figures that met their gaze. There was Henry the Eighth in red tights and a spangled cloak. There was Guy Fawkes wearing a black mask and holding a barrel of gunpowder. There was Mary Queen of Scots in a very elaborately anachronistic crinoline with an executioner who carried a real axe. There was Perkin Warbeck in a suit of armour. There was Rufus wearing a red beard and an arrow through his heart. And there were the little princes in the Tower in black velvet suits and much befeathered hats.

"Crumbs!" gasped Douglas, "they're fine, aren't they? I bet they're *exactly* like what the real ones were.

They look jus' as if they were, anyway. I say, William would like to see 'em, wouldn't he?"

He addressed this remark to Ginger. Ginger was staring at the nearest little prince in the Tower, open-mouthed, open-eyed. An idea had come to Ginger—an idea so daring that for a minute it took away his breath. Then:

"I—I've *got* it!" he said hoarsely.

"What?" said the other Outlaws and gathered round while he told them. Then they said "Crumbs!" in awe-stricken whispers.

*   *   *

Very, very cautiously they approached one of the little princes in the Tower. Then they stopped and looked around. The tent was still empty. The voice of the showman could be heard outside, still vociferously informing the world that the show would be open in half an hour's time. Very gently, very cautiously, they lifted the little prince, Ginger holding his head and Douglas his feet, and carried him under the flap of the tent. Still no one was about. They laid him on the grass.

"He's about William's size, isn't he?" said Ginger.

They all considered him carefully and agreed that he was.

Then they rolled him up in their overcoats and carried him through the hedge and along the road towards the school. Fortune favoured them. They met only a few people and those few people took little or no interest in them. The identity of the little prince was completely concealed by his covering.

When they reached the school, Ginger left Douglas and Henry and, going round to the front door, rang the bell as loudly as he could. Cramps, a depressed-looking individual with long whiskers, came to answer it.

Meanwhile Douglas and Henry were tapping gently at the window of the headmaster's form room where William was sitting before a Latin grammar (upside down) and imagining himself at the fair with such vividness that when their signal roused him it seemed almost incredible to him that he was still in school.

He came to the window, and with a cautious glance at the glass panel in the door said:

"Well, what's it like?"

" 'S all right," said Douglas.

"What 've you got there?" said William, leaning further out and looking with interest at their overcoat-shrouded burden.

Without a word they unwrapped the little prince. The little prince smirked his waxen smirk at William. William glared his freckled and ferocious glare at the little prince.

"What *ever*——?" he gasped.

"It's Ginger's idea," said Douglas with apprehension and admiration mingled in his voice. "It's all Ginger's idea. We didn't stop to think. We jus' did it. It *oughter* turn out all right but——" Evidently the sheer daring of the idea was beginning to weigh on Douglas. It was Douglas who possessed the least share of that glorious optimism for which the Outlaws were famous.

"But what *is* it?" said William.

They revealed Ginger's daring plan to him. William's eyes gleamed. It was a plan after William's own heart.

In a few minutes the little prince, garbed now in William's tweed suit, was propped up at a desk before a Latin grammar, his elbows resting on the desk, his head on his hands, while William was hastily drawing Henry's overcoat over a rather skimpy black velvet suit with a lace collar, and crushing the black velvet feathered cap into his pocket. They crept down to the road and Henry gave the whistle that was to inform Ginger that the coast was clear. Ginger, who had been leading the grumbling but conscientious caretaker round cloak-rooms and class-rooms in a search for an alleged lost purse, heard the signal with relief. It had been rather a strain drawing out the search to the required length, going from room to room and gazing intently at empty spaces of floor and cupboard as if he thought that if he stared long enough the purse would materialise before his eyes.

"Well, I don't know," he said to the grumbling but conscientious caretaker. "Now I come to think of it I jus' *may've* lost it at home. I'd better go'n' see before I trouble you any more."

"That's just like you boys," said the caretaker, "always losing your things and saying you left them in school and in the end finding them at home all the time. Seems to me you boys never will learn sense. Giving such a lot of trouble all round. I've got one of you now upstairs in Mr. Markson's room and it's time I went up again to see he wasn't up to any of his tricks. Full of tricks you boys are. It's one person's work looking after each one of you. Amazing to me that you don't learn more sense."

Ginger murmured perfunctory apology and took a hasty departure.

The caretaker went round to Mr. Markson's class-room and glanced anxiously through the glass panel. Then he nodded to himself, reassured. It was all right. The little devil was still there, sitting at his desk and learning his Latin verbs. The caretaker had been rather anxious at being left in charge of this particular little devil because he knew that he was a more devilish little devil than most of the little devils, but he seemed to be turning out quite harmless on this occasion. Satisfied, the caretaker took himself back to his own quarters.

"WHAT ON EARTH HAVE YOU GOT THERE?" WILLIAM GASPED.

Meanwhile, William, clutching Henry's overcoat tightly round him to hide his black velvet suit and lace collar, was walking down the road with his followers. Ginger was jauntily elaborating his plan. Its success so far had gone to his head.

"An' you know ole Markie *never* goes back, so it'll be all right. You can have a good look round an' we'll be back by the end of the hour an' it'll be all right an' it

"IT'S GINGER'S IDEA," SAID DOUGLAS; "IT'S ALL GINGER'S
IDEA. WE DIDN'T STOP TO THINK! WE JUS' DID IT!"

looks *jus'* like you from the door."

"I think it was *jolly* clever of you to think of it," said
William generously, giving honour where honour was
due, then, opening the overcoat to glance down at his
costume, added dispassionately, "Queer sort of clothes
it wears."

"We got in by a hole in the tent," said Ginger. "They're jolly fine, the others. You'll like 'em. There's Guy Fawkes."

"P'raps William 'd better not go in," said Douglas cautiously. "If anyone happened to see his suit there'd be an awful fuss. They might take us to prison for stealing."

"We didn't steal anything," said Ginger hotly, "we only borrowed it. Well, there's no law against borrowing, is there?"

"No, but I think William'd better not go into the waxworks," persisted Douglas. "There'd be a fuss if they saw he was wearing their clothes. He can go round the stalls and go on the roundabout."

"Oh, *can* I?" said William with heavy sarcasm. "*Thanks*. Thanks *awfully*. Well, let *me* tell *you*, I'm jolly well *going* to go to the waxworks." Suddenly he stopped and drew in his breath. An inspiration had just visited him. "Tell you what?" he said breathlessly. "I'll go an' *be* a waxwork. What about that? I bet I'd make a fine one. I bet it would be fun. I'll go an' *be* a waxwork. Then I'll see 'em all right with no one saying I stole anything. An' it'll be fun standing there with all the people lookin' at me an' listenin' to what they say. I bet I can do it all right. I've got its hat here."

The suggestion rather took the Outlaws' breath away. William, having started on the path of adventure, never seemed to know when to stop.

"I bet I make a jolly good waxwork," he went on self-admiringly. "I bet that no one spots I'm not a real one. I'm wearing its clothes so it seems silly not to have a try at what I can do at being a waxwork. And then we can have a waxwork show of our own. . . ."

Douglas murmured disapprovingly, "Well, I bet you'll go an' make a mess of it," but Ginger and Henry, fired by William's enthusiasm, said: "All right. Go on and have a try. I bet they spot you're not a real one. We'll come in and watch you. It'll be fun."

They went round to the back of the tent, lay on the ground and cautiously lifted up the back flap. The inside was still empty of human beings. A little prince in the Tower stood solitary with an empty space beside him. Evidently no one had noticed his brother's disappearance. From outside came the raucous voice of the showman informing the world that the show would open in four minutes *honly* from now.

William dropped his overcoat and, holding his feathered head-dress in his hand, slipped under the tent flap into the tent. There he put on his feathered velvet hat and took his place in the empty space next to the solitary prince, faithfully copying its attitude, one leg slightly forward, hands down by his side. He was only just in time. As he took his stand with a last wink at Ginger's face, just visible under the flap of the tent, the showman announced the show open and a gaping crowd surged in the wake of a bored-looking youth with a straw in his mouth. The bored-looking youth had been hired by the showman to introduce the exhibits to the public while the showman remained outside and tried to draw the public in by sheer lung power.

"Ladies and gentlemen, walk *hup* and see the finest show of waxworks in the world. Here for one night only, ladies and gentlemen. Shown before hall the crowned 'eads of Europe. Wonderful historical panorama. Hentertaining and hinstructive. Best sixpennyworth of hentertainment and hinstruction of its kind to be found hanywhere. Walk *hup*, ladies and gentlemen. Walk *hup!* Walk *hup!* WALK HUP"

The bored-looking youth did not know much about the waxworks and cared less. He had been merely told to announce their names. He was a local youth and had not seen them before. His eye flickered over William with the same careless contempt with which it flickered over Perkin Warbeck and Rufus and Mary Queen of Scots.

William stood rather in a fortunately dark corner. His velvet-feathered hat threw a shadow over his face. The rope that kept the spectators from approaching too near was about five feet away from him. Both the bored-looking youth and the spectators accepted him without suspicion.

"Li'l' princes crulely murdered in the Tahr," announced the bored-looking youth monotonously through his straw.

The crowd of spectators inspected William and his companion with interest.

"Why do they have one pretty one and one ugly one, mother?" piped the youngest spectator. "I like that one," pointing to the waxwork, "but," pointing to William, "I don't like that one. Why did they get such a *nugly* one?"

"Perhaps they couldn't afford two pretty ones, dear," said the youngest spectator's mother, "and they got this one cheap."

"Yes," said the youngest spectator, satisfied. "I expect they got it *very* cheap."

And they passed on to Mary Queen of Scots.

A negligent youth in plus-fours now approached. He had brought with him a party of which he was evidently the admired centre, and spoke languidly with the accent that is generally supposed to hail from Oxford. He took up his stand just in front of William and began to hold forth to the admiring group.

"Of carse," he said, "to anyone who knows anything about anatomy these things are frightfully amusing. Doing medicine, of carse, one knows anatomy from A to

Z. These models are made without any regard to anatomy at all. Look at that one, for instance." He pointed languidly at William. "It's quite absurd to anyone who knows anything about anatomy. Legs and arms entirely wrong. Out of proportion, set at wrong angles, and—well, the muscles that *are* represented are quite wrong ones. For instance," he pointed to William's leg, so nearly touching it that it was all William could do not to flinch, "you can see that they've made an attempt to reproduce a muscle just heah in the moulding of the figure, but the amusin' thing is that there *is* no muscle just heah in a human being's leg. Ha, ha! Most amusin', by Jove!"

And he passed on to Perkin Warbeck.

William was already tired of being a waxwork. The lace collar tickled his neck and the feather in his hat tickled his ear and he was fighting against an almost irresistible temptation to scratch both. Also he'd got pins and needles in his arm and something was crawling up his leg. More than that, it was galling to anyone of William's proud spirit to have to listen meekly to personal abuse without retaliating.

He breathed hard when two women stood and stared at him for some minutes in silence and then one of them said dispassionately, "No wonder they murdered 'im if 'e looked like that."

It was just after that that Hubert Lane and his friends entered the tent. They glanced round at the other waxworks without much interest, but when they came to the little princes in the Tower their interest seemed to quicken.

Hubert pointed to William and said excitedly:

"I say, look at that one. Who does he remind you of?"

His companions looked long and searchingly at William's feather-shadowed face and then began to giggle.

"William Brown!" they said, "he! he! It *is* a bit like him."

"Poor old William," said Hubert. "We'll tell him to-morrow. We'll tell him there was a waxwork jus' like him."

"Poor ole William," repeated his companions, "swotting Latin verbs instead of coming to the fair. It was a joke, wasn't it, Hubert?"

They giggled together. There came a gleam to the eye of the little prince in the Tower. Then one of Hubert's followers leant forward and said in jeering challenge to the little prince in the Tower:

"Hello, William! Hello, poor ole William Brown. Swotting Latin verbs instead of coming to the fair. Poor ole William Brown."

It was an exquisite jest to the Hubert Laneites to bait this waxwork, which resembled William Brown, to its face as they dared not bait William Brown himself.

"Hello, silly ole William Brown. Catch me if you can, William Brown. Yah! William Brown! Who's got to stay in swotting Latin verbs instead of going to the fair? Yah! Yah! Yah! Little Lord Fauntleroy."

This last taunt was more than William's proud spirit could brook. In a second he had leapt over the rope and was pursuing his amazed foes to the entrance of the tent and across the fair ground. The Hubert Laneites, so startled as hardly able to believe the evidence of their senses, were yet not too paralysed by fear to turn to flee before this avenging fury. Even William's lace collar and feathered hat did not make him at that moment less terrible in their eyes.

The spectators stood motionless and the straw drop-ped from the mouth of the bored-looking youth. One of the waxworks had suddenly come to life, leapt over the rope, and fled headlong out of the tent. The youngest spectator suddenly pointed to Henry the Eighth and said, "*He's* beginning to move, too. I *sor* him movin'. They're *all* comin' alive," and the whole body of spectators suddenly made a rush for the doorway.

The people in the fair ground also stood spell-bound with astonishment. They had seen no waxwork come to life, but they had seen a boy strangely attired in a black velvet suit and lace collar and a black velvet feathered hat dashing across the ground in fierce pursuit of a little crowd of normally attired boys. The waxwork show spectators followed. The showman and the bored-looking youth followed them. The youth had shed his boredom with his straw and was leaping along, uttering shrill cries of excitement. At the end of the fair ground the showman gave up the chase and returned (still running) to his tent. It had perhaps occurred to him that what had happened to one might happen to another, and he had horrible mental visions of Guy Fawkes with his gunpowder, or the executioner with his axe, running amok through the fair ground. The bored-looking youth followed him, eager to be in at the coming to life of the next waxwork. The Outlaws, who had been standing in a little crowd at the door of the tent where they could just see William, followed in the wake of William's strange figure across the fair ground. Outside the fair ground William forgot the Hubert Laneites and the uncontrollable fury that had sent him after them. He found himself in a public road wearing a humiliating costume that would attract scorn and ridicule from all beholders, and thought only of escaping from the public gaze. He left the Hubert Laneites to go panting and puffing but unpursued down the lane that led to Hubert's home, while he turned into a lane and ran by devious ways till he reached the barn which was the Outlaws' meeting place. His pursuers had given up the chase (William was

**WILLIAM TRIED HIS UTMOST TO LOOK UNCONCERNED, BUT A
GLEAM CAME INTO HIS EYE.**

a fleet runner), but the Outlaws had made straight for
the old barn knowing that William would take refuge
there. They found him, purple-faced and panting. He
glared at them furiously. His mental picture of his
appearance was a horrible one. That "Little Lord
Fauntleroy" rankled deeply. But to his relief the
Outlaws did not collapse upon each other in helpless
mirth. They looked at him gloomily.

"I *said* you'd make a mess of it," said Douglas.

"YAH! YAH! YAH!" JEERED HUBERT LANE. "LITTLE LORD
FAUNTLEROY!"

"Oh, shut up," said William fiercely. "I'm jolly well
goin' to get into some decent clothes." He glanced
coldly at Ginger. "Can't think what made you think of a
thing like this."

Ginger defended himself with spirit.

"It'd have been all right if you'd kept the overcoat on
'stead of messin' the whole thing up pretendin' to be a
waxwork."

But William was too much depressed to argue.

Moreover, Henry had lent him his overcoat again and the overcoat had restored something of his self-respect. At least the black velvet suit and lace collar that had earned him the opprobrious taunt were no longer visible.

"Well, I'm goin' back to get my own clothes now," said William, and added earnestly, "I'd almost sooner go *nakid* than wear things like these."

"The hour 'll be up now," said Henry soothingly, "it'll be all right. We'll jus' go an' get it an'—an' "- —tamely—"take it back an'——"

The difficulties of the situation were becoming more and more evident to them at every minute. The excitement and admiration that had greeted Ginger's conception of the plan were paling into apprehension and disapproval. Ginger, feeling that his popularity was on the wane, said spiritedly:

"Well, *he* messed it all up pretendin' to be a waxwork. It was a jolly good plan before *he* started messin' it up."

"Oh, shut up and come on," said William, hugging Henry's overcoat around him and fiercely pushing down a bit of the lace collar that showed above it. "Come on and let's get back to my clothes. I'm *sick* of these things. I tell you I'd sooner go *nakid*."

They made their way down to the main road and walked silently towards the school.

A man was walking in front of them. So depressed were they that at first they did not recognise him. Then suddenly something familiar in his gait made Ginger stand rigid and draw in his breath.

"Crumbs!" he breathed. "Ole Markie!"

The Outlaws stared aghast at the figure that was striding on ahead of them towards the school.

"He *can't*——" gasped William.

"*Shurely* he isn't——" gasped Ginger.

"He *never* has before——" gasped Douglas.

"Well, of all the——" gasped Henry.

But they could do nothing but walk on behind him, apprehensive and aghast.

The school gates were now in sight.

"P'raps he's jus' goin' for a walk," suggested Henry hoarsely. "P'raps——"

His sentence faded away.

Mr. Markson had turned in at the school gates.

"Crumbs!" breathed all the Outlaws in horror.

"Quick!" said William breathlessly, "let's run round to the window. P'raps we'll jus' be in time——"

They ran round to the window. But they weren't just in time. Already Mr. Markson was entering the door of his class-room. The waxwork still sat as they had left it, garbed in William's tweed suit, propped up at the desk, its head on its hands, before an open Latin grammar. Its face was hidden by its hands and the sleeves of its suit.

The Outlaws crouched in the bushes just outside the open window and watched and listened, horror-struck.

"Well, my boy," said Mr. Markson, "have you learnt it?"

His boy continued to pore over the Latin grammar without moving or replying.

Mr. Markson raised his voice. "I'll—er—hear you now, my boy. You've had your hour."

Still the figure did not move. Mr. Markson went across the room and touched its shoulder.

"Don't you hear me, my boy?" he said.

The figure collapsed on to the desk, head down, arms outstretched, as if abandoning itself to despair.

Mr. Markson (who was rather short-sighted) was evidently surprised and distressed at this.

"Come, come, my boy," he said. "No need to despair like that. No need at all. If you can say your verbs properly no more will be said about the matter. Very childish to behave like this. Be a man. Be a man."

The figure refused to be a man. It remained in its tragic attitude of despair, its head on the desk, its arms outspread.

Mr. Markson, still surprised and distressed, approached it and laid his hand again on its shoulder. It collapsed in a heap on the floor. Mr. Markson rushed to the door and called loudly for the caretaker, "Cramps! Cramps! Ring up for the doctor at once and bring some water to my class-room. There's a boy here fainted."

Then he approached the prostrate figure and lifted it carefully in his arms. . . .

The Outlaws, of course, should have disappeared before that, but horror and surprise had literally deprived them of the power of movement, and when Mr. Markson had laid down his burden with considerably less tenderness than he had shown in raising it, and had looked around him, his eye ablaze with lust for vengeance, the first object it fell on was William, standing outside the window, his eyes and mouth wide open, his unbuttoned overcoat disclosing a black velvet suit and a lace collar. The power of movement returned to William, but too late. With surprising agility Mr. Markson had flung himself across the room and through the open window and his hand closed on William's neck just as William's power of movement was returning.

* * *

The crisis was over. The Outlaws assembled again in the old barn to discuss the matter. They had taken back the waxwork to its proprietor, prepared for a scene almost as unpleasant as the one in which William and Mr. Markson had played the leading parts. But the proprietor of the waxwork show was unexpectedly benign. His waxwork show was being an unprecedented success. Queues stood half-way down the fair ground waiting to come in. Various rumours were afloat about it. One was to the effect that one of the waxworks was alive and that you got £10 if you guessed which one it was. Another was that they all came miraculously to life every twenty minutes and if you were lucky you might catch them at it. It was generally understood that even if neither of these things were true, there was something unusual about the waxwork show and that it should not be missed. The showman had doubled his entrance fee and still they came. The bored-looking youth (now strawless and no longer bored) was giving wildly exaggerated accounts of the coming to life of the Little Prince in the Tower. A woman in very large spectacles and a dress of hand-woven tweed was saying that she could tell by the atmosphere that elementals were at work here and that someone ought to send for the Psychical Research Society.

The showman examined his figure, found it uninjured and dismissed the Outlaws with a "You try it on again, my boys, and you'll hear something."

They didn't feel like trying it on again, however. They'd heard something already.

They went to the old barn to discuss the affair in all its aspects.

Ginger, Henry and Douglas sat on the ground. William, of his own choice, stood, for Mr. Markson, sacrificing himself to the noble cause of discipline, had deliberately brought on one of the worst attacks of arthritis in his right arm he'd had for a long time.

"Well, what I say about it is," said William, "that in spite of the crule way people treat boys nowadays I'd sooner live nowadays than then. I'd sooner be treated in the crule way they treat boys nowadays jus' when it happens than have to wear collars that tickle your neck and feathers that tickle your face all the time. Well, that's what I think anyway, and I oughter know; I've tried both."

Chapter 5

William the Showman

"I think," said William, "that it's time we did something a little more exciting than some of the things we've been doing lately."

"They seem exciting enough to *me!*" retorted Ginger.

"Oh yes," admitted William, "they're excitin' in a *way* all right, but they're the sort of thing we've always done. What we want is somethin' *new*. You know. Somethin' we've never done before." "Yes," said Douglas sardonically, "some of your things are a bit *too* excitin' for us. That time you had greyhound racin' with Jumble, an' that time you pretended to be a waxwork."

"Now *that's* a thing we've never done an' I've always thought it would be nice to do," said William, "have a waxwork show. What about havin' a waxwork show? It's quite a long time since we had any sort of a show. People 'll be thinkin' we can't think of anythin' else to do an' I shun't like people to get thinkin' things like that about us."

"You mean have a waxwork show an' let people come an' watch it?" said Henry with growing interest.

"Make 'em pay, of course," said William; "we'll have it in aid of somethin', same as grown-ups do."

"In aid of us," suggested Ginger.

"No, we can't do that," said Douglas; "they keep a bit for expenses, but they give the rest to something."

"The worst of givin' money to things," said William slowly, "is that one doesn't get anythin' out of it oneself. I'd like it if we could find a way of givin' money to somethin' an' still gettin' somethin' out of it ourselves."

"Well, we can't," said Ginger; "we've jus' got to choose somethin' to give it to and give it to it."

"What'll we give it to?"

"Oh, there's lots of things to give it to. Societies they call 'em. Lookin' after old people an' givin' socks to fishermen—that sort of thing."

"I don't feel as if I could get up much interest in anythin' like that," said William. "All the old people I know can look after themselves a jolly sight too well an' I don't see what fishermen want with socks."

"Well, those aren't the only two," said Ginger irritably; "there's heaps more. There's one for sendin' children to the sea."

"I've always wanted to go to sea," said William with interest, "but I didn't know there was a Society——"

"Not that sort of goin' to sea," said Ginger. "Goin' to the seaside, I mean."

"Well, I never see why people want to go to the seaside," said William. "Nothin' but sand. I jolly well get fed up with sand in a day. And the water tastes nasty an' everyone's cross. Well, I bet we don't give any money to any of *those*. What others are there?"

"There's—oh, there's lots, but I don't remember 'em. I know that one of 'em belongs to Mr. Peters, at The Elms, you know. It's somethin' for old people, or children, or animals, or fishermen, or somethin': I know he goes round gettin' money for it."

"We'll give it to that one, then," said William finally; "then he'll have to let us play in his shrubbery 'stead of chasin' us out same as he does now. Yes, I bet that would be a very good Socity to give it to. We'll keep half the money ourselves for expenses, an' give half to Mr. Peters for his Socity to let us play in his shrubbery. Don't you all think so?"

"Oh yes," said Douglas sarcastically, "let's give 'em half. Half of nothin's nothin'. Let's give 'em nothin'. If *you* think anyone's goin' to pay *money*—well, think of all the other things we've done, that's all. When 've we ever made any *money*?"

"Oh, shut up!" said William wearily, "we never should for all you do to help, that's *cert'nly* true. Why, I tell you we've never *done* a waxwork show before. I bet we'll make heaps of money with a waxwork show."

"Well, what'd we have to do?"

"Oh, jus' dress up as people, that's all. People in history. Then I'll make a speech about you an' say you're made of wax. An' you've not gotter do anythin' but jus' stand starin' in front of you an' not movin'. It's quite easy; you jus' stand starin' in front of you and not movin' an' they jus' pay money an' look at you."

"What history people?" said Ginger.

"Oh, any," said William carelessly.

"We haven't got any history people's clothes," objected Douglas.

"Haven't you got *any* sense?" said William irritably. "Cert'nly to hear you talk anyone 'd *think* you hadn't. *Anyone* can make up history people's clothes. History people jus' wore tablecloths and long stockings an' funny things on their heads. Anyone c'n get those. You can make crowns out of cardboard for kings, an' other people wore waste-paper baskets or—well, p'raps not saucepans," ended William thoughtfully, remembering an occasion when a saucepan had slipped down over his head during his rendering of a dramatic part in a play and refused to be removed. "No—p'raps jus' waste-paper baskets an' crowns made of cardboard. An' we'll put on beards an' whiskers an' things with cork an' then we'll look *jus'* like history people."

"What history people shall we be?" said Ginger.

They were passing the gate of the Hall. The Hall had lately been taken by a famous actress and according to rumours fabulous sums had been spent upon its redecoration. The actress and her little girl had only come into residence the week before and as yet the neighbourhood had seen little of them. The Outlaws glanced up at the chimneys that could be seen through the trees.

"Pity it's a girl," said William dispassionately, "they're never any use."

As they reached the gate, a little girl about the Outlaws' age, accompanied by a governess, was turning into it. She was a very pretty little girl, but William was immune against the wiles of feminine charm. He looked at her scornfully. She looked at him with interest. They passed each other. She went into the gate with the governess. When William had gone a few yards he looked back. He could still see her. She too was looking back. He pulled a face at her. She did not burst into tears or turn haughtily away as he expected her to do. Instead she pulled a face back at him—a face so perfect in its suddenly assumed hideousness that William was startled into relaxing his own efforts.

"Soppy-looking kid," said Ginger who had not noticed William's facial challenge and its spirited acceptance.

"No, she isn't," said William; "she's all right," and added hastily, "all right for a girl, of course, I mean."

*   *   *

The Outlaws met in the old barn to discuss the waxwork show in greater detail.

"We've gotter think of famous history people," said William.

"All right," said Ginger, "you start."

"Oh, there's heaps of 'em," said William carelessly, "you jus' say one or two."

"S'pose you jus' say one or two first," said Ginger.

"Anyone 'd think," said William, "hearin' you talk, that you thought I di'n' *know* any history people."

"I don' think you do," said Ginger simply.

After an exhilarating but indeterminate scuffle the argument was resumed.

"Well, I'll say one if you'll say one," said William.

"Alfred and the cakes," said Ginger, whose brain had been stimulated by the contest.

"That one sounds all right," said William carelessly, secretly rather impressed.

"Well, now you say one," challenged Ginger.

William's brain still remained empty of historical characters.

"Robinson Crusoe," he said at last uncertainly.

Ginger had a vague impression that there was something wrong with this, but did not like to commit himself too definitely.

"I think we'd better stick to English history people," he said; "he was a foreigner."

"All right," said William, and with a burst of inspiration, "what about Bruce?"

"Who was Bruce?" said Ginger suspiciously.

"It tells about him in copy-books," said William vaguely. "He kept spiders."

"Well, I've kept spiders myself," said Ginger, "but they aren't very interestin'. They don't turn into anythin'. I don't think much of an history person what only kept spiders."

"All right," said William, annoyed, "think of another yourself then."

He was rather relieved thus to be able to detach himself with dignity from further historical research.

"Oh, well, there's lots of 'em," said Ginger, "there's all the kings such as Charles an' George——"

"What did they do?" challenged William, stung by Ginger's academic manner.

"They fought in wars an' went to the Crusades——"

"What were they?"

"Crusades?" said Ginger vaguely. "Oh, they were jus' things people went to wearin' armour an' such-like. There wasn't much goin' on at home those days, you see. It was before cinemas an' things were invented. They'd gotter do somethin'."

"Well, we're not much nearer a waxwork show," said William irritably (he objected to being taught history by Ginger), " 'cept Alfred and the cakes. . . . Oh, an' I suppose we can have King George goin' to the Crusades. Wasn't there somethin' about a dragon too? I seem to think that King George did somethin' to a dragon."

"No," said Ginger, "we'd better leave that part out. We haven't anyone to be a dragon, anyway. We'll just have him goin' to the Crusades in armour."

"That'll be quite easy," said William thoughtfully, "trays an' things tied round him an' a saucepan on his head. I won't be him," he added hastily, "I'm the showman. Besides, I never have any luck with saucepans. They always seem too big when they're on my head an' then when they've slipped down over my face they seem too small. They nearly tore off all the front of my face gettin' the last one off. I went on feeling the feeling of it for ever so long afterwards. Well, then, we'll have Alfred and the cakes an' King George goin' off to the Crusades. What did King Charles do? Somethin' about oak trees, wasn't it?"

"He was killed," said Ginger.

"I bet he wasn't," challenged William, with spirit, "I bet it was somethin' to do with oak trees."

"Oh, well, never mind," said Ginger wearily. Ginger was tired of historical discussions, and in any case felt rather unsure of his ground. "It doesn't much matter what they did. We've only gotter dress up as them, anyway. It doesn't matter what you say about 'em either. No one'll know any different whatever you say."

"How d'you know?" said William. "Sometimes they do. Sometimes there's someone there that knows things an' keeps on contradictin' you."

"Smack his head," said Ginger simply, "or else learn up the history first so's no one can contradict you."

"There's so many pages out of my history book," said William, "it makes it more muddlin' readin' it than not readin' it. I'd better not start 'em all fightin' either. There always seems to be trouble when everyone starts fightin'. You know, their mothers all comin' round to tell your father afterwards. No, if anyone starts contradictin' me I'll jus' *reason* with 'em. I'm good at reasonin'!"

"Well, then, it's nearly settled, isn't it? You the showman an' Douglas Alfred and the cakes. He can easy get some cakes an' burn 'em. An' me King George goin' to the Crusades in tin trays and things. An' Henry King Charles. It ought to be all right. An' how much shall we charge?"

"I wonder if they'd pay a penny?" said William hopefully.

"You *bet* they won't," said Ginger bitterly. "I've never met such a mean lot of people as the lot of people that lives about here. I bet they'll only pay a half-penny. Or a farthin'. I bet they try to get in for a farthin', or a cigarette card. An' bring ones you've got at that."

But subsequent enquiries among the Outlaws' contemporaries elicited the fact that the potential patrons of the show had no intention of paying anything at all. They were willing to come if the show was free and they were equally willing to stay away if entrance fee was charged. William reasoned with them.

"Kin'ly tell me," he said with dignity, "anyone else what gives shows free an' without people havin' to pay money to go in."

"Kin'ly tell us," retorted the potential patrons, "anyone else what gives such rotten shows as you do."

The argument then shifted from the plane of reason to the physical plane, and the main problem was forgotten in the exhilaration of the contest. It was, of course, William who had a brilliant idea next day.

"Tell you what," he said to the Outlaws, "tell you *what*, let's give it free the first day and charge the second day an' be diff'rent history people the second day. See? They'll have enjoyed it so much the first day that they'll all want to come the second day an' pay money."

The others were not quite so optimistic as William, but his plan was, as usual, adopted. As William said, "Anyway it'll be fun doin' it twice as diff'rent people."

* * *

William was a glorious sight as showman. He wore his red Indian costume and had corked a luxuriant moustache and an imperial upon his face. He wore also a pair of horn-rimmed spectacles that for no particular reason generally formed part of any character he impersonated.

Douglas as Alfred was slightly unpopular. Ginger, by the exercise of much skill and ingenuity, had managed to abstract two slightly burnt cakes from the cook's last batch. Douglas had turned up at the rehearsals with these and they had given an atmosphere of verisimilitude to the whole affair that had greatly impressed the others. It was annoying therefore to find on the day of the performance that Douglas had been overcome with hunger in the early morning and had eaten them. Ginger, after having tried without success to abstract two more, had brought two potatoes to take their place, but it was felt that the potatoes were less convincing, and Douglas, despite his gorgeous appearance, was under a cloud. He wore a long pair of white silk stockings (borrowed by him from his sister without her knowledge), and over these his trousers were rolled up as far as they would go. On the upper part of his person he wore a mauve jumper (also borrowed from his sister). On his head he wore a waste-paper basket of rather a gaudy pattern and at his eye a monocle, which belonged to his father. On his feet he wore brown brogues—the property of his brother—so large that his feet came out of them at every step. Despite all this, however, he was, as I have said, under a cloud for eating his cakes, and the potatoes, though submitted to an elaborate blackening process by Ginger who mixed together ink and black paint for the purpose, were felt to be wholly inadequate.

Ginger as King George on his way to the Crusades was the *pièce de résistance* of the whole show. He wore six tin trays, two fire guards, seven saucepan lids and a saucepan. Although a whole ball of string had been used to secure his equipment, trays and saucepan lids were continually falling off him and when he stooped to recover them others followed. William, who had continually to return from the arrangement of the others every other minute to pick up pieces of Ginger's panoply, grew irritable.

"Can't you stop dropping things all over the place?" he said.

"I can't help it," returned Ginger, "they drop off when I breathe."

"Well, then, you needn't breathe so hard," said William, "surely you needn't breathe so hard that trays and things drop off you all the time. Other people don't."

"You'd like me to die with not breathin', I s'pose," said Ginger indignantly, "and then I'd like to know what you'd do for King George."

"Oh, shut up," said William who was wrestling with King Charles's head-dress.

Henry as King Charles was magnificent in a fringed tablecloth and a paper crown that was just a little too big for him, and moustaches that arose with a flourish from either lip to perform symmetrical revolutions just under his eyes.

*   *   *

The audience was seated on turned up boxes in various stages of insecurity on the floor of the old barn. Douglas, Ginger and Henry were posed in suitable attitudes behind a string that was tied from wall to wall to prevent a too near approach of the audience. William as showman made his speech.

"Ladies an' gentlemen," he began, "I've gotter message first of all for you from Ginger an' Henry an' Douglas. They're very sorry not to be able to be here. They'd all hoped they'd be able to be here, but they all of them aren't very well an' have to stay in bed havin' their temperature took an' such-like. Well, I've got three very good waxworks for you here. Made by the best waxwork maker in the world an' sent down from London jus' for the performance."

The sheer impudence and ingenuity of this deprived the audience temporarily of breath and he continued unchallenged. "The first waxwork you see before you, ladies an' gentlemen, is Doug—is King Alfred, I mean, what burnt the cakes. You see the waxworks of the cakes too."

"Looks like potatoes to me," said a member of the audience sceptically, "dirty potatoes with bits of their skin scraped off."

Ginger's ink and black-paint treatment had certainly been less successful than he had imagined.

"Those are the sorts of cakes people had in those days," said William coldly; "it was before the sort of cakes people have nowadays was invented. D'you think that people ate the sort of cake people have nowadays in anshunt times? How could they when the modern sort of cakes people have nowadays weren't invented? It was very expensive gettin' a waxworks of an anshunt sort of cake, but we wanted to have everythin' jus' like what it was in anshunt times."

The audience stared suspiciously at the potatoes, but were momentarily silenced by the severity of William's voice and expression.

"He burnt the cakes, you know," said William vaguely. William had meant to borrow a history book with its full complement of pages to read up the careers of the historical characters that figured in his show, but he'd been so busy preparing his waxworks that he hadn't had time. "He burnt his cakes, you remember. Let 'em fall into the fire jus' when he was eatin' 'em. Got 'em burnt up, you know. Pulled 'em out, but they were too burnt to finish eatin'. Got insurance on 'em," he ended uncertainly with vague memories of a hearth rug onto which some coal had fallen out at home the week before, and added hastily, "Now let's look at the next one. The next one's made very speshul for this show. At very great expense. It was a jolly expensive one this one was. It's King Charles."

"Which King Charles?" said an earnest seeker after knowledge in the front row.

"The one what had to do with an oak tree," said William coldly and hastened on. "His clothes is made exactly like the real one's clothes were like. He's a very expensive one indeed."

"Wasn't he killed?" went on the earnest student in the front row.

"Yes," said William, assuming an air of omniscience, "killed fallin' out of the oak tree," and hastily proceeded, "his crown's made of gold same as the real one's was."

"I thought he was put to death with an axe by Parliament for doin' something wrong," protested the student.

"Yes, he was," agreed William, trying to accommodate his story to this fount of knowledge. "He was, but it was all to do with the oak tree. He was trespassin' in the oak tree. The oak tree was in someone's field an' they had him up an' put him to death for it, same as they did in those days. The lor was different in those days——"

"But I thought——" began the student.

William ceased trying to accommodate his story to the facts of history as revealed by the student and turned to simpler methods.

"You can jolly well shut up or get out," he said to the student.

"All right," murmured the student pacifically. "All right. All I meant was that it says in my history book——"

"Well, your history book's *wrong*," said William. "Do you think I'd be havin' a waxwork show of history people like this, if I didn't know all about 'em? Your history book's *all* wrong. It was written ever so many years ago an' I've found out a lot of things about history what no one knew when your history book was written. So you'd better listen to me or get out."

So impressive was William's tone and mien that that young student subsided and ever hereafter regarded his history book with deep distrust.

"Looks to *me*," said another critic, "jus' like Douglas dressed up."

"Yes," said William, unperturbed, "I had it made like Douglas. I thought it would be more int'restin' to have it made like someone we all knew. It was more expensive, of course, but I thought it'd be more int'restin' for you all."

"Made of wax, did you say?" said a red-headed member of the audience, peering over the dividing string.

"Yes," said William, "very good wax."

"He's winkin' his eyes."

"Yes. I had 'em made to wink their eyes," said William, "so as to look more nachural. It costs more to have 'em made that way, but it looks more nachural. More like what the real person must 've looked like. Real people always wink their eyes, so that's why I had my waxworks made to wink their eyes—so as to look more nachural—more like the real person must 've looked like—winkin' their eyes like what the real person did. Look at 'em. They all wink their eyes." Ginger, Henry and Douglas promptly began to blink with great violence. "There's speshul machinery inside 'em makin' 'em wink their eyes. Very expensive machinery."

"They're *breathin'*," said the investigator leaning yet further over the string. "I can see 'em—breathin'——breathin' an— movin'."

"Yes, I had 'em made to breathe an' move," said William calmly. "There's speshul machinery inside 'em makin' 'em breathe—so as to make 'em look more nachural." Then he proceeded hastily with his lecture.

"The nex' one, ladies an' gentlemen, is King George goin' off to the Crusades."

"What are they?" said the red-headed investigator.

"Things people went to in armour."

"I bet you're thinkin' of Saint George."

"Some call him one an' some the other," said William with dignity. "I call him King George," and continued hastily: "He lived in anshunt times an' he went out to the Crusades."

"What were the Crusades?" demanded a member of the audience.

"Islands," said William with a burst of inspiration, "like the Hebrides what we learnt in Geography las' week. He went out to 'em wearin' armour an' such-like."

"What for?" said the red-headed boy simply.

"Oh, shut up," said William wearily.

"I thought he had something to do with a dragon," said the student, recovering something of his poise. "I've seen a picture of him with a dragon."

"Oh yes," said William carelessly, "he had a dragon all right. There were lots of dragons in the Crusades. He tamed this one and took it about with him—sort of makin' a pet of it."

"But he was fightin' it in the picture I saw," objected the student.

"Yes, he *did* fight it," conceded William. "He fought it all right. It turned savage on him one day an' bit him an' he had to fight it"—then, wishing to bring the story to a conclusion—"an' it killed him. That's how he died—fightin' his dragon what'd turned savage on him out in the Crusades——"

"What d'you say they're made of?" said the red-headed boy, leaning so far over the string that it broke. "Wax?"

"Yes, wax," said William. "Very good wax. You really couldn't tell the difference between that wax and a real person. It's so nachural."

"It wouldn't feel it if I pinched it, seein' it's wax?" said the red-headed boy.

"Course not," said William; "but you'd better not go spoilin' my waxworks or——"

His warning was too late. The red-headed boy had given Ginger a sharp, experimental nip. With a yell of fury and a clatter of tin trays and saucepans Ginger hurled himself upon him. Henry and Douglas joined the fray. The audience, too, joined the fray except for the student, who went home to consult his history book. William stood in the background and murmured pathetically, "I had 'em made to fight like that. There's speshul machinery inside 'em makin' 'em fight like that."

   * * *

The Outlaws were holding another meeting in the old barn to discuss the next day's waxwork show.

"I bet they enjoyed this one so much they'll pay to come to the nex' one," said William optimistically.

"I bet they won't," protested Ginger. "I bet you anythin' you like they won't."

"Well, but we'll all be diff'rent people," said William, "it'll be quite a fresh show."

"I've heard 'em sayin' they won't come again," said Douglas sadly.

"Well, I can't understand why not," said William with spirit. "I simply can't understand why not. It seems to me it's jus' like the sort of waxwork show people do pay money to see. It's the *meanness* of folks round here——"

They hastily pulled him down from his favourite hobby-horse.

"Never mind that," said Ginger. "Let's try'n' think what we can do to make 'em pay to come in."

"Have animals as well. I mean dress up as waxwork animals," suggested Henry.

This suggestion was dismissed as impracticable. Then Douglas said, "Of course most waxworks have ladies in. Queens an' such-like. P'raps that's why they don't want to come. P'raps if we had ladies in——"

"All right," said William, "I'll dress up as a lady if you'll be the showman. I had jus' about enough of bein' the showman yesterday. I'm sick of people askin' questions an' pretendin' to know such a lot. An' then everyone startin' fightin'."

"You don't *look* much like a lady," said Ginger, eyeing William's countenance doubtfully.

"Well, I can *disguise* myself to look like a lady, can't I?" said William. "Anyone can shurely *disguise* themselves to look like a lady."

"Yes, but they always have to be *beautiful* ladies for waxwork shows an' such-like," said Douglas, "not the ordinary sort."

"Well, shurely I can *disguise* myself to look like a beautiful lady, can't I?" challenged William with spirit.

Nobody accepted the challenge. They merely gazed incredulously at William's freckled homely countenance.

" 'S easy enough," said William carelessly; "you jus' put on a sort of soppy look. The sort of soppy look Ethel's got."

William here rolled up his eyes and assumed the

expression commonly attributed to a dying duck in a thunderstorm. The others blinked and blenched, but, not wishing the discussion to descend to the physical plane before some agreement had been reached, refrained from comment.

"What about clothes anyway?" said Douglas, "it's harder to get ladies' clothes than men's."

"Tell you what," said William, "Ethel had a dress once when she was smaller than what she is now. She went to a fancy-dress dance in it. It's Mary Queen of Scots or somethin' like that. I know where it is. I could borrow it from her. I'd put it back afterwards an' no one 'd ever know."

"All right," said Ginger, "we'd better put up a notice about it."

"Yes, we will," said William. "I'll make it up. An' we won't pretend to be *reel* waxworks this time 'cause they know now we aren't. We'll jus' pretend to be people pretendin' to be waxworks. An' we'll have a notice about the lady. I bet they'll all want to come and see her. An' I bet they'll none of them know it's me. I bet when I'm dressed up as a lady an' put on my soppy look they'll none of them know it's me."

William's notice was the result of much hard labour and deep thought. He broke three nibs (William was rather hard on nibs) and dyed all his fingers black to the bone in the process. It ran as follows:

"there will be annuther sho of wonderful yuman beings actin waxworks so you cudent tell the diffrance tomorro the most wonderful acters of waxworks in the world no one can tell the diffrance there will be a new lady acter with them to-morro the most wonderful lady acter of waxworks in the world speshully butiful come from along way of at grate expence to be in the

sho the most butiful lady acter of waxworks ever none
ax before kings and queens in speshully butiful clos
william brown."

"That's all right, isn't it?" he said with modest pride
as he showed it to the Outlaws.

"I bet it's spelt wrong," said Ginger, irritated by
William's superior manner.

"What's spelt wrong?" challenged William.

"Lots of it," said Ginger, not liking to commit himself
too definitely; "you've never wrote anythin' yet that
wasn't all spelt wrong."

"Neither 've you," said William. "I don't see that it
matters. I know that to me there always seems to be
more sense in my sort of spelling than there is in the sort
of spelling you find in books. Seems to me people ought
to be let spell the way that comes easiest to them."

"So do I," said Ginger, retreating from a position
which in view of his own spelling capabilities he felt to be
untenable. "So do I. I think so, too. Yes, I think it's a
jolly good notice but I think all our names ought to be on
it, too."

"All right," said William obligingly, "I'll put your
names on too."

"An' you oughter begin, 'We the undersigned,' that's
what they always do."

"We the what?"

"The undersigned."

"How do you spell it?"

"I don't know. But it's the proper way to begin a
notice. What are you goin' to be doin' as Mary Queen of
Scots? Bein' killed or somethin'?"

"No, I'm not," said William, "I'm goin' to be jus'
lookin' soppy same as Ethel does. I'll be holdin' some
flowers. There's a photograph of Ethel in our drawing-

room lookin' soppy holding flowers what everyone says is very beautiful. I'll be lookin' jus' like it."

Again Ginger gazed doubtfully at William's countenance, but again, for the sake of peace, refrained from comment.

William successfully "borrowed" the Mary Queen of Scots costume from Ethel's bedroom in her absence.

It had been made for Ethel many years ago, when she was at school and taking part in some theatricals, and it fitted William fairly well. It cannot be said that it suited him. William's bullet head with its shock of wiry hair and William's stern, homely, freckled face emerged strangely from the elaborate ruff. He "borrowed" a boudoir cap of Ethel's to enhance the general effect, but his face looked more unromantic than ever when framed in cascades of lace and baby ribbon. Even William could not pretend that he was satisfied with his appearance, nor could he deceive himself so far as to believe that it would be accepted without protest by his audience as that of the most beautiful actress in the world. It was still William—shock-headed, carroty, lacking in almost every element of beauty. But William was a born optimist. Flowers. Ethel in the much-admired photograph was holding flowers. Flowers would probably make all the difference. It was useless to try to get flowers at home. Relationships between William and the gardener were more strained than usual owing to the fact that William had recently "borrowed" some of the gardener's plant stakes to use as arrows. It would be useless to ask the gardener for flowers and it would be more useless still to try to get them without asking the gardener, because the gardener had formed the habit of watching William's every movement when William was in the garden. William therefore changed into his actress's dress and, clad in a long mackintosh, made his

way as unobtrusively as possible to the old barn where
the performance was to be held, arriving half an hour
before the time advertised for its opening. The gardens
of The Hall ran alongside the field where the old barn
was, and from their garden William hoped to cull the
armful of flowers that was to dower him with beauty.

He got through the hedge and wandered for some
time through the shrubbery looking for flowers and
finding none. At last he saw a blaze of bloom just beyond
the shrubbery across a gravelled path. It was farther than
he meant to venture, but William never liked to
relinquish any undertaking half performed. He ventured
cautiously on to the gravelled path, darted forward
and—collided with the little girl who was just coming
round the corner. Both sat down on the gravel very
suddenly and stared at each other in breathless surprise.

The little girl's surprise needs no accounting for.
William's appearance has already been described. William's surprise will be understood when I say that the
little girl, too, was in fancy dress—an elaborate affair of
satin and pearls—and that her fancy dress was obviously
meant to impersonate Mary Queen of Scots. She looked
very pretty in it. William gaped at her.

"Hello," she said, "what are *you* doing in our
garden?"

"Jus' lookin' round," said William loftily as he
straightened his boudoir cap.

"You're the boy that pulled a face at me."

"I know," said William and did it again.

She retaliated.

"That's a good one," said William condescendingly.
"How do you do it?"

"You start with your nose and then you do your
mouth," said the little girl. "Like this."

William tried it.

WILLIAM COLLIDED WITH THE LITTLE GIRL. BOTH SAT DOWN ON
THE GRAVEL SUDDENLY. "HALLO," SAID THE LITTLE GIRL.

"Yes, that's right," she said, "you do it jolly well,"
and added admiringly, "you *are* an ugly boy. Why are
you dressed up?"

"Why shouldn't I be? Why are you, anyway?"

"I hate it. I've got to go to a silly place they've made
for me in the garden and be talked to by a stupid
woman."

"Don't you want to be?"

"No, I hate it. I hate everything. There's only one

thing in the whole world I want and that's to go to a boarding school and they won't let me. Now why are you dressed up? You *are* ugly."

William accepted this—as indeed it seemed to be meant—as a compliment.

"Oh, I'm all right," he said modestly; "I'm dressed up for a waxwork show."

"Oh what *fun!* You *are* lucky!" said the little girl.

William looked at her in silence for a minute and his eyes gleamed suddenly as if with a brilliant idea. No doubt at all about the little girl's beauty. Surely anyone would pay to see *her.* . . .

"You can go 'stead of me if you like," he said carelessly.

"Oh, *may* I?" she said excitedly, then her excitement faded; "but I'm s'posed to be going to that silly place to be talked to by that stupid woman."

"I'll do that for you," volunteered William. "I'm dressed same as you—well, *nearly* same as you. Only—I s'pose she'd know I wasn't you."

The little girl's eyes were gleaming.

"She *wouldn't*," she said, "she's never seen me. She's come to ask me a lot of stupid questions in a silly place they've made for me that I *hate*. Then there's going to be a silly photograph, but I'll be back in time for that. Oh, I'd love to go and play at being a waxwork."

"All right," said William, "you go. It's over in that barn in that field. There's a hole in the hedge. You'll find three boys there. Tell 'em I've sent you 'stead of me to be Mary Queen of Scots. What about flowers? Oh, but *you* don't need 'em. Well, I'll go to this place you say. What sort of questions she goin' to ask. Not lessons?" suspiciously.

"Oh, no . . . just *stupid* questions. It will be fun. I'll go now before anyone comes along and stops me——"

She flitted through the shrubbery, through the gap in the hedge, and disappeared across the field. William was left alone on the garden path. The zest with which he had originated the plan was fading and he was beginning to see some of its disadvantages. His mackintosh had fallen off in the shrubbery. He had an uncomfortable suspicion that his appearance was not such as to inspire confidence should he meet anyone in this garden. Where was this "silly place" the little girl had mentioned? He proceeded cautiously down the path, ready to turn tail and run into the shrubbery if he met anyone. He didn't meet anyone. At the end of the path he found an elaborate little garden house with two small but luxuriously furnished rooms. William entered one of them and sat down. A middle-aged woman with very large spectacles and carrying an attaché case was approaching from the opposite direction.

Miss Perkins had been sent by her paper, *Woman's Sphere*, to interview Rosemary, the daughter of Clarice Verney, the famous actress. At a series of tableaux lately given in London by the children of famous actors and actresses Rosemary had appeared as Mary Queen of Scots and her appearance had created something of a furore. *Woman's Sphere* had at once conceived the plan of an illustrated interview and had approached Rosemary's mother. Rosemary's mother had no objection at all, provided that she herself figured largely in both interview and illustration. Miss Perkins had already interviewed Rosemary's mother, and the photographer was now engaged in posing Rosemary's mother for the photograph. Miss Perkins had been told that she would find Rosemary in the dress in which she had appeared in the tableaux in the beautiful little garden house that had been her mother's last birthday present to her, and that was her favourite haunt. Miss Perkins approached the little house, wearing her most engaging smile. She saw the flicker of a fancy dress, and the smile broadened.

"So *this* is the little——"

Then her mouth dropped open. She had come face to face with the little occupant of the garden house in fancy dress. She blinked and blenched and swallowed. *Extraordinary* how standards were changing all the world over. That this child should be considered beautiful! It was amazing. The effect, of course, of jazz and cubism, thought Miss Perkins. Miss Perkins put everything down to the effect of jazz and cubism. This child—Miss Perkins met its unblinking stare and again blenched and swallowed. She was, she knew, short-sighted, but —*this*—well, short-sight or no short-sight, *this* would never have been called beauty when she was young. With an almost superhuman effort she summoned back the ghost of her engaging smile.

"And this is Rosemary, is it?" she said.

"Uh—huh," said the child in a gruff voice. Miss Perkins shuddered again.

"And is this the garden house we've heard so much about?"

"Uh—huh," said the child again in the same voice. The dress wasn't at all what she'd been led to believe it was going to be, either, thought Miss Perkins. It was really rather a cheap-looking affair of sateen and imitation lace. She'd heard that it was the most exquisite Mary Queen of Scots costume in miniature. People seemed to be losing their standards about everything nowadays. What a funny head-dress, too. She'd never have thought it was meant to be a Mary Queen of Scots head-dress.

"And this is where you spend nearly all your time, isn't it, dear?" she went on.

"Uh—huh," said the child again, in the same gruff voice.

"And what are your favourite games?" went on Miss Perkins heroically, taking out a little note-book.

"Red Indians," said the child in the same unbeautiful voice. "Red Indians an' Pirates."

Miss Perkins shuddered.

"You like playing with your dolls here, don't you, dear?"

"*Me?*" said the child fiercely and with a glance before which Miss Perkins quailed. She hastily passed on to the next question.

"You love to be alone here with your books, don't you?"

"No," said the child succinctly.

"What sort of books do you like best? Your mother said you love everything beautiful. You read a lot of poetry, don't you?"

"No," said the child. "Soppy stuff."

Again Miss Perkins shuddered. These were not the answers she had come to write down in her little note-book. She made another great effort and assumed a roguish air.

"Ah," she said, "but your mother told me a secret about you."

"Uh—huh," said the child without interest.

"You believe in fairies," said Miss Perkins, still more roguishly.

"*Me?*" said the terrible child again, so terribly that Miss Perkins hastily passed on to the next question.

"What's your favourite story, dear?"

"Dick of the Bloody Hand," said the child.

Miss Perkins wrote down "Cinderella." One did, after all, owe a duty to one's readers.

"What do you like doing best of all?" went on the interviewer.

"Jus' messin' about," said the child, "messin' about an' goin' in woods an' makin' fires an' climbin' trees an' such-like."

Miss Perkins hastily closed the note-book. She was feeling rather faint. To her relief a distant clock struck, marking the end of the interview.

"It's time for the photograph now, dear," she said to the terrible child. "It's to be in the arbour by the yew hedge. That's just along here, isn't it? I'm sure you just *adore* this beautiful garden, don't you?"

"No," said the child coldly. They walked slowly down the path towards the arbour by the yew hedge.

"Don't you *love* the sound of the birds?" said Miss Perkins as they walked along, making a last attempt to reach any beautiful child soul that might underlie this unprepossessing exterior.

"Noise of the birds?" said the child; "birds don't make any noise. Not worth speakin' of, that is. I had a thing once that was s'posed to make a noise like a canary an' I got so's I could do it so's you could hear it a mile off. People said it went through their heads. It was fine."

"And the scent of the flowers?" persisted Miss Perkins faintly in a dying effort.

"Flowers don' smell, not to call a *real* smell," said the child. "I once found a dead cat in a hedge. You should 've smelt *that*."

They had reached the arbour by the yew hedge now. A camera stood in place before it and behind the camera was a young man with a harassed expression. In the arbour by the yew hedge sat Clarice Verney, the actress, very carefully posed. It had taken the young man with the harassed expression over an hour to pose her to her complete satisfaction. He had acquired the harassed expression in the process. But now Clarice Verney was posed to her complete satisfaction in such a way to show to best advantage her hair and eyes and nose and teeth and chin and figure and legs and ankles—all of which she considered to be her chief good points. She was bending forward so as to show off her figure and chin and neck, and smiling so as to show off her teeth. She was bending forward and gazing toward the right because she considered the left side of her face to be the better one. Miss Perkins and the child approached from the left. The actress did not move her head or look towards them for fear of upsetting the pose.

"You just sit down on the little footstool that's at my feet, darling," she said, and added, afraid lest the smile should lose its freshness, "quickly."

The child sat down obediently on the footstool at her feet.

The young man with the harassed expression was gaping at the child, his eyes and mouth wide open. His harassed expression became almost wild.

"This isn't—isn't ——?" he stammered to Miss Perkins.

"Yes, it is," said Miss Perkins stonily.

He too blinked, blenched and swallowed. The child, now seated on the footstool, fixed him with a stern gaze.

"Do be quick," said the actress, still smiling dreamily into the distance.

"Y—yes," stammered the young man diving beneath his black cloth. He'd have dived anywhere to escape from the sight of the child.

There came a sound of a little click.

"Finished?" said the actress still without moving.

"Y—yes."

"Well, I want you to take another of me just like this, but alone. I'm keeping this pose exactly as it is because I

"YOU JUST SIT DOWN ON THE LITTLE FOOTSTOOL AT MY FEET, DARLING," SAID MISS VERNEY.

WILLIAM SAT DOWN OBEDIENTLY.

THE YOUNG MAN WAS GAPING AT WILLIAM. "THIS
ISN'T—ISN'T—?" HE STAMMERED.
"YES, IT IS," SAID MISS PERKINS STONILY.

think it's such a good one. You run away now, darling."

The child arose and ran away. The second photograph was taken. Three more were taken. Then the actress relaxed and looked about her.

"My little Rosemary's gone to change, I suppose?"

Miss Perkins supposed so.

"Isn't she a *beautiful* child?" said the actress.

"Exquisite," said Miss Perkins, rising nobly to the occasion.

"People say," said the actress, "that she's *exactly* like what I was at her age."

Miss Perkins made no comment.

*   *   *

William scrambled through the hedge and ran across the field to the old barn.

A small stream of children was issuing from the old barn. A queue was lined up outside.

"It *reelly* is like what it says on the notice," said a small child just emerging; "it *reelly* is a mos' beautiful actor lady, what we've never seen before got special for the show."

"It isn't any of *them*—William or Douglas or Ginger or Henry?" said the queue anxiously.

"No."

"Worth a halfpenny?" asked the queue still more anxiously.

"Yes. *Reelly* worth a halfpenny," said the small child earnestly.

*   *   *

William and the Outlaws were coming home from a happy day spent in Mr. Peters' shrubbery. Mr. Peters had watched them anxiously from an upstairs window. He would have liked to have sent them away but lacked the courage. William had arrived the week before with a handsome contribution for his "society", and so Mr. Peters knew that at any rate for the next few weeks he would have to allow them to riot unchecked in his shrubbery. He watched them in an agony as they made fires and climbed his favourite trees, longing for the time when the few weeks should be up during which the moral effect of their contribution might be supposed to last.

"It's a *jolly* good place to play, isn't it?" said William happily, "an' he can't stop us for a bit yet, seein' we gave him three an' elevenpence three farthin's——"

"Let's see the letter she wrote you again," said Ginger.

William drew from his pocket a grimy piece of paper already worn to shreds from its sojourn in his pocket.

Dere William,

I did so enjoy being a waxwork in your sho and its luvly that they've sent me to a bording scule. Mother had a nurvus brakedown when she saw the foto, to late to stop it in the papers, an is stil having it. I luv being at bording scule.

Luv from,

Rosemary.

"She did it jolly well," said Ginger.

"An' I did *her* thing jolly well too," said William complacently, "talkin' to that woman an' havin' my photo taken an' lookin' soppy."

"Huh!" said Ginger. "I'd like to've seen you. I bet you looked jolly funny."

"I looked all right," said William coldly.

He went indoors to the drawing-room where his mother sat with Ethel idly turning over the pages of an illustrated paper.

"Look at this," she was saying: " 'Miss Clarice Verney, the actress, with her beautiful little daughter Rosemary, who is wearing the Mary Queen of Scots costume she wore in the children's tableaux in London.' They were at The Hall for a short time, you know, but I never saw them. Now," handing the paper to Ethel, "would you call her a pretty child? Of course these newspaper photographs don't do anyone justice, but to my mind she's downright plain."

Ethel took the paper and studied it.

"Awful," she commented at last, "and what a queer erection on her head. It isn't at all the sort of head-dress I'd have thought suited the costume at all."

"The costume's rather like that Mary Queen of Scots costume you had once, isn't it, Ethel?" said Mrs. Brown.

"Yes, I've got it somewhere still."

"It shows it was a very good one because of course this child's sure to have had the best. I always thought that that costume was a very good one. Don't you think that the child has just a look of William?"

"Oh, not *quite* as bad as that, surely?" said Ethel.

But William, rather to her surprise, refused to rise to this. He stared out of the window as if he had not heard, wearing his most enigmatic expression.

Chapter 6

The Outlaws
Deliver the Goods

William and the Outlaws sat on the back row of the
School Hall, carelessly cracking nuts and surreptitiously
scattering the shells under the bench on which they sat.
Cramps, the school caretaker, hated the Outlaws with a
deadly hatred because he knew that the nut-shells and
ink-soaked blotting-paper bullets that made his life a
perpetual burden to him could usually be traced to them.
However, he was a morose, gloomy type of man in
general who'd have been miserable without his
grievances, and anyway he doesn't come into this story.
The headmaster was on the platform and had been
speaking quite a long time, but the Outlaws had not been
listening to him. The Outlaws never listened to the
headmaster when he was making a speech. His speeches
were generally exhortations to lead a better life, and the
Outlaws considered that this did not concern them
because they'd often tried leading better lives and had
found them even more fruitful of complications than
their normal lives of evil-doing. So instead of listening
they engaged in various quiet diversions among themselves. William and Ginger had each brought a mouse
which, in the intervals of eating nuts, they tried to put

down each other's necks, and Henry and Douglas were dipping bits of paper into an inkpot and flicking them at each other with rulers. And so, despite the headmaster's speech, the afternoon was passing quite pleasantly till a more forcible inflection than usual in the headmaster's voice suddenly riveted their attention on him.

"I think," he was saying, "that you would all like to help with the new wing and therefore I suggest that in the next fortnight you all do what you can to raise funds for it. I propose that you split yourselves up into groups of, say, four or five boys, and work hard this next fortnight to bring in the funds. Solicit subscriptions from your friends and relatives and do little services for them for cash—helping in the garden and in the house. They will, I am sure, when they know the object, be ready to pay you by the hour or piecework. In their interests I suggest the latter. Ha, ha. . . ."

Then he continued after the fashion of his kind to enlarge upon all these points and the Outlaws returned to their nuts and mouse and blotting-paper battle. It never even occurred to them to identify themselves with the great money-raising campaign thus initiated by the headmaster. They knew nothing and cared less about the new wing and they had no money and no chance of getting any. They had solicited subscriptions from friends and relatives for purposes of their own so frequently that their friends and relatives became abrupt and disagreeable before they had even broached the object of the solicited subscriptions and, as they had frequently discovered, their families were the sort of families that expect you to do little services for them without payment. So convinced were the Outlaws of this that they would never have given the headmaster's suggestion another thought had it not been for Hubert Lane and his followers.

The headmaster had drawn his speech to its long delayed conclusion and the school trooped out into the road. The Outlaws' thoughts were wholly concerned with a mouse fight that they were organising in the old barn. The two combatants were William's mouse and Ginger's mouse. The first round had already taken place and the only drawback to it as a fight was that the combatants persisted in fraternising and refused, despite all the efforts of the organisers, to display any signs of hostility.

"I'm goin' to try wavin' a red handkerchief at 'em as they do in bull fights," said Ginger.

And just then they passed Hubert Lane's house. The Hubert Laneites never attempted verbal hostilities except when within easy reach of the parental roof, because the Outlaws were fleet of foot and sure of hand and in open warfare they had no chance against them.

"Yah!" jeered Hubert Lane from half-way up the drive, his plump body already poised for flight. "Yah! A lot o' money *you'll* get for the new wing! *You* with your twopence a week!"

It was well known that Hubert Lane received five shillings a week.

William foolishly stopped to reply to this challenge despite the efforts of the other Outlaws to drag him on. William always hated to leave a challenge unanswered. He answered it with a scornful laugh.

"We'll jolly well get more'n' *you*," he said contemptuously.

"Oh, will you?" said Hubert Lane with a snigger; "p'raps you don't know that we're goin' to get five pounds for it."

William's laugh was yet more scornful.

"Only five?" he said. "What a bit. We're goin' to get ten."

And he walked on with a swagger leaving the Hubert Laneites gaping.

The Outlaws didn't recover the power of speech till they'd reached the end of the road. Then Ginger said faintly:

"Crumbs, William, what'd you say *that* for?"

"I dunno," said William, who was also feeling rather aghast at his temerity; then with the ghost of his old spirit added: "Well, I wasn't goin' to have 'em going on like that."

"Well," said Ginger, "they'll jolly well go on like that at the end of the fortnight when they find out that we've got nothin' an' they've got their five pounds. They'll tell everyone, too."

"Well," said William, trying to carry off the situation but without much conviction in his voice, "we—we've jus' got to get ten pounds then."

" 'S easy to *talk*," said Ginger, and added darkly, "Talkin's what's wrong with you. You talk too much."

"Well, what would you've done?" said William indignantly, "jus' lettem go on an' not said anythin'?"

"Jus' punched his face," suggested Ginger.

"Yes," said William scathingly, "an' him standin' jus' outside his front door. He'd 've been in before we'd opened the gate an' sent the gardener round to us same as he did last time."

"Well, we've jus' gotter make the best of it, I s'pose," said Douglas with a deep sigh, "jus' try'n' keep out of their way at the end of the fortnight when they find that they've got five pounds an' we've got nothin'. That's all we can do."

"Yes," said Henry gloomily, "an' it won't be so easy to keep out of their way. They'll be carryin' on at us all the time an' they'll *tell* everyone."

"Well," said William aggressively but still without

conviction, "we've jus' gotter get ten pounds. There *mus'* be ways of gettin' ten pounds. If there isn't, how do people that do get it get it?"

The logic of this was of course unassailable.

"Well," said Ginger with heavy sarcasm, "if you c'n find a way, find it."

"And I can," said William airily. "Lots of people get ten pounds. Well, that shows there mus' be ways of gettin' it, doesn't it?"

"All right, go on an' find a way," encouraged Ginger coldly. "It was *you* what said you could. Not us."

"All right," said William aggressively, "I jolly well will, then. Ten pounds isn't much. I mean"—in answer to their gasp of incredulity—"it isn't much when you think of a hundred pounds or a thousand pounds or a million pounds. Why, when you think of a million pounds, ten pounds is hardly anythin'."

"An' when you think of twopence, which is all we get for pocket money," said Douglas gloomily, "it's a jolly lot."

This reflection brought William down to earth.

"All right," he said irritably, "it's nothin' for *you* to get fussed up over. It was me who said I'd do it."

But they weren't going to leave William in the lurch. With William they would stand or fall as they'd always done. In this particular case they'd probably fall. After all, it was generally more exciting falling with William than standing alone.

"We'd 've prob'ly said it, if you hadn't," said Ginger carelessly. "We'll all try'n' get it anyway. An' if we don't we can fight the ones that start talkin' about it. It won't be so bad, anyway. How'll we start?"

"We'll start with easy ways," said William, secretly touched and cheered by their loyalty, "we'll start with the ways he said. S'lic'ting subscriptions an' doin' services an' such-like. We'll start with s'lic'tin' subscriptions. That's his way of sayin' askin' for money, of course."

"Why can't he say askin' for money?" said Henry rather irritably. The magnitude of their undertaking was weighing heavily upon his spirit.

"They never do," said William indulgently. "They've gotter say things in a way that's harder to understand than the ornery way or else they'd never get to be headmasters. It's a spechal sort of langwidge that gets 'em to be headmasters. . . . Well, let's start goin' round our relations askin' for money an' we'll meet tomorrow night an' see how we've got on."

So they spent the next day going round their relations asking for money and they didn't get on very far. They met in fact with a coldness and a lack of response that would have made their opinions of their relatives even lower than it was, had that been possible.

"I went round to them *all*," said Ginger mournfully, "an' my Aunt Emma she said 'Certainly not, after your ball comin' in through my landin' window like it did last week'; an' my Uncle John said 'Cert'n'ly not after you goin' over my lawn with your scooter the way you did yesterday.' An' my Aunt Jane said 'Cert'n'ly not after you chasin' my dear Pussy as I saw you last week,' an' my Uncle George said 'Cert'n'ly not after you throwin' stones up at my walnut tree like I saw you doin' yesterday,' an' my Uncle John said 'Cert'n'ly not after you climbin' my rose pole an' breakin' it'; an' all the others said things like that." . . .

"So did all mine," said William sadly.

"An' so did all mine," said Henry and Douglas, and Douglas added:

"Seems sort of extr'ordin'y to me the sort of mem'ries they've got. If ever they say, p'raps they'll take you to the pantomine nex' Christmas, you'll jolly well never find 'em rememberin', but if you do jus' a little thing like breakin' a window quite by accident, well, you'll jolly well never find 'em forgettin'."

"Well," said William with a sigh of disappointment, "we'll try doin' little services for them for cash next, then, like what he said."

Again the expectations of the Outlaws were low, nor did events prove them wrong.

They tried at first to persuade their parents and relations to engage them in some capacity at a definite salary, and were so far successful that William's elder brother promised him twopence if he would clean his bicycle, but subsequently not only refused to pay him but committed violent physical assault upon him because William, who considered it his duty in the interests of science to dismember it before cleaning (William loved taking anything to pieces), misplaced several vital parts in reassembling it.

The experiences of the others were similar.

"Said he'd give me sixpence for weedin' his garden," said Ginger indignantly, "an' then said all the things I'd pulled up was all plants an' all the things I'd left in was weeds. Well, how was I to know? They looked like plants. They were quite pretty, too, some of 'em with little flowers on 'em. I don't call 'em weeds when they've got little flowers on 'em. He ought to 've labelled 'em if he's so particular. I wouldn't be a gardener not for anything. They mus' have a rotten time tellin' which is plants an' which is weeds."

Douglas had been engaged by an aunt to saw some logs, but he had put the saw out of action on the first log.

"It mus' have been a jolly *weak* sort of saw," grumbled Douglas. "Well, it *mus'* have been. All those little tin spiky things went crooked almost as soon as I started, an' it kept sort of stickin' in the wood. Well, that can't 've been *my* fault, can it? She said I'd runed her saw an' it would cost her a lot of money to get it put right. I said that it mus' have been a jolly *weak* sort if it went wrong the minute anyone started sawin' with it, but she seemed so mad that I didn't stay to argue with her."

Henry, however, had made the sum of twopence. His brother had—somewhat foolishly—paid him in advance for taking a note to the present object of his affection. Henry had faithfully taken the note, but on the way he had met an errand-boy who had rashly mimicked his gait and expression. Henry had resented this and after a spirited exchange of verbal insults a contest had ensued in the course of which Henry had received a black eye and the errand-boy a burst nose. The note which Henry had dropped in the thrill of battle had received the first evidence of the errand-boy's burst nose. It was that that brought Henry's spirit down from the proud height to which it had soared. He picked up his note, the errand-boy picked up his basket and they parted amicably, the errand-boy as proud of his burst nose as Henry would have been of his black eye if it hadn't been for the note. For Henry knew that it was no fit note to present to anyone's ladye love—trampled underfoot by muddy boots and dyed in an errand-boy's gore. He handed it to the housemaid with a muttered apology and the evident horror with which she received it did nothing to lessen his misgivings. He was sure that the appointment suggested in the note would not be kept by the lady and that his brother would find out the reason and lay the blame on him. He was already engaged in composing as an explanation the story of a gigantic man who had leapt upon him from behind a wall and cruelly assaulted him, trampling him in the dust and bursting his nose. He hastened, however, to put his twopence into William's charge before his brother could demand its return.

William regarded it with perhaps over-optimistic cheerfulness.

"Well, it's a *beginnin'*," he said, and added in a challenging tone, "no one can say it isn't a *beginnin'*."

"Not much of a beginnin' to ten pounds," said Douglas mournfully.

"It's as much a beginnin' to ten pounds as it would be to anything," said William spiritedly and with truth.

"*Why* did you say ten pounds?" said Douglas again mournfully.

"Doesn't matter what he said," said Ginger, "we'd still be as far off it whatever he'd said. We'd be as far off it if he'd said a shilling."

"No, we'd only be tenpence off it if he'd said a shilling," said Henry the literal. "With him sayin' ten pounds we're nine pounds nineteen shillings an' tenpence off."

"An' we've only two days left," said Ginger.

Their hunting for employment from reluctant employers had taken some time and they all realised with surprise and dismay that the fortnight had almost elapsed.

"*They've* got their five pounds," said Douglas mournfully. "Ole Hubert Lane yelled out to me that they had this morning. That and a lot more cheek. An' I felt so—sort of fed up that I can't even run after 'em."

"Fancy!" said Henry wistfully. "They've got their five pounds!"

"Well, we'll get our ten pounds," said William. "I bet there's lots of people that have got ten pounds in two days."

"How?" said Ginger simply.

"Oh, there's lots of ways of gettin' money," said William vaguely and irritably. William always disliked

having his soaring optimism brought down to earth by
such questions. "Look how rich all grown-up people
are. Well, they mus' get their money *somehow*."

"They pass exams. an' then start off bein' doctors an'
clergymen an' things like that an' people pay 'em money
for it, an' we can't do that because we haven't passed
any exams.," said Douglas.

"I nearly passed one once," murmured Ginger
modestly. "If I'd 've got ten more marks I'd 've passed
in Arithmetic last term."

"Oh, shut up," said William, "an' let's try'n' think of
a way of gettin' money. All grown-ups haven't passed
exams. I bet there's lots of rich grown-ups that haven't
passed exams. What about shopkeepers? There isn't any
exam. for shopkeepers. People can jus' set up a shop an'
get money without passin' exams. That's the best way of
makin' money, too. You buy a thing for, say, a half-
penny an' you sell it in your shop for a penny. You sell
everythin' for double what you pay for it an' so you get
richer an' richer till you're a millionaire."

"Yes, but *we* can't do that," said Henry gloomily;
"you gotter have some money to start with to buy the
shop an' the stuff to sell in it. An', anyway, it'd take
more'n two days settin' up a shop an' makin' ten pounds
in it."

"They don't always buy a shop before they start
sellin' things," said William. "Sometimes they jus' have
a stall in the road. I've often seen people havin' a stall in
the road an' sellin' things. I bet that they're much richer
than the ones who buy a shop 'cause a shop mus' cost an
awful lot of money."

"Yes, I've often seen 'em," said Ginger. "I've seen
'em havin' refreshment stalls sellin' buns an' lemonade,
an' such-like."

"*That's* what we'll do," said William, his freckled

face illuminated by a sudden flash of inspiration. "We'll have a refreshment stall."

*   *   *

The refreshment stall stood by the roadside awaiting patrons. It consisted of a large packing-case turned up on end sideways and covered by a newspaper. Upon this chaste covering reposed four buns, a jug of lemonade and a tin mug together with a notice unevenly printed in ink, "buns a penny lem'nade a penny." Behind it, gazing with eager, expectant faces down the empty road, stood the four Outlaws. The lemonade had been made from a tin of lemonade powder that William had found in his mother's larder. The jug and mug were Ginger's contribution. The buns were four halfpenny buns that had been honestly purchased with Henry's twopence.

The system upon which the refreshment stall was to be run had been fully explained by William.

"You see," he said, "as soon as anyone buys a bun one of you run down to the village with the penny an' buy two more halfpenny ones with the penny. An' so on. It's ever so easy. We'll be rich in no time."

Their spirits rose. . . . They waited, their eyes fixed on the bend in the road.

"S'pose no one buys anythin'," said Douglas dejectedly. Douglas was always rather inclined to look on the black side.

At that moment a cyclist appeared. He dismounted by the stall and read the notice gravely. Then he took twopence out of his pocket and asked for a mug of lemonade and a bun. Eight eager and none-too-clean hands flashed out to serve him.

Just as this was happening Bertie Franks passed. He gazed with goggle-eyed amazement and interest at the scene. Bertie Franks was Hubert Lane's chief supporter.

THE CYCLIST BOUGHT A MUG OF LEMONADE AND A BUN. BERTIE FRANKS GAZED WITH GOGGLE-EYED AMAZEMENT AT THE SCENE.

"How's business?" said the cyclist.

"Fine," said William exuberantly.

The cyclist mounted and rode off again.

"Bertie saw us," said William with satisfaction. "*He'll* begin to feel a bit small at their mingy ole five pounds now."

"We've only got twopence yet," put in Henry mildly.

"Yes," said William, "but it only took about a second gettin' it. An' there's all the rest of the day. Hours an' hours. About a second gettin' twopence. An' there's sixty seconds in an hour. That's sixty twopences. That's——" William wrestled for a moment with the mighty sum and finally gave it up. "That's ever so much money. We'll soon have the ten pounds."

Henry and Douglas had run down to the village with the twopence and now returned with four more half-penny buns which they placed upon the packing-case. "It's a jolly easy way of makin' money," said William thoughtfully. "I wonder more people don't go in for bein' shopkeepers. You'd get rich this way ever so much quicker than any other. . . ."

He stopped. An old lady was coming down the road. Alas! The Outlaws should have been prepared for treachery once Bertie Franks had seen their wayside stall with all its evidences of prosperity. But they had not been invited to Bertie Frank's Fancy Dress dance in the winter when Hubert Lane had won the first prize as an old lady. Hubert's podgy little figure even normally suggested that of an old lady. He wore a long full skirt and a cape. His bonnet was tied under his ears. A veil hid his face, showing only rosy cheeks (his usually pasty cheeks were heavily rouged), and grey side curls. He spoke in an assumed high-pitched voice.

"I've been watching you, my dear boys, from my house up the road. I'm sure that you're both tired and hungry, and I'd be so pleased if you'd go up to my house and have something to eat. I've left a nice tea for you on the verandah. I'll look after your stall for you and you needn't be away a minute, need you?"

Alas for the Outlaws! They didn't know that this was Hubert Lane. They didn't know that the Hubert Laneites surrounded them, crawling slowly along the dry ditch on either side of the road. They hesitated, they weakened, they fell.

"Thanks awfully," said William. "Yes—we wouldn't mind havin' tea. We've been so busy that we forgot all about tea. No, we needn't stay away more'n a minute an' if you'd kindly look after our stall for us——"

"Cert'n'ly, dear boys," said the old lady, "mine's the first house on the right an' you'll find a nice tea laid for you on the verandah."

Hubert's plan was a deep and cunning one. At first he had meant to decoy William from his post by the description of a non-existent tea, but on the way down the road he had noticed a tea laid for four on the verandah of a house down the lane. There were no signs of hosts or guests. It occurred to him that it would be fun to involve the Outlaws in the terrible complications that would ensue from an unauthorised consumption of this inviting and evidently carefully prepared meal.

"Thank you very much," said William politely and set off with his Outlaws down the road.

Only Douglas felt slight misgivings. "I dunno as we ought to've gone," he said anxiously.

William defended their action with spirit.

"Well, we've gotter *eat*, haven't we? We'd die if we went on an' on without food, an' it wouldn't be much good gettin' ten pounds an' then dyin' of starvation gettin' it an' not bein' able to see old Hubert's face when it's read out."

It was well for their peace of mind that they could not see old Hubert's face at that moment as, still wearing the semblance of a venerable old lady, he stood with his followers around the Outlaws' refreshment stall, drinking the lemonade and eating the buns with gloating haste.

The Outlaws hesitated for a second at the gate of the house the old lady had mentioned, "first on the right," then summoned up their courage and entered. After all

they were invited guests. . . . They walked round to the
side of the house and there they found a tea laid for four
on the verandah, just as the old lady had said. It was a
most sumptuous tea, spread upon a dainty lace
tablecloth—cups and plates of eggshell china, tea in a
silver tea-pot, cream in a silver cream jug, wafer-like
bread and butter, buttered tea-cake, iced cakes, choc-
olate biscuits and a big currant cake all arranged taste-
fully upon lace d'oyleys. They sat down weakly upon the
four wicker chairs that were ranged round the table and
gazed at it open-mouthed.

"I *say*," gasped William in a faint voice. "How—how
jolly decent of her! You—you don't find many ole ladies
as decent as this nowadays."

They all looked at the feast eagerly and yet with
compunction.

"She needn't have took so much trouble," said
Ginger, his voice throbbing with gratitude. "We would-
n't've minded a bit havin' it plainer, would we?"

At that moment they heard voices. Four people were
coming round the house to the verandah. And in a flash
some sixth sense informed the Outlaws that these were
the four people for whom the feast was intended. Like
four rabbits making for their burrow they dived into the
only refuge available—through the open French window
just behind them into a small but—mercifully—over-
furnished drawing-room. There with looks of frozen
horror upon their faces they cowered in the only corner
that was invisible from the window.

Their suspicions were only too correct. The four newcomers sat down at the table. Apparently the hostess
after preparing the meal had gone to the post and had
there met her three visitors on their way to her house.
One of them was talking in a thin, plaintive wail:

"I nearly didn't come, my dear. I'm so wretched that I

simply don't know what to do with myself. I don't think
that *anyone's* ever gone through what I'm going through
to-day."

"What's happened?" said one of the others.

"It's Toto. . . . Hadn't you heard, dear? He's lost. He
got lost last night. I haven't seen him." The voice
quavered into tears. "I haven't seen him since four
o'clock yesterday afternoon. I've lived an eternity since
then. Every second as long as an hour. You don't know
what he is to me. To you, of course, he's just a dog, but
to me he's—he's everything." The bereaved one was
abandoning herself luxuriously to her grief—"everything in the world. He's really valuable, of course, but
that's not what upsets me so much. It's he himself. He's
my little friend and comrade, you know. I always call
him that—my little friend and comrade. And he's go-o-
o-o-o-one!"

Apparently Toto's mistress here abandoned herself
yet more luxuriously to her grief. William peeped out
cautiously. She was a small woman with red hair, a
ludicrously grief-stricken expression and a green hat that
was too small for her. Her hostess had evidently heard
her tale before and was making strenuous efforts to
divert the stream.

"Yes, it is *terribly* sad, Mrs. Hoskins, and we all
sympathise with you. Now we want to tell Mrs. Peters all
about our little society."

But Mrs. Hoskins was not to be diverted thus from her
elegy of grief.

"I keep ringing up the police station. Hardly a minute
goes by but what I ring up the police station to see if
they've heard anything yet. They aren't a bit
sympathetic. I'd always heard that the police were such
nice men, but they aren't a bit. They're most
unsympathetic about my poor little Toto. I've just sent

notices round to all the newspapers with descriptions of
him. . . . He's so *appealing*. I expect that someone met
him and simply couldn't resist him. He *is* like that—*irresistible*. I keep thinking about him. He must miss me so
terribly. . . . I do so hope that he's not been stolen by
anyone cru-u-u-u-uel!"

Again the bereaved one buried her face in her
handkerchief. Her hostess seized the opportunity to
change the subject—

"Now let us tell Mrs. Peters about our little society."

William craned forward again.

Mrs. Peters had earnest eyes and an earnest mouth
and an earnest nose. She quivered with earnestness from
head to foot. Every word she uttered thrilled with
earnestness.

"Oh *do!*" she said, "I'm so *interested*. I'm so
honoured to be chosen."

"He was so *beautiful*," moaned Toto's mistress. "I
wouldn't have come out of course if I hadn't felt that I'd
go *mad* if I'd stayed at home alone thinking of Toto any
longer."

Her hostess ignored her and continued talking to the
earnest lady.

"I'm sorry none of the other members could come to
tea to meet you, but Tarkers down at Breenside are
selling off their stock half price so most of them have
gone down there. They say that there are some quite
good silk stockings to be got for three and eleven three."

"How *marvellous*," said the earnest lady earnestly.
"How *too* marvellous, but *do* go on and tell me about
the society."

"Well," said the hostess hastily, with an anxious eye
upon Toto's mistress who was waiting open-mouthed for
an opportunity to re-enter the conversation, "it's a sort
of society for *discussing* things. We meet for tea and

discuss things once a week. We discuss the burning things of the day such as Communism and Vivisection and the Longer Skirt and things like that. Then when we've finished we give the rest of the time to tea and ordinary conversation. Of course an intellectual discussion oughtn't to last too long because it's so exhausting to the intellect. Sometimes we get a book out of the library to read it up beforehand, but we've discussed most of the subjects there are books about in the library now so we have to rely upon the light of Nature."

"How *wonderful*," breathed the earnest lady earnestly.

"Toto's always——" began the lady in the red hat determinedly but her hostess unceremoniously broke in.

"They are always *intellectual* discussions, of course. *Most* intellectual. We discussed the *drama* last week. Some of us had been up to see that sweet new musical comedy at the Gaiety, so we felt quite *au courant*. It's too sweet for words, you know. Such smart dresses and the sweetest tunes. Have you seen it?"

"No," said the earnest lady earnestly, "but how *marvellous*."

"Toto's always——" began the lady in the red hat, but no one took any notice of her and her hostess broke in again:

"We give tea in turns after the discussions, and we all pay a small subscription which goes to *social* work. We do *social* work locally, you know. Last year we presented the Cottage Hospital with an Encyclopædia. So useful, you know, for convalescents doing crossword puzzles——"

"How *wonderful!*"

"Toto's always——"

"——and this year we sent one or two of the village boys down to the seaside for a day. So *educational* for them, you know. Fishes and the sea and that sort of thing. We gave them a little money each to spend on some little souvenir of their visit and they bought rock and were sick on the way home. We didn't *go* with them, of course, you know, but we provided the funds. We're having another meeting next week at which we hope to discuss *Art*. It's always such a wonderful subject to discuss, I think, don't you?''

"*Marvellous*," said the earnest lady earnestly.

"Totosalwaysbeensosweetandcompanionable," said Toto's mistress all in one breath in a determined tone of voice.

The Outlaws, deeply interested in the party, had drawn gradually nearer and nearer the window and now suddenly met the eye of the fourth guest—a large, stout woman who had as yet contributed little to the conversation and who was the only one in their range of vision. In silence they gazed at each other for a few minutes, then she turned to her hostess and said dispassionately:

"There are four boys in your drawing-room."

"Four b——" said her hostess. "There can't be, dear."

"But there are," said the stout lady. "Unless, of course, I'm seeing spirit visitants."

"You must be, dear," said the hostess, "because there certainly aren't any boys in my drawing-room." She turned to the earnest lady and said, "We had a most interesting discussion on that last month. Spirit visitants, you know, and that sort of thing. Most interesting."

"How *marvellous!*" said the earnest lady earnestly.

"Can you still see them?" said the hostess.

"Yes," said the stout lady, still staring at the Outlaws. "I can still see them quite plainly."

"Do they remind you of any dear ones of yours who have passed over?"

"N—no," said the stout lady, still gazing with frowning concentration at the Outlaws. "N—no. Not strongly. My father had a brother that died when he was a boy. One of them may be him."

"Does any of them remind you of your father?"

"Not strongly," said the stout lady. "He was supposed to have been a beautiful child and these are all very plain."

"Surely, dear," said the hostess reproachfully, "surely they have a sort of *spiritual* beauty."

"N—no, I don't think they have," said the stout lady.

"Toto isn't with them, is he?" said Toto's mistress anxiously.

"No," replied the seer, "I don't see Toto anywhere. Just the four boys."

"No. . . . I'm sure," said Toto's mistress in a quivering voice, "that if Toto had passed over it would be to *me* he'd have paid a spirit visit. He was always my little friend and comrade, you know. Always." The voice broke upon a high note.

"I'm so glad that we've got someone with psychic vision," said the hostess complacently. "Mrs. Merton interprets dreams *marvellously* and Mrs. Barmer has a wonderful gift for trimming hats and Mrs. Franklin recites like—like Shakespeare himself, but I've always thought that we needed someone with psychic vision to make our little circle complete. . . . Can you still see them?" she said to the stout lady.

The stout lady's gaze was still fixed upon the Outlaws, who returned it, rooted in horror to the spots on which they stood.

"Yes," said the stout lady, "I can still see them."

"Do they seem to grow fainter or plainer," said the hostess with interest. "I'd go to get a note-book but I'm afraid that if I moved it might disturb the—the *waves*, you know, and they'd vanish."

"They seem to stay just about the same," said the stout lady, keeping an unblinking stare upon the Outlaws, and added, "or perhaps they get a bit plainer."

"I'm sure that Toto was psychic," said Toto's mistress tearfully; "I'm *sure* he was. Somehow he used to snap and bark for no reason at all. I'm sure he saw things."

The stout lady took her eyes off the Outlaws to gaze with interest at Toto's mistress, and they took advantage of that moment to take a hasty step backwards.

"Are they still there?" said the hostess.

The seer looked again.

"No," she said, "they've vanished."

"Something must have disturbed the waves," said the hostess.

But unfortunately at that minute the Outlaws, trying to get farther away from her range of vision, knocked a table over. At the sound the stout lady craned her head into the room.

"I can see them again," she said. "and they're real boys. They must be. They've just knocked a table over."

"*Real* boys!" said the hostess in horror. "How annoying! Who *can* they be? Oh, perhaps they're the boys we sent to the seaside. I told them to come here as soon as they were able and tell us all about it. They must have come to-day and the maid must have forgotten to tell me. . . ."

She went to the French window and flung it wide.

"Come out here, boys," she said. "How *stupid* of you to stay in there without saying anything. And pick up that table. How clumsy you are. I didn't want you

"COME ALONG," SAID THE HOSTESS. "TELL US ABOUT THE
TREAT YOU HAD LAST SATURDAY. NOW, WHAT WAS THE FIRST
THING YOU SAW?"

to-day, but now that you've come you'd better tell us
about your treat. Come along."

She motioned them on to the verandah. They stood
and gazed at her in helpless bewilderment. They had
caught only fragments of the conversation and did not
know whom she took them for, nor what she expected of
them.

"Come along," she said sharply to William, rightly

"LIONS," SAID WILLIAM. "OH, NO; WE SAW ELEPHANTS FIRST.
WALKIN' ABOUT ALL OVER THE PLACE!"

taking him for the leader. "Tell us about the treat you
had last Saturday."

William sent his mind searching into the recesses of
the past and remembered that an aunt had taken him to
the Zoo last Saturday.

"Now," said the hostess more kindly, "tell us what
was the first thing you saw when you got there."

"Lions," said William.

"*Nonsense!*" said the lady sharply.

"Oh no," said William, "we saw elephants first."

"You *untruthful* little boy," said the hostess sternly, "how *dare* you say such a thing."

"*Where* were those elephants you say you saw?" said the earnest lady with the air of a famous K.C. cross-examining a prisoner.

"Walkin' about all over the place," said William. "Camels, too."

"*Nonsense!*" put in the hostess. "How *can* you expect us to believe such wicked stories?"

"What did you see next?" said the earnest lady, still with an air of judicial cunning.

"Tigers," said William, "an' bears an' wolves an' hyenas an' snakes."

"Perhaps he's psychic," said the stout lady suddenly. "Perhaps he sees places as they were before the pre-historic animals were driven out. Perhaps they were *spirit* animals."

"You didn't see a dear little dog among them, did you?" said Toto's mistress anxiously.

"You're a wicked, untruthful boy," said the hostess severely. "I know for a fact that there isn't a *single* lion in Belton-on-Sea."

"I didn't go to Belton-on-Sea," said William. "I went to the Zoo."

The look of severity on the hostess's face deepened so much that William did what he had been longing to do ever since he entered the house—dashed down the drive to the gate in precipitous flight, followed by his gallant band.

In the road, seeing that they were not being pursued, they stopped to draw breath.

"*Crumbs!*" said Ginger faintly, "what a *norful* time."

"Yes, an' think of all the time we've wasted when we might 've been makin' money," said William.

"Wonder what the ole lady meant," said Douglas thoughtfully, "wonder if she jus' made a mistake an' meant first house on the left or somethin' like that."

"Yes, I wonder," said Henry.

But they didn't wonder long. They retraced their steps to the refreshment stall and found it emptied of buns and lemonade. Only their notice was left, turned upside down with something written on the other side. There was no sign of the hospitable old lady. Wide-eyed with horror they approached and read the notice:

"Many thanks for buns and lemonade—

"Hubert Lane.

"P.S. Aren't I a nice old lady!"

"It was *him!*" cried the Outlaws with mingled fury and despair. "It was *him! He's done it again*. What 're we goin' to do now?"

But nobody answered for nobody knew. They stood, a drooping, disconsolate group around their empty stall.

"We can't even fight 'em," said Ginger mournfully, " 'cause they'll take jolly good care not to come out of their garden gates."

"An' I don't see *how* we can get ten pounds now," said Douglas. "It's after tea-time an' he wants the money in to-night to read out at prayers to-morrow mornin'."

"An' we haven't even had any tea," said Henry, "an' I'm feelin' jolly hungry."

"Well, there doesn't seem anythin' to stay here for," said William, eyeing the empty stall distastefully. "I votes we go home to tea anyway. It's no good goin' without tea on top of everything else."

They set off down the road, walking slowly, dejectedly and in silence. Suddenly Ginger, who was walking at the side of the road, said:

"I think there's a rat in the ditch. I saw something move."

Even their dejection, great as it was, was not proof against that. They brightened and hung over the ditch, peering down.

"Where?"

"There! It moved again."

They dived down to investigate. It was not a rat. It was Toto—Toto, most minute of minute toy dogs. Toto, jaunty, abandoned and debauched-looking, making his rollicking way homewards through the ditch after his night out.

Ginger held it up by the scruff of its neck.

"It's a dog," he said doubtfully.

Toto leered at them and emitted a sound like a snigger.

"It's got a name on its collar," said William. "See what it is."

Ginger read it out.

"It's the house jus' up the hill," he said. "P'raps it's that woman that was carryin' on at tea."

And it was. It was a large, rich-looking house with a large, rich-looking garden and a large, rich-looking door was opened by a large, rich-looking butler, and the Outlaws were shown into a large, rich-looking room. The lady was there still wearing the red hat. She had just come in. She screamed when she saw Toto, and then, holding him to her breast, went into hysterics, till Toto brought her out of them by biting her ear.

Then she held out both hands to the Outlaws.

"My dear, dear boys!" she said and kissed them.

They blushed with shame to their very souls.

Then she went to a writing-table and brought them a sheet of paper on which something was written.

"Read that!" she said dramatically.

But the writing was so wild that they couldn't read anything but the word "Reward." Then she took an envelope and thrust it into their hands. On it was written "For Toto's Finder."

"I've had it ready and waiting," she said, "ever since I sent that notice to the papers, and it's yours by right, dear boys. Yours by right. Toto is worth hundreds of pounds to *anyone* but to me he's worth millions because he's my dear little friend and comrade."

Bewildered they went out to the road.

There they opened the envelope she had given them.

In it was a ten-pound note.

* * *

It was the next morning. The school was assembled in the big hall. The headmaster began to read out the sums earned by the various groups for the new wing.

The youngest boy in the school—aged seven—had alone and unaided collected ten shillings. He had gone round to his friends and relations asking them in all good faith for money for new wings for the headmaster and so had met with a better response than he probably would have done had he had a clearer conception of the object of the fund.

The headmaster read the list slowly and impressively. He came to the group of names headed by "Hubert Lane" and he read "Five Pounds." There was a faint burst of applause. Then he came to the group of names headed by "William Brown."

The Hubert Laneites turned round to the Outlaws with jeering grins of anticipated triumph.

The headmaster read out "Ten Pounds." The applause was the more deafening because the Outlaws were popular and the Hubert Laneites were not. The mouths of the Hubert Laneites dropped open weakly. The Outlaws stared in front of them with looks of calm and superior aloofness.

But the best was yet to come. The Outlaws and the Hubert Laneites met face to face on the playground.

"We didn't half pull your leg," said William, "pretendin' not to know who you were yesterday. We were laughin' fit to burst inside all the time."

And whatever inflation had been left in the Hubert Laneites departed.

Chapter 7

Fireworks Strictly Prohibited

"We've got to have fireworks this year," said William in his most Napoleonic manner, "we've simply *got* to."

In previous Novembers the pyrotechnical attempts of the Outlaws had been doomed to frustration by various unkind strokes of fate. On several occasions they had had all their fireworks confiscated on the very Fifth itself in retribution for what the Outlaws considered trifling misdemeanours. On one occasion Douglas, who was carrying them to the scene of the display, had fallen into the stream while executing a dance of anticipatory exultation on the plank that served as a bridge. The other Outlaws had immediately concentrated all their energy on rescuing the fireworks, leaving Douglas to his fate, but all the virtue had gone out of them when rescued, and though the Outlaws used upon them half a dozen boxes of matches ("borrowed" from Ginger's mother's store cupboard) they refused to function.

But last year had been the most glorious fiasco of all. Last year, inspired by a chapter in a book called "Things a Boy Can Do," that someone had given to Henry, they had decided to make their own fireworks. They had managed to secure some gunpowder, and though they persisted that they had followed most faithfully the directions given in the book, the shed in which they were manufacturing them had been completely wrecked, and the Outlaws themselves had narrowly escaped with their lives.

"How're we goin' to get any?" said Henry.

"Let's save up," suggested Ginger. "Let's start savin' up at once."

This suggestion roused very little enthusiasm. Henry's pocket-money had been stopped indefinitely to pay for a broken window. Douglas was, under strict parental supervision, saving up to buy a birthday present for his godmother (his resentment at this was made more bitter by the fact that his godmother's last birthday present to him had been a copy of "Pilgrim's Progress"). Robert, William's elder brother, was receiving weekly so large a proportion of William's pocket-money in payment for a pocket compass of his that William had "borrowed" and lost that it didn't seem worth while to do anything with the residuum but spend it on sweets. And Ginger, despite his suggestion of saving, was one of those unfortunates who never have any money. It didn't matter whether he received his pocket-money or not. He never had any money. Near to the front gate of his house there was a little shop where lollipops and darts and squibs and toy pistols were sold, and if there was any money at all in his pocket Ginger could never pass this shop without going in.

Hence the lack of enthusiasm with which William's suggestion was received.

"What about makin' some?" said Ginger tentatively.

"We tried that last year," said William gloomily, "don' you remember?"

"Yes," said Ginger slowly, "I remember. They said that when they heard the bang they thought we were all killed an' you'd 've thought by the way they went on at us when they found we weren't that they'd *wanted* us to be."

"We'd better not do it again," said Henry. "It was fun, but it was such a trouble gettin' the gunpowder an' it wasn't the right sort when we got it. It cun't 've been the right sort, 'cause we did it jus' like it said to do it in the book, and it oughtn't to have gone off like that."

"No, we've jus' got to either get some money to buy them or get them given us," said Douglas.

"Who'd give 'em us?" asked Ginger simply.

"Let's ask people," said William hopefully, "let's ask our fathers. I bet they used to have 'em when they were our age."

"I jolly well *bet* they did," said Ginger, "though I bet they'll say they didn't if we ask 'em. If they'd *reelly* been the sort of boys like what they pretend they were they must 've been jolly funny, that's all I can say, an' I'm jolly glad I didn't go to the same school as them."

"We'll ask 'em anyway," said Douglas and added, "I wonder why it's called Guy Fawkes Day."

" 'Cause a man called Guy Fawkes tried to blow up the House of Commons," said Henry. Henry was always the best informed of the Outlaws.

"Why?"

" 'Cause he di'n' like 'em, I s'pose."

"Why di'n' he like 'em?"

"People don't like 'em. You should hear my father goin' on about 'em. I bet he'd blow 'em up if he knew how to."

"Why di'n' this man—this Guy whoever he was—blow 'em up?"

"Dunno. I expect they sold him the wrong sort of gunpowder same as they sold us. The sort that goes off too soon."

"Well, anyway, I don't see why people have fireworks

every year jus' 'cause he di'n' blow up the House of Commons."

Henry thought over this for some minutes in silence. Henry never liked to own himself at a loss.

"I know," he said at last. "They felt so sick at him not doin' it. You see it 'd 've been such a jolly good sort of thing to watch. The House of Commons shootin' right up into the air like that. So they started havin' fireworks to sort of comfort themselves with. You know—tryin' to see a bit what it 'd 've been like if he hadn't made a mess of it. An' "—with a rush of inspiration—"that's why they burn him. 'Cause they're so fed up with him makin' such a mess of it."

"I see," said William, completely satisfied with the explanation. "Course we'll have to have a guy too. We mustn't forget a guy."

"Who'll we have?" said Ginger.

"We'll wait to see nearer the time who's been worst to us," said William with an air of calm, judicial impartiality.

*   *   *

William approached his requests for fireworks with over-elaborate tact.

He went into the morning-room after lunch when his father was there alone reading the paper, and sat down in an arm-chair opposite him on the other side of the fireplace.

"Father," he said brightly, "I expect you used to have a jolly good time when you was a boy, didn't you?"

"Uh?" said his father without looking up from the paper.

"I say, I expect you used to have a jolly good time when you was a boy, di'n' you?"

"Were a boy," said Mr. Brown absently. "You were a boy. I was a boy."

"Yes, I know," said William patiently, "that's jus' what I'm tryin' to talk about. About when you was a boy."

Mr. Brown groaned but said nothing.

William tried again.

"I expect you used to have a jolly good time," he said.

"Uh?" said his father again, absently turning over a page of his paper.

"I say I expect you used to have a jolly good time when you was a boy."

Mr. Brown, who was once more lost in the financial news, emerged from it again, vaguely aware that someone was addressing him.

"What did you say?" he said irritably.

"I say I expect you used to have a jolly good time when you were—was a boy."

"I thought you'd said that once," said Mr. Brown.

"Yes," said William, "I did. I was—I was jus' sayin' it again."

"What do you want?" said Mr. Brown shortly.

"Fireworks," said William, abandoning finesse.

"Well," said Mr. Brown with a simplicity as beautiful as his son's, "you won't get any out of me. Or out of anyone else if I can help it. When I remember——"

At this point William, rightly suspecting that a highly coloured description of his abortive career as a firework manufacturer was about to follow, crept from the room.

He met the other Outlaws in the old barn.

"Wasn't any good with *mine*," he said morosely. "Simply no good at all. He jus' started rememberin' that time when they gave us the wrong sort of gunpowder. Jus' as if it'd been *our* faults."

"So did mine," said Henry.

"So did mine," said Douglas.

"So did mine," said Ginger.

"I hope," said Ginger sadly, "that it won't come to jus' tryin' to watch ole Colonel Masters same as it had done some years."

Colonel Masters was a choleric old gentleman who lived with his sister at the other end of the village. Every November he had an elaborate firework display to which he invited a small band of his intimate friends, among whom he did not include the Outlaws. Moreover, he disliked the Outlaws and strongly objected to them as uninvited spectators. The back garden where his firework display was always held was surrounded by a high wall, and during his firework display he always kept a hose in readiness for any small boys' heads that might appear above it. The Outlaws had been dislodged from posts of vantage by this means on several occasions.

"Yes," said William gloomily, "an' get nee'ly drowned an' then have our mothers goin' on as if it was *our* fault. An' not see anythin' at that. No, this year we're jolly well goin' to have a firework show of our own. At least we are if I know anything about it."

So very impressive did William sound that for a moment the Outlaws felt as if the whole thing were settled down to the smallest detail. Then Ginger said:

"How're we goin' to get 'em?"

"That's what we've gotter decide now," said William.

"I *know*," said Ginger suddenly. "My aunt. She's coming to stay with us. She's goin' home the day before firework day. She always gives me five shillin's."

The Outlaws turned cartwheels exultantly in the middle of the road.

"There," said William, sitting up panting and covered with dust on the spot where he had overbalanced, "I *knew* we'd hit on somethin'."

"It's *my* aunt," said Ginger, thinking that due importance was not being given to him as originator of the suggestion.

"Yes, an' if it's the one what wears the feather thing round her neck you can *keep* her," said William.

Ginger assumed a truculent attitude and expression, then, as if thinking that his aunt was not really worth fighting for, pretended that he had not heard.

"Well, *that's* all right then," said William, disappointed of a scrap with Ginger, but cheered at the thought of the fireworks that were to be bought with Ginger's aunt's five shillings. "We'll wait till the day before when Ginger's aunt gives him his five shillin's an' then we'll buy 'em. We can get a jolly good lot for five shillin's. I bet we can get some of all the sorts in the world for five shillin's. An' we'll wait till nearer the time to see who's been worst to us before we fix on who we'll have for a guy."

They watched Colonel Masters with interest during the days that followed. The thought of his firework display fascinated them. They were convinced that their own display would be superior to it in every way and yet they were consumed with curiosity to see what his was to be like. They dogged his footsteps as he went to and fro in the village—a conspicuous figure in his grey bowler hat and brown overcoat. They followed him whenever he set forth from his gate, hoping that he was going to the village shop to buy his fireworks. They began to feel that it was absolutely imperative that they should know what fireworks Colonel Masters was having, in order to surpass them. There was, they felt, nothing in the world in the way of fireworks that couldn't be bought for five shillings. They even had glorious visions of Colonel Masters creeping near to watch their display and their turning the hose pipe on to him. It was, of course, useless to approach him directly and ask him what fireworks he was going to have. He possessed an excessively military temper and went purple at the mere sight of the Outlaws. He had first made their acquaintance in his orchard, and had met them subsequently on several occasions in his strawberry beds. So terrible had he been on those occasions that they fled him now on sight, following him very discreetly on his expeditions to the village and scattering whenever he turned round. His sister—a little old lady as mild as she was choleric—lived with him and kept house for him. She was of a nervous temperament and spent her life cherishing him. She was easier to approach, of course, than her brother, but she was uncommunicative. She refused to enter into conversation with the Outlaws. All she would say to them was "Go away, you naughty little boys. I know all about you. Go away."

The Outlaws' spirits rose, however, when they heard that she was going to tea with William's mother. William promised to put in an appearance at tea-time and bring back full particulars of the Colonel's fireworks.

William did not usually take tea with his mother when she was entertaining visitors and she was as surprised as her visitor when William—a radiant vision of cleanliness and neatness (it had taken him nearly an hour to effect the miracle) and wearing his smuggest expression—entered the drawing-room at tea-time and began to hand round the cakes. So amazed were they that a dead silence fell upon them and they gazed at him helplessly. William took this as a silence of admiration, and the smugness of his expression deepened. He handed the cake-stand to the visitor with a courtly bow, fell over the hearthrug, upset the sugar, and then, choosing the largest bun within his range of vision, returned with it to the corner of the room to listen to the conversation. His mother and his mother's visitor gradually recovered from their paralysis and continued the conversation where it had been ruthlessly cut off by William's spectacular appearance. The conversation lacked its pristine verve and ever and anon they threw helpless glances at William, who sat smug and clean and shining in his corner munching his bun. His mother was hoping that the visitor would think that William always looked like this, and the visitor was wondering whether this was some member of the family that she'd never seen before. She was rather short-sighted, but she thought that he bore a strong family resemblance to the dirty little boy who'd annoyed her brother so much by trespassing in his garden. That reminded her of her brother and she began to talk about him again. She seldom talked about anything else for long.

"I'm so nervous about it all," she said plaintively. "I think that these firework displays are so dangerous. One reads of such terrible things in the newspapers. But he *will* have them—every year—though I *beg* him not to. You've no idea what I go through beforehand. After all, the things are made of gunpowder, and it's a notorious fact that gunpowder is highly explosive. *One* of those catherine wheels and things can do untold damage. Just a slight flaw in the manufacture and *hundreds* of people may be killed. Gunpowder, you know. I *tell* them so. I *beg* him every year not to have them, but he takes no notice of me."

The highly-polished figure of William spoke ingratiatingly and in its best company voice from its corner.

"Has he got his fireworks yet?" it said.

Miss Masters turned her short-sighted eyes vaguely in his direction.

"Yes," she said despondently, "I'm afraid he has. In

spite of all I've said to him I'm afraid he has. He's got them from Tanks' in London. I've refused to have them in the house, though. He's keeping them in the shed at the bottom of the garden."

Then the conversation tailed off to the rummage sale that Mrs. Brown was getting up and to which Miss Masters had promised to send an old hat and coat of her brother's, and while that was going on the sleek and radiant figure of William was seen to creep quietly from the room. A close observer might have noticed that its pockets now bulged considerably where it had, with a deftness acquired by long practice, unobtrusively secreted cakes for the other Outlaws.

"What a nice little boy," said Miss Masters when the door had closed on him.

"Y—yes," said William's mother uncertainly. She was wondering helplessly why William had come and where he had gone.

Outside in the road William distributed his largess, then turned head over heels in the dust several times in order to rid himself of the revolting and unfamiliar feeling of spruceness.

"Well," said the Outlaws indistinctly from behind half-masticated buns, "did you find anything out?"

"Yes," said William triumphantly as, still sitting in the dust, he carefully stroked his hair up the wrong way. "Yes, I did too. I found out that he's gottem from London an' that they're in the shed at the bottom of the garden."

The Outlaws hastily swallowed what remained of their buns and stood up. "Come on," said Ginger succinctly, "let's go'n' have a look at them."

The inside of the shed was plainly visible from the top of the garden wall. Balanced precariously upon the top of the wall the Outlaws craned their necks to see through the little window.

"I can see a box of catherine wheels," chanted William.

"I can see a box of rockets," said Ginger.

"I can see some Roman candles," said Douglas.

But what they didn't see was the figure of Colonel Masters, who had espied and recognised them from afar, creeping up behind the shed with his garden hose. They didn't see it, in fact, till the stream of water hit them full and square on the face and dislodged them precipitately into the road below. For some time they sat there, gasping and spluttering, bereft of the power of speech. Then William, damp but impressive, said slowly, "Well, that *settles* it. There isn't any doubt about it at *all* now. We're goin' to have *him* for our guy."

They separated their several ways homewards, each intent upon the problem of how to enter his home unseen.

William thought that he had succeeded. He reached his bedroom door without meeting anyone, but with the usual perversity of fate met his mother there just as he was thinking himself safe. She was carrying a brown overcoat and a grey bowler hat.

"*William!*" she gasped.

But William's eyes were fixed upon the hat and coat.

"Whose are those?" he said.

"Colonel Masters'," she said absently, "at least they're for the rummage stall. But what *have* you been doing?"

"A crule man turned the hosepipe on us," said William pathetically.

"What were you doing?"

"Jus' sitting on a wall."

"What wall?"

"Jus' a wall," said William, "jus' sittin' on a wall for a rest same as anyone might. Well, no one can go on walking for ever an ever without a rest. You've gotter sit down an' have a rest sometimes. An' we sat down to rest on this wall 'cause," with a sudden burst of inspiration, " 'cause we didn't want to spoil our clothes sittin' on the ground. It was our clothes we was thinkin' about. You're always tellin' us to take more care of our clothes.

"I CAN'T GET IN MY HOUSE," GINGER EXPLAINED, "'CAUSE MY MOTHER'D SEE ME COMIN' IN AT THE GATE."

"BAD LUCK," SAID WILLIAM. "I SAY," HE ADDED
EXULTANTLY, "IT'S ALL RIGHT ABOUT THE GUY!"

So that's what we was tryin' to do. Well, as soon as we'd
sat down on the wall jus' for a rest so as not to get our
clothes dirty with sittin' on the ground along comes the
crule man with a hosepipe and turned it on to us all. You
ask Ginger if it wasn't like that, if you don't believe me.
He'll tell you it was. Jus' sitting on a wall to rest so's not
to get our clothes dirty sittin' on the ground, when along
comes this——"

"William, *will* you stop talking and go in and change.
You're soaking."

William went into his bedroom and closed the door. A
small pebble hit the window. He went to it and opened
it. Ginger, a disconsolate and still dripping figure, was
below.

"I say," whispered Ginger, "can you throw me down

somethin' to dry with? I can't get in my house 'cause my mother's sittin' jus' at the drawin'-room window an' she'd see me comin' in at the gate."

William carelessly threw down his bath towel and proceeded to dry his own person on his counterpane, standing at the window. Thus engaged, they conversed.

"I say," said William exultantly, "it'll be all right about makin' *him* the guy. I've found out where I can borrow some of his clothes."

* * *

The first setback the Outlaws received was a sudden and unexpected parental ban on any firework display at all. It happened that William's father and Ginger's father and Douglas's father and Henry's father travelled to town in the same carriage one morning, and it happened that they mentioned and discussed last year's firework fiasco and finally agreed that the safest plan would be to forbid fireworks at all this year. As William's father put it, "The young scoundrels are sure to blow the place up if we don't," and as Ginger's father still more succinctly put it, "After all, we know them and it's foolish to take risks."

This parental ban did not very seriously disquiet the Outlaws. "What I'm goin' to take it to mean," said William, "is that we've not gotter let off any fireworks where they can see or hear 'em. Well, that's nacherally what they mean, isn't it? I mean, you don't mind anythin' you can't see, do you? You nacherally don't. So it's jus' that that they mean. They don't like lookin' at fireworks an' they don't like the sound of 'em and so that's why they've told us not to have 'em. But it'll be all right nacherally if we have 'em where they can't see 'em or hear 'em. That's what they mean. Well, anyway," he ended shortly, "that what's *I'm* goin' to think they mean."

The other Outlaws agreed that that was what *they* were going to think they meant too.

The days before November the Fifth were spent in preparation. The Outlaws had decided to hold their show in the field behind the old barn and preparations were made in the old barn. The chief preparation consisted in the making of the guy. William had successfully "borrowed" from the box-room, where the rummage goods were being stored, the brown overcoat and grey hat that had been the property of Colonel Masters. Moreover, they had secured a mask with very red cheeks and an upturned moustache that bore a strong resemblance to the military gentleman himself, and from these materials they had manufactured a guy truly worthy of the magnificence of the occasion.

"No one can see it an' not know who it's meant to be," said William gazing at it with deep satisfaction, "and it's all right about the clothes 'cause the sale isn't till a week after Fireworks Day an' we're only borrowin' them. We needn't reelly burn them. At least," he said slowly, "If they sort of catch fire we won't be able to help it. They'll be mad, of course, but," he ended simply, "after a firework show like what ours is goin' to be it won't matter much what happens to us afterwards. It'll be worth it."

Although the five shillings that Ginger's aunt was to give them was not yet in their possession, they had allotted every penny of it in imagination. They had discussed its expenditure for literally days together. They had spent whole mornings and afternoons with their noses glued to the window of the village shop. They had decided on their purchases down to the smallest squibs.

They could hardly believe that they weren't actually in possession of them. As William said:

"It'll only jus' be a case of goin' out to fetch 'em.

We've got 'em settled on all right. It won't take a minute once Ginger's aunt's given us the money. We've as good as got 'em now."

Meantime they prepared the old barn and sat round their guy gazing at it proudly.

"Of course, if it catches alight," said William again dreamily, "I don't see how we can help it. It's only ole clothes for a rubbish sale. Well, it'll be savin' my mother the trouble of sellin' 'em if they do happen to catch fire. It'll look jolly fine all burnin' up."

On the morning of November the fifth they were in a state of barely concealed exuberance.

William's father looked at him suspiciously during breakfast.

"You haven't forgotten what I said about those fireworks, have you?" he said.

William hastily assumed his smug expression and said with perfect truth, "No, father."

"A silly, childish habit," said Mr. Brown. "I'd grown out of it long before I'd reached your age. Noisy and dangerous and extravagant and of no earthly use to anyone."

"Yes, father," agreed William. "That's what I think."

"I'm very glad to hear it," said Mr. Brown grimly, "very glad indeed."

"Yes, father," said William.

It was Mr. Brown, not William, who felt that the conversation had been vaguely unsatisfactory.

At the same moment Henry's father and Douglas's father were holding similar conversations with their sons.

"It's a stupid, uncivilised habit," said Henry's father. "It's amazing to me that any intelligent boy can give a thought to it."

And Henry agreed.

"When I was your age," said Douglas's father, "my mind was too much taken up with my school work to have room for such foolishness as fireworks."

Douglas implied that his was, too.

But it was Ginger's father who produced the bombshell.

"Your aunt has given you five shillings, as usual," he said, "but I am taking charge of it for you till after to-day. I'll give it to you at the end of the week. I didn't want you to be exposed to the temptation of spending it on fireworks."

Ginger, aghast, hastened to convey the news to his friends.

"He's got it an' he's not givin' it me till the end of the week," he said.

For a moment the Outlaws were speechless with horror. Then they ejected "*Crumbs!*" in tones of helpless horror.

" 'S not my fault," said Ginger weakly; "I told him I wanted it to-day *most* particular, but he di'n't take no notice. I told him I wanted it for a pore old man what might be dead to-morrow. That wasn't a very big story 'cause I was thinkin' of the guy. But, anyway, he di'n't take no notice even of that. If it *had* been a *reel* old man I'd wanted it for," he went on with stern and righteous indignation, "an' he'd starved to death to-day it'd serve him right if he'd got put in prison for murderin' him."

"Yes, but what're we goin' to *do?*" said William.

Douglas's suggestion of postponing the firework display till the next week was dismissed as unworthy of them. As William said:

"You might as well put up holly an' stuff for New Year's Day or have pancakes on Ash Wednesday. There wouldn't be any *sense* in it."

Henry's suggestion of merely burning the guy without any accompaniment of fireworks was also dismissed contemptuously. "There wouldn't be any sense in that either," said William.

For several minutes the Outlaws contented themselves with a hymn of hate against Ginger's father, in which Ginger joined whole heartedly.

"*Mean*. That's what it is."

"Stealin', I call it."

"People can get put in prison for takin' other people's money."

"Serve him right if we went to the police."

"An' that poor ole man starvin' to death," said Douglas vaguely.

They felt a little better after a few minutes of this and turned to face the future more courageously.

"Well, what 're we goin' to *do*?" said Ginger.

"We're goin' to get some fireworks *somehow*," said William firmly.

In the silence that followed their thoughts all turned in the same direction.

"He keeps the shed locked, dun't he?" said Ginger thoughtfully.

"Yes," said William, "windows and all."

"But he's gone to London to-day," said Douglas. "I saw him goin' down to the station. He'll prob'ly not come back till jus' before time to get his fireworks ready."

There was another long silence. Then Ginger said to William:

"Didn't you say she was nervous of 'em?"

"Yes," said William.

And the plan leapt like Aphrodite, full grown, into the brains of both William and Ginger, simultaneously. They never even quarrelled as to who had thought of it first because they knew that both of them had thought of it in the same second.

* * *

Miss Masters moved restlessly from room to room. She'd be thankful when this terrible day was over. November the Fifth was always as long as a week to her. One read of such dreadful things in the paper. A knock at the front door bell startled her. She went to answer it. A small boy with his arm in a sling and his face bandaged stood there and asked her with exquisite politeness what the time was. She told him, gazing at him anxiously.

"What have you done to yourself, my little man?" she said kindly.

"I was jus' helpin' my father get the fireworks ready for to-night an' some of them went off," said her little man.

"Poor *child!*" said Miss Masters deeply moved; "and was your father hurt?"

"Yes," said the child, "he was hurt very bad. They've took him to the hospital."

"Dear, *dear!*" said Miss Masters anxiously. "I've always said they were nasty, dangerous things."

"Yes, they are," said the child whole heartedly. "I feel I never want to see one of 'em again anyway. Eleven o'clock, did you say? Thank you very much indeed. I'm sorry to have troubled you. Good mornin'."

Still with exquisite politeness the child took his leave and Miss Masters watched him pitifully as he walked down the garden path.

"Poor little chap!" she murmured as she closed the door.

Her restlessness increased. November the Fifth seemed a more terrible day than ever. The poor little chap. And his father in hospital. The fireworks going off as they were getting them ready. Nasty, dangerous things. She'd *begged* Alexander not to have them this year, but he was so obstinate. She had terrible visions of Alexander with his face bandaged up and his arm in a sling like this poor boy, or being carried off to hospital like this poor boy's father. Just went off as they were getting them ready. . . . Terrible. There came another knock at the front door. She went to answer it. Another small boy stood there. He leaned heavily upon two sticks and his face was bandaged. He too spoke with exquisite politeness.

"I hope you'll kin'ly excuse me for troublin' you," he said, "but would you kin'ly tell me the way to the doctor's?"

"Good gracious!" gasped Miss Masters.

"It's not for me," said the boy, "it's for my pore uncle. We were jus' gettin' the fireworks ready this mornin' an' they went off. My uncle's in bed hurt very bad indeed. Doesn't think he'll ever be able to walk again."

"Good heavens!" gasped Miss Masters, "how terrible, how *very* terrible!"

"I'm only hurt a bit, of course," said the boy modestly; "the doctor says that I'll be able to walk without sticks quite all right in about three months, but my uncle's hurt very bad indeed. I'm goin' to the doctor's now for some more medicine for him. But I don't live here. I'm only stayin' with him. So that's why I don't know the way to the doctor's, so I came to ask you very kin'ly to tell me."

In a faint voice Miss Masters directed him to the doctor's, received his exquisitely-polite thanks and watched him hobble slowly and painfully down the drive. He hobbled beautifully till he had turned the corner of the road and then, like the other boy, he began to leap and run and tear off his bandages. An observer would have supposed that that corner of the road possessed miraculous healing powers. Miss Masters, of course, did not see this miraculous cure. She watched the hobbling form with tears of pity in her eyes and then turned to pace her drawing-room, distracted. She had visions of Alexander hobbling like that with both his arms in slings and his face covered with bandages. It was terrible . . . terrible. She must do something. She must do something at once. It was no use pleading with Alexander. She'd pleaded with him already. He was deaf and obdurate. Wringing her hands, she went down the garden path to the shed where the fireworks were kept. She unlocked the door and stood gazing at them in horror. Suddenly she saw an eye looking down at her from the top of the wall. It was only an eye. Bandages completely concealed the face and head it belonged to. The bandaged head reposed on the wall like a pudding in a cloth, except for the eye that gleamed through a slight aperture. William, who did nothing on a mean scale, had used half a dozen bandages ("borrowed" from Douglas's mother's bandage box) on himself. He had even taken off his collar and tie and bandaged his neck till it was almost as large as his head.

Miss Masters gazed with helpless horror at this apparition. It looked like something out of a nightmare. After fixing her with its eye for some moments in silence, it proceeded to address her in a muffled, indistinct voice.

"I jus' happened to be passin'," it said, "an' I jus' happened to see all them fireworks in the shed, an' I got up here to see if I could see anyone to speak to about it."

So bewildered and horrified was Miss Masters that she did not stop to wonder how this boy, who happened to be passing, had happened to see the fireworks in the shed through a high brick wall.

"H—have you had an accident, boy?" she said faintly.

"Yes," said the apparition in its muffled voice, "a norful accident. I was jus' gettin' our fireworks ready for to-night." Miss Masters groaned. "An' a lot of 'em went off sudden, without any warnin' at all. Our doctor says there's been a norful lot of accidents to-day 'cause of that. He says that ever so many people 've had orful accidents with them. He says that he thinks there's somethin' wrong with the gunpowder people 've made the fireworks out of this year, an' that other people oughter be warned about it. That's what he says. I look somethin' orful under this bandage. You've no idea. All blown up." Miss Masters shuddered and closed her eyes. "Somethin' orful," went on William, pleased and encouraged by her expression. "Well, I was jus' passin' like what I told you, an' I saw your shed with the fireworks in an' I thought that I'd better warn the person they belonged to, to save her bein' blown up like what I was. I thought that I'd better warn the person they belonged to that there was somethin' wrong with the gunpowder what was bein' put in fireworks this year. Do they belong to you?" ended the muffled voice innocently.

"No," said Miss Masters wildly, "they don't. They belong to my brother. I know that what you said is true because I have already seen two other victims of the terrible accidents you describe. My poor boy. Does it hurt much."

"Somethin' terrible," said the muffled voice, "worse than toothache. But I don't care about myself. I wanted to save other people from sufferin' agony like what I'm sufferin'. You'd better ask your brother not to let off his fireworks else he'll have an orful accident same as me an' the others."

"But I've begged him not to," wailed Miss Masters. "He won't listen to me. . . . Oh, what *shall* I do?"

"Tell you what," said the muffled voice suddenly; "I've jus' thought of somethin'. Let me take 'em away from you an' throw 'em into the stream so that no one 'll be able to let 'em off. I'll do that for you. Jus' to save anyone else going through the orful agony what I'm sufferin'. I feel as if I don't ever want to see 'em or touch 'em again, but jus' to save your brother from sufferin' the orful agony I'm sufferin', I'll do that for you. I'll take 'em all down to the stream an' throw 'em in so that they can't go off sudden an' make anyone else suffer the orful agony what I'm sufferin'. Jus' to help you save your brother from orful agony, I'll do that, though I feel I never want to see 'em or touch 'em again."

The whole eye gazed expectantly at Miss Masters through the aperture in the mass of bandages.

"But I daren't," moaned Miss Masters. "I really daren't. He'd be so angry. No, I daren't do that. It would be wrong."

The eye gazed at her speculatively for a minute, as if in deep thought, then brightened.

"Tell you what," said the muffled voice, "there wouldn't be any harm jus' unlocking the shed door an' chancin' 'em gettin' stole, would there? That wouldn't be the same as givin' 'em away to someone, would it? Well, that's what I'd do if I was you. I'd leave the shed door open an' chance 'em gettin' stole. Mind you, maybe no one 'll steal 'em with all these accidents about. They'll all know about the wrong sort of gunpowder bein' used in 'em this year. Still, *p'raps* some tramp 'll take 'em. Anyway, that's what I'd do. I wun't give 'em away to someone to put in the stream either. I don't think that's right. But I think that leavin' the shed door unlocked and chancin' 'em gettin' stole's quite different. I'd do that all right. I wun't do the other either, but I *would* do that. I don't think there'd be anything wrong in that. Well, I wun't s'gest it if I thought it was wrong," the muffled voice ended anxiously.

Miss Masters wrung her hands again. "It doesn't seem—it doesn't seem *quite* right," she said, "but I think I *will* . . . it seems the only thing to do short of throwing or giving them away, which I daren't. Yes, I'll do that. I'll leave the shed door unlocked for just half an hour and if they haven't been stolen by then, I'll know that fate doesn't *mean* them to be. Thank you, dear boy, for——"

But the eye was already disappearing down the other side of the wall.

Miss Masters wrung her hands again and moaned. "But how *awful* . . . how *terrible!*" Then she went to the shed door, unlocked it, and returned to the house to lie down for half an hour. She felt that she needed rest. She returned to the shed at the end of half an hour. The fireworks were no longer there. Miss Masters inferred that fate had *meant* them to be stolen.

* * *

The Outlaws never discovered who betrayed them, but they suspected their old enemy, Hubert Lane. It happened that the fathers of Ginger, William and Douglas and Henry were walking up from the station together, when they learnt that despite the parental ban the Outlaws were holding—or rather were just about to hold—a firework display in the field behind the old barn. Aflame with righteous indignation, the four fathers left the high road and proceeded over the field to the scene of the crime.

The display was just on the point of beginning when they arrived. The guy stood in the middle—an impressive figure with his grey bowler, brown overcoat and upturned military moustache. Around, affixed to trees, were catherine wheels of every size, and William already held a rocket in his hand. The four fathers had walked to the scene prepared to exact summary retribution, but the minute they arrived on the scene something happened. They had been boys together.

"Catherine wheels," said Ginger's father. "I say—they're about twice the size of the ones we used to have."

"And the fools have got them fixed up all wrong," said William's father, proceeding to fix them up all right.

"And look at the way this idiot's holding the rocket," said Douglas's father, taking it from William and proceeding to hold it the right way, absently applying a light to it as he did so.

William's father had set off one of the catherine wheels, Ginger's father was setting off the rockets, Henry's father was just preparing a Roman candle, and Douglas's father was opening another box of rockets.

"I say," Douglas's father was saying, "do you remember that Fifth when you——?"

And Ginger's father was saying at the same time, "Do you remember that Fifth when we——?"

They seemed suddenly to notice the presence of the Outlaws. "Clear off, you kids," they said shortly, "what are you hanging about for? Clear *off!*"

Dumbfounded and aghast at the turn events had taken, the Outlaws cleared off.

They walked slowly down the road away from the field. From behind came the voices of their parents raised excitedly, "I say, I remember letting one like this off that year that——" came bangs and fiery sparks.

"*Well!*" said William bitterly, "think of that. Jus' *think* of it . . . an' after all the trouble we took to get 'em.

"I SAY," DOUGLAS'S FATHER WAS SAYING, "DO YOU
REMEMBER THAT FIFTH WHEN YOU——?"

I still feel choked with all those things round my neck
and it's a wonder I'm not dead having no place to
breathe through. An' to think of sufferin' all that orful
agony jus' for *them* to let 'em off——"

"I wun't have minded if they'd 've jus' been mad an'
thrown 'em away. I wun' 've minded what they'd 've
done to us," said Ginger. "But to go an' do them
themselves—well, it seems too mean to be true."

THE OUTLAWS WATCHED, DUMBFOUNDED AND AGHAST.

They walked drearily, silently, despondently. Life simply didn't seem to be worth living.

Then suddenly at a bend in the road they met Colonel Masters. He carried a stick and was purple with fury.

"Here, you!" he bellowed, "have you seen anyone about here with any fireworks? Fireworks in green boxes. I've had all mine stolen and I'll"—he choked with passion and then continued—"I'll show 'em. I tell you I'll show 'em. I'll find the thieves if I have to walk all night an' I'll—I'll *show* 'em."

The Outlaws brightened.

"There's four men havin' a firework show over there," said William with his blankest expression;

"we've jus' been watchin' 'em. They've got fireworks out of green boxes with 'Tanks, London,' on them."

"They're *mine*, then," yelled the Colonel, dancing about with mingled excitement and fury; "they're *mine*. I'll show 'em. Where are they?"

"They've got a guy jus' ready to burn," went on Ginger with an expression that in blank innocence almost rivalled William's. "It's got a grey hat jus' like yours an' a brown overcoat and moustache that turns up an'—now I come to think of it—it *is* you—it mus' be you they've got for their guy."

"WHAT?" yelled the warrior, his purple deepening to a rich plum shade. "WHERE are they?"

"Over there," said the Outlaws pointing in the direction of the old barn. Bangs could still be heard and sparks be seen.

Roaring with fury the Colonel began to hasten in its direction.

The Outlaws followed. They walked brightly, expectantly, joyfully. Life was worth living, after all.

Chapter 8

The Outlaws Fetch the Holly

It was not without misgiving that the Vicar's wife commissioned the Outlaws to go into the woods and get some holly for the Christmas decorations. She would not, of course, have done it had other material been available, but most of the juvenile population of the village had succumbed to an epidemic of mumps that the Outlaws, with the proverbial good fortune of the wicked, had escaped. The Vicar's wife would have preferred almost any of the others to have escaped, but she was a good woman and accustomed to make the best of untoward circumstances, so she summoned the Outlaws to the Vicarage in order to tell them exactly what she wanted. She hoped by an appeal to their better natures to ensure that they should fulfil their mission as well as any of the infant Samuels who usually gathered the holly, but who now occupied beds of sickness in the village. The Vicar's wife was a great believer in herself as an appealer to people's better natures.

The Outlaws arrived looking so neat and clean and wearing expressions of such utter vacancy that the Vicar's wife was reassured. Perhaps, she thought, she'd done them an injustice. Perhaps they weren't, after all, quite as bad as she'd believed them to be. . . .

She made one of her beautiful little speeches appealing to their better natures. It lasted nearly twenty minutes. She impressed upon them what an honour it was for them to be allowed to collect holly for the Christmas decorations. She painted in glowing colours their pride and pleasure on Christmas morning, when they should see the holly they had gathered adorning the pillars and the choir stalls. She painted in lurid colours the envy of those who were prevented by mumps from performing this service for her. It was, she thought, a speech calculated to inspire anyone to pious effort. She'd have been amazed and horrified had she known that the only definite impression the Outlaws gained from it was that they were to be allowed a whole day in the woods with the Vicarage wheelbarrow.

*   *   *

They called for the wheelbarrow the next morning, still looking repellently clean and tidy and wearing exaggerated expressions of virtue. They knew the Vicar's wife. She was a terrible woman. At any sign of levity she would have thought nothing of cancelling the whole expedition. Solemnly, silently, with faces of set, stern virtue, the Outlaws departed, trundling the Vicarage wheelbarrow before them. The Vicar's wife saw them off at the front gate. Her final admonitions floated after them down the road.

"*Quietly*, boys, remember, and *industriously* . . . Keep in mind the great work you are helping in . . . and as many berries as possible, please."

Once round the corner and out of sight of the Vicarage, the tension of the group relaxed. They set down the wheelbarrow and clustered round it, examining it.

"It's a jolly fine one," said Ginger, "I bet we can play all sorts of games with it."

"We've gotter get her holly," said Douglas.

Douglas, generally speaking, possessed a more highly-developed conscience than the other Outlaws.

"Oh yes, of course," said Ginger hastily. "Of *course*, we'll get her holly. But I meant that we could have a few games *first*. We don' want to get her holly all droopin' an' dead with pickin' it too soon. I votes we have a few games first an' *then* start gettin' her holly."

The idea appealed to the others.

"Yes," said William, "that's the best thing to do. We've got to try'n' do it prop'ly like what she said about it bein' a good work an' that sort of thing. Well, we won't be doin' that if we bring home a lot of dead droopin' holly at the end of the day, with gettin' it too soon. We shan't feel those feelin's she says we ought to feel when we see our holly all dead an' droopin' round the pillars an' things. No, I think we'd better have a few games first an' *then* get the holly. Well, that's how it seems to *me*," he ended with an unconvincing air of modesty. That apparently was how it seemed to all of them. Even Douglas's conscience, that tender but easily appeased organ, was satisfied.

"Where'll we go?" said Ginger who was lying full length in the wheelbarrow with William.

"She said Mells' Wood," said Douglas tentatively.

"Yes, but everyone goes there," objected Ginger. "No one minds you goin' there. It isn't even a trespass wood. I mean—well, there's nothin' *about* Mells' Wood."

"Crown Wood's better," suggested William.

Crown Wood had the allurement of (almost) impenetrable barbed wire barriers, frequent notice boards that warned trespassers of prosecution, and a ferocious keeper armed with a gun and a dog that, the Outlaws firmly believed, would rend them limb from limb if ever he caught them. Moreover, Crown Wood belonged to an elderly professor of science who was reported to be eccentric and, according to the juvenile population of the village, used trespassers found on his land for "human experiments."

"Yes, that's more excitin'," agreed Ginger, his spirits rising.

So they marched along the road to Crown Wood, singing joyously and inharmoniously, and wheeling each other in turns in the wheelbarrow. Near one of their private entrances to it they met the keeper with his dog and gun. Their song died away and they hastily assumed expressions suitable to those who are quietly and industriously engaged in the work of the Church.

"Where are *you* off to?" he challenged them sternly.

"Jus' doin' a little errand for the Vic'rage," said William unctuously.

The man passed on growling.

The Outlaws executed a war dance in the middle of the road.

"I bet he's goin' over to Marleigh," chanted William. "I bet he won't be comin' home till to-night. I bet we'll have all day there with no one to stop us."

"An' we'll be able to get some jolly fine holly," put in Douglas, who evidently still felt faint stirrings of his conscience.

"Oh, yes," said William, "we'll be able to get some jolly fine holly. That's why we're goin' there, of course."

The morning passed quickly. They lit a fire and played Red Indians, adorned with the feathered headdress that they always carried with them. The wheelbarrow played the parts successively of fortress, wagon, cave and mountain top. Even Douglas forgot the holly till they were on their homeward way. Then he said in a voice of pained surprise:

"Why—why—we haven't got any holly."

"No," agreed William hastily from the wheelbarrow where he was lying recumbent in the character of a mortally wounded chieftain, "No . . . you know we thought we'd better not get it in the mornin' case it got dead an' droopin', you know, cause we wanted it to be the best holly an'—an' worthy of the Church, same as what she said."

"So we'll start gettin' it this afternoon," said Douglas.

"Oh, yes," said the wounded chieftain, "course we will."

After lunch they approached the keeper's cottage, whose front door fortunately opened on to the lane bordering the wood, and William tactfully ascertained from the keeper's youngest child (who was sitting at the door engaged in watching the effect of its saliva upon the newly whitened step) that the keeper had gone into Marleigh and would not be back till evening. The Outlaws danced another dance of exultation in the lane, then crawled once more through the barbed wire fence, after throwing the wheelbarrow over it. Then they proceeded into the heart of the woods.

"What'll we do this afternoon?" said Henry. "Red Indians again?"

But William felt that one morning's Red Indians was enough.

"Let's think of somethin' else," he said, "somethin' more excitin'."

"Pirates," suggested Ginger.

"Robbers," suggested Douglas.

"Smugglers," suggested Henry.

William shook his head.

"We've played them so often," he said. "Let's think of somethin' quite diff'rent. I know!" His freckled face lit up with inspiration. "I know . . . *Arabs!*"

"*What?*" said the Outlaws.

"*Arabs!*" said William excitedly. "Arab chiefs fightin' each other in the desert with camels an' things. Come on . . . *Arabs!*"

At the mention of Red Indians the Outlaws had taken out their feathered head-dresses. Now they looked at them rather regretfully.

"I s'pose," said Henry, "Arabs don't wear anything like this."

"No," said William, "only Injuns."

He frowned thoughtfully. He saw the difficulty.

"What *do* they wear?" said Ginger and added, with vague memories of the Tower of London, "Coat o' mails an' armour an' such like, I s'pose."

"No, they don't," said William. "I've seen pictures of them. They wear sort of dressing-gowns an' bath towels round their heads."

"Why?" said Douglas.

"Oh, shut up always wanting to know why," said William. "What does it matter why if they do? . . . the dressing-gowns don't really matter, but they have things wrapped round their heads like bandages. That ought to be easy enough. Tell you what," again his freckled face shone with inspiration. "*Tell* you what . . . I'll go home'n' get some things like that. My mother's gone out for the afternoon," he added simply, "so I c'n get what I want."

Secure in the absence of the keeper he set off gaily through the wood homewards and reappeared in less than half an hour with a bundle under his arm.

"I've got some fine things," he called as he came. "She'd locked the linen cupboard but I got some things that were in the rag bag. An' I've got some corks and matches to make whiskers an' beards for us too."

They crowded round him eagerly to share in the division of the spoil. He had indeed found some treasures. There was a tattered bedspread and a sheet with a hole in the middle that did admirably as a head opening. There was an old pair of pants of his father's and a pair of ancient pyjamas that had once belonged to his elder brother. There were—marvellously—two old bath towels that, torn across, would furnish headgears for all four of them.

They set about accoutring themselves. William appropriated to his own use the sheet with the hole in the middle. He made two further holes for his arms, taking off his coat and shirt so that bare arms might protrude. His robe flowed about his feet in a way that made him almost decide to give up the Arab idea altogether and be someone out of the Old Testament. He wrapped his half bath towel about his head and plentifully adorned his face with burnt cork. As he had no mirror and was anxious to make his general appearance as impressive as possible, he erred on the side of generosity as far as the burnt cork was concerned. In fact, when he had tied about his waist a girdle from a derelict dressing-gown of Robert's, there was no doubt at all of his fitness to play the part of Chieftain. The other Outlaws, though less gloriously apparelled, were striking enough figures—Ginger in the tattered pants, Douglas in the bedspread and Henry in the old pyjamas, all of them with plentifully-corked beards and moustaches and with bath towels round their heads. They gazed at each other with deep satisfaction. They did not see each other quite as an impartial observer would have seen them. They saw each other as commanding figures, handsomely robed, fit lords of the desert. The wheelbarrow, of

course, was a camel, and at first William as chieftain
rode upon it while the others in turn guided its course.
William occasionally put up his hand as if to shade his
eyes from the glaring sun and gazed about him slowly
from side to side. He did not see the bushes and trees
that actually surrounded him. He saw a vast expanse of
sand, stretching as far as the eye could see. At last,
however, he proclaimed that he had espied an oasis, and
following his direction the company made their way to it.
There they rested under the shade of a palm tree that to
the impartial observer would have suggested a hawthorn
tree, and refreshed themselves with small red dates that
grew upon it. Then they made a fire to protect them from
prowling beasts and lay down to sleep, leaving Ginger on
guard with a bow and arrow that he had improvised for
the purpose. During the night (which was of short
duration) Ginger occupied himself by shooting the
innumerable wild animals that drew near to attack the
camp. Some he wrestled with and throttled with his bare
hands in order to vary the monotony of shooting. In the
morning the space about the camp was entirely covered
by the dead bodies of hundreds of wild animals killed by
Ginger. They breakfasted on dates, then left the oasis
and set off again over the boundless desert, Ginger
riding the camel and the others guiding it in turn. During
the day they met and vanquished several hostile tribes
and large bands of wild animals. Finally they reached
another oasis where they spent the night. They spent a
day or two more in this way, but the imaginary dangers
were beginning to pall and they decided to split up into
two hostile tribes, scout each other over the desert, and
join in combat whenever they met. They were to share
the camel, having him for a day each. They drew lots as
to how they should separate their forces and the result
ranged William and Henry against Douglas and Ginger.

Douglas and Ginger departed, leading the camel that had fallen to their lot for the first day, and that seemed more likely to be an incubus than a help to them in their scouting operations.

William and Henry found an oasis where they rested and refreshed themselves with dates. Then they set out on the task of tracking down the hostile tribes.

"I bet I can see them from yon tall tree," said William, who fitfully tried to invest his speech with such dignity as befitted an Arab chief. "Methinks I'll have a jolly good try anyway."

The tall tree was an evergreen oak, thickly leaved and easy of ascent, that had more than once served William, in his rôle of pirate, as a ship on his previous lawless expedition in the wood. Henry was enjoined to stay to guard the camp; an elaborate system of signs in whistles was arranged between them and William set off jauntily to his tree, his sheet trailing about him. Garbed thus, he was finding the ascent more difficult than usual but was accomplishing it quite creditably when to his horror he heard voices just beneath the tree—feminine voices speaking with the indefinable intonations of those who are not trespassers but have every right to be where they are. William froze into silent immobility, and peered down through the branches. He could just see them. There was a girl with fair hair and a girl with dark hair. They were talking earnestly and in low voices, but their words reached William quite plainly in his leafy bower.

"But why must he come *here?*" said the girl with fair hair.

"I told you, didn't I?" said the other, "he's *brilliant* in every way except for this extraordinary bee that he's got in his bonnet about Mars. You know he's *convinced* that he's been getting messages from Mars. And what's

**WILLIAM PEERED DOWN THROUGH THE BRANCHES. THE GIRLS'
WORDS REACHED HIM QUITE PLAINLY.**

more, he's *convinced* that the messages say that an
inhabitant of Mars is going to visit him to-day and that
he'll meet him just here. He was out all yesterday doing
most complicated measurements to find the exact spot
where he was going to meet him. He says that the
messages were very involved but that at last he's worked

them out and that the place arranged for the meeting is just here under this tree."

"But—but how does he think that the—the Mars person will get here?"

"He's no idea, but he's certain that he'll come. I'm afraid that the poor old man will be terribly disappointed. He's been simply living for it, you see, all the time that he's been getting these messages, as he imagines."

"BUT WHY MUST HE COME *here?*" SAID THE GIRL WITH FAIR HAIR.

"Of course," said the girl with fair hair, "there *may* be something in it. 'More things in heaven and earth' you know, and that sort of thing."

"I'm *afraid* not," said the other. "So many people have thought they've had messages from Mars, and there's never anything in it. It's such a pity, because you know he's not really potty. It's just this one subject he's got a bee in his bonnet about. Here he is!"

Still peering down from his leafy retreat, William saw an elderly gentleman armed with rulers and other measuring instruments drawing near.

"It should be just about here," he said excitedly, "I've verified all the measurements. There can't possibly be any mistake and," he took out his watch, "if I've interpreted the messages correctly it should be within the next five minutes."

"B-but, grandfather," said the dark-haired girl, "I—I think you'd better—better not expect too much. You know it *may* be a—mistake."

"You ought to be prepared for disappointment, I think, Professor," said the fair-haired girl, "because so many people have been mistaken. The whole thing's so incalculable."

"Nonsense," said the old gentleman, "I've calculated it most carefully. I've given months—*years* of work to it. I'm sure I've made no mistake." He knelt down and busied himself with the measuring instruments, then drew a small square on the ground with his walking stick.

"He should arrive upon this planet at this spot exactly within the next few minutes," he said, "assuming, of course, that my calculations are correct . . ."

William, greatly interested, bent forward to see what the elderly gentleman was doing, overbalanced and fell—exactly into the square that the elderly gentleman had traced with his walking stick.

He sat up blinking, then looked up at them aggress-ively, expecting to be fiercely denounced, if not actually assaulted as a trespasser. The three faces gazed at him open-eyed, open-mouthed, slowly paling. Then the old gentleman spoke in a faint voice.

"This—this is a very great moment in my life," he said.

"Where have you come from?" said the fair-haired girl sharply to William.

The elderly gentleman smiled.

"My dear," he said, "it's no use addressing him in our tongue. He has his own language, of course. I have had no opportunity of studying that. The signals were flashed to me by code."

William had grasped the situation and decided to sustain the only character in which he would not be subjected to vituperation or personal violence. He stood up silently, arranged his robe around him, and con-tinued to glare aggressively at the three amazed faces. The elderly gentleman drew a notebook from his pocket.

"I must get down the salient points about him," he said eagerly, "in case—in case his visit is not of long duration."

He made a hasty and not very flattering sketch of William and wrote underneath, "small stature—flowing robes confined at waist—face painted (cf. Ancient Britons)."

Then he slipped the book back into his pocket and said:

"But the intrepid explorer must be weary. We do not know what dangers he has faced to reach us, only we may be sure that the way was not easy. We must take him home for rest and refreshment. I will beckon to him.

Doubtless he will understand the sign."

He beckoned, accompanying the gesture by a smile of invitation, and then turned to go along a narrow path through the wood that led by a short cut to his house. Every few minutes he turned and repeated his beckoning gesture and inviting smile. The Martian, wearing an inscrutable and slightly forbidding expression, followed, his long robe trailing about him. The amazed girls brought up the rear.

On reaching his house, the Professor led his protégé through the French windows into his study and there, still smiling reassuringly, invited him to take an armchair. The Martian, still retaining his inscrutable and forbidding expression, and preserving complete silence, took it. The Professor immediately brought out his little book again and wrote: "Chairs and furniture similar to ours evidently found in Mars. Visitor expressed no surprise at seeing them. Action of sitting upon chair performed as if familiar one."

He then rang the bell and ordered an astounded housemaid to bring refreshment. Meantime, the reassuring and apologetic smile much in evidence, he examined his visitor from a polite distance, wrote in his notebook and expounded his views to the still speechless girls.

"It's what I've always said," he said, "the main features of life are the same as ours. The material from which his robe is made," he touched it, glancing up at its wearer with the reassuring and apologetic smile, "is, I should guess, made by a process roughly similar to the process by which we make such materials in this country. I have always insisted that the main feature of life upon the two planets are the same. Ah, thank you, Jane," as the housemaid entered with a tray, "thank you. Put it by that gentleman, will you? He is a traveller from a distant planet who, I hope, will be an inmate of my house for some little time."

The housemaid stared at William, more amazed than ever. Then she withdrew to the kitchen to tell the cook that she'd never worked in a lunies' asylum before and wasn't going to start it at her time of life, and she'd give in her notice that very day.

Meanwhile William raised the glass of wine to his lips with gusto, thinking that it was blackcurrant tea of which he was very fond, then hastily set it down with an expression of acute nausea.

The Professor took out his notebook and wrote: "Alcohol evidently unknown in Mars."

He ordered the housemaid to bring some grapes, and these William consumed with evident familiarity and relish. The Professor wrote: "Grapes evidently known and eaten as fruit but not fermented to make wine."

He addressed the girls:

"And I only hope, my dears, that we shall not corrupt this civilisation, as we have corrupted so many others, by teaching them the use of alcohol. It is a wonderful thing to look at this inhabitant from a distant planet—small but sturdy and virile—and notice his natural aversion from the degrading liquid. Look at him."

They gazed in silence at William, who was zestfully consuming the sandwiches and biscuits that were on the tray. The elderly gentleman watched his every movement, making frequent and copious notes in his little book. Finally he said in wistful tones to the two girls:

"What I'm *hoping*, my dears, is that when he has refreshed himself he will speak a few words in his own language. I hope to be the man to make the first known record of the speech of the Martians."

William, who was feeling much stimulated by his little meal and was beginning to enjoy being a Martian,

decided to please the old gentleman by saying a few
words in the Martian language. He turned his fixed,
unflinching stare upon him and said:

"Flam gobba manxy pop gebboo."

Trembling with eagerness, the old gentleman wrote it
in his little notebook:

"Flam gobba manxy pop gebboo."

"It may not be *spelt* right, of course," he said to the
girls, "but I think that using our native spelling I have
more or less correctly reproduced the sounds. I think
that I have actually obtained the first phonetic record in
our language of the Martian speech. . . ."

William, who was warming to his performance, rose
from his seat and began to wander round the room,
uttering strange sounds and making strange gestures, all
of which the elderly gentleman, whose excitement was
steadily increasing, noted in his book. Some of them he
interpreted to the still paralyscd girls.

"That's the clock. He's never seen a clock before.
Evidently they don't have them on his planet . . . he's
probably asking what the bureau's for. He means, I
think, that he likes the flowers . . . different flowers
probably from the ones that grow on his planet. Did you
hear that? 'Crumbs.' By 'Crumbs,' he evidently means
the window. I must get that down."

By "Crumbs," however, William didn't mean the
window. He meant that he had distinctly caught a
glimpse of his father in the wood that surrounded the
house.

"His expression has changed," said the old man. "Do
you notice that a look of weariness has come over his
face? All this must be most exhausting for him. He must
have passed through a most exhausting time coming
here at all. I think that he should have a rest before we
continue our investigations any further. I'd like to

"FLAM GOBBA MANXY POP GEBBOO," SAID WILLIAM.
TREMBLING WITH EAGERNESS, THE OLD GENTLEMAN WROTE IT
IN HIS LITTLE NOTEBOOK.

discover whether the painting of the face is common to all the Martians or whether it is the mark of a particular rank or class. However, all that can come when we have correlated our two languages better. At present I am sure that he needs rest more than anything."

He turned to William with the reassuring smile and beckoned. William followed him out of the room, up the stairs and into a bedroom. There the Professor waved him to a bed and disappeared. William gazed about him distastefully. He was suddenly tired of being a Martian and his only desire now was to return to his own character. He looked out of the window, but the room was on the third floor and there was no drain-pipe or tree near the window by which he might escape. He went to the door, and opened it very slightly. The Professor sat just outside, so as to be ready to receive his guest immediately on his awaking. He was writing in his little book and had not noticed the opening of the door. William hastily closed it again and considered the situation. There didn't seem anything to do at present but follow the line of least resistance and wait for Fate to find some way out for him. The bed looked inviting, and William, as Red Indian, Arab Chief and Martian, had had a tiring day. He climbed upon it, composing his robes about him and laying his corked cheek upon a snowy linen pillow. He had a hazy impression of the Professor's opening the door and gazing at him with a proud and beatific smile before he drifted off into a doze. He was awakened by the sound of voices—his father's and the Professor's.

His father was speaking.

"I'm sorry to trouble you, but the boy's friends say that he's completely disappeared. They were playing in the wood and they say that he vanished, leaving no trace. They'd no right to be there at all, of course. I expect the young ruffian's hiding somewhere but his mother's got worried about him so I said I'd have a look round. I suppose you've seen nothing of him?"

"No," said the Professor absently. "I've seen no boys at all, "but," he added mysteriously, "as you're the first person who's come to the house since he arrived I—I'll *show* you him."

"Whom?" said William's father.

"A Martian," said the Professor.

"A *what?*" said William's father.

"A Martian," said the Professor, "an inhabitant of the planet Mars. I've been in communication with it for some time. He's asleep at present, but——"

Cautiously he opened the bedroom door. The Martian leapt from the bed, tore past them with lowered head, dashed down the stairs and out of the door.

The Professor and Mr. Brown followed.

"Into the woods," gasped the Professor, "we came that way."

They ran out of the little gate that led to the wood and gazed about. There was no sign of the white-robed figure.

"I'm afraid he's gone," said the Professor sadly. "I've been afraid of this from the beginning. You see the atmospheric conditions may possibly be different. I mean, a Martian may only be able to breathe this atmosphere for a short time. I'm afraid that he's gone back."

"How do you think he's gone back?" said William's father.

"The same way as he came," said the Professor mysteriously. "I don't know what way that was. Nor does anyone except the man who came by it. . . ."

"And you *really* believe—" began William's father.

"I *know*," said the Professor solemnly, "I don't

expect anyone else to believe me. In fact I know they won't. No further developments may take place in this particular branch of research for years—probably not till after my death. I do not expect to be recognised as a pioneer in my life-time—but I have my notes—they will still be here after my death and in future years I shall be recognised as the pioneer of communication between the two planets. You saw him, didn't you?"

"Y-yes," said William's father and added thoughtfully, "there seemed to be something—something familiar about his face."

*   *   *

The Outlaws were assembled in the tool shed at the bottom of William's garden. The wheelbarrow was turned upside down to represent a stage and upon it William was precariously executing a clog dance. The others were sitting around him on the floor, watching admiringly. So energetically did William perform his dance and so unsteadily balanced was the wheelbarrow that it seemed that every moment the whole thing must collapse. William had as usual thrown himself so completely into his rôle of music hall artist that he had entirely forgotten that he had already that day been Red Indian, Arab Chief and Martian. Suddenly Ginger said warningly:

"I say, your father's coming, William, with the old man."

William stopped and listened. Through the open window they could hear William's father's voice.

"Well, I just want you to look at him and see if it's the same. I don't suppose you'll get anything out of him. I've already questioned him but one gathers from his answers that he's never heard of either Crown Wood or

Mars. However—just have a look at him. I'm afraid you'll find it is so. I saw the face quite clearly."

The door opened and they entered.

"This is the boy," said William's father, pointing to William.

William hastily descended from his platform and assumed his most expressionless expression. The Professor looked him slowly up and down—William, rough-headed, freckled, frowning, in his school suit. He'd retrieved his coat and shirt from the wood and he'd washed his face. The Professor burst out laughing.

"It most *certainly* isn't the same, my dear sir. Hardly any resemblance at all. My—my visitor was at least a foot taller and altogether more—more mature. Though of small stature he had an intelligent and thoughtful face. He moved with dignity and grace. This—excuse me, my dear sir—this is an ordinary uncouth English schoolboy."

William's face was still drained of expression as he met his father's gaze.

"Well," said his father, "I'm glad to hear you say so. It certainly simplifies the situation as far as I'm concerned."

Then they departed.

"Go on dancing, William," said Ginger as soon as they'd gone.

"I've forgotten where I was," said William, "with everyone interrupting."

But no sooner had he mounted his platform to continue than there came yet another interruption. It was the Vicar's wife. She entered, wearing her brisk bright smile.

"I've been waiting for the holly, boys dear," she said. "I meant you to bring it to the Vicarage, but perhaps you misunderstood me. Where is it?"

The Outlaws gazed at each other open-mouthed. Then: "*Crumbs!*" gasped William, "we quite forgot the holly."

Chapter 9

The Sentimental Widow

William had very few adult friends but Mrs. Roundway was one of them. Mrs. Roundway was small and fat and pleasant-looking, and she lived in a little cottage just outside the village. She was a woman of few words and many smiles. William had known her ever since he could remember. Always when he passed down the lane where she lived she would nod and smile at him from the window and then come running down the garden path to him with a cookie boy. She made cookie boys better than anyone William had ever known. The efforts of William's mother and her cook were puerile in comparison. She made them out of both gingerbread and dough. They had currants for eyes and buttons. They had arms and legs and fingers and toes. Some of them even had hats. There was an amazingly lifelike air about them. At the age of four or thereabouts William had almost lived for them. To nibble them slowly bit by bit from toe to head or from head to toe afforded him a sensation that nothing else on earth could ever afford him.

In his more ruthless moods he was a cannibal chief and the cookie boy a rash white man who had ventured into his territory. In his milder moments he was merely a lion and the cookie boy a jackal or an antelope. Now that he was eleven and a leader of men, of course, he pretended to regard the cookie boys with amused indulgence, but secretly they gave him almost as much pleasure as ever, and he wandered just as often past Mrs. Roundway's cottage, wearing a rather inane expression of absent-mindedness that was meant to indicate that the last thing he expected to see was the sight of Mrs. Roundway smiling and beckoning from the window and holding a cookie boy in her hand.

He was surprised and slightly embarrassed one morning when Mrs. Roundway, instead of thrusting the cookie boy into his hands and running back to her cottage as usual, suddenly began to talk to him. She seemed very much excited. She told him that her sister was coming to live with her. Her sister, she said, was a widow who had been a housekeeper in Sydney and whose employer had just died, leaving her a handsome legacy.

"I ain't seed her for nigh on twenty years," ended Mrs. Roundway breathlessly. "I'm that excited I can't tell you, dearie. There you are—though I'm afraid that what with the excitement an' all his legs isn't quite straight, but he'll taste all right."

William walked down the road, thoughtfully nibbling his cookie boy. He was wondering how the arrival of Mrs. Roundway's sister would affect his supply of cookie boys. It would be too much to hope that she should be another Mrs. Roundway. William had a large experience of elderly ladies and most of them were as unlike Mrs. Roundway as it is possible to imagine. Mrs. Roundway was, in fact, in William's eyes a sort of oasis in a desert.

He threw a very cautious glance at the cottage window when he passed it the next week.

"Shouldn't be surprised," he muttered to himself

morosely, "if she even stops her making cookie boys."

But that cautious glance reassured him. It was as if there were two Mrs. Roundways standing at the cottage window—both nodding and smiling and beckoning. They came down together to the cottage gate.

"This is my sister, William," said Mrs. Roundway, smiling, "and this is William, Maggie. He's the friend of mine I told you about who likes cookie boys. Here it is, love. She helped to make it. Isn't he a beauty? Look, she's put buttons on his boots."

Mrs. Roundway's sister was exactly like Mrs. Roundway to look at—small and round and fair and smiling. But she talked. She was as garrulous as Mrs. Roundway was silent. On the whole William didn't like her quite as much as he liked Mrs. Roundway. She insisted on telling him all about Sydney, and he didn't want to know about Sydney. And she made the cookie boys too elaborate.

He was relieved to find Mrs. Roundway alone at the window the next time he passed the cottage. She nodded and smiled and beckoned and came running down with the cookie boy as usual.

Then she pointed down the road, where the figure of her sister could be seen disappearing in the distance in company with a stalwart-looking male.

"It's George," said Mrs. Roundway, smiling mysteriously. "He's always been fond of her. He'd have had her when she was a girl but for Bert. No, not the one she married, Bert isn't. He had curly hair, and I never could abide him though she nearly married him. It was all his hair. Golden curls he had, like a girl. She couldn't resist 'em—till, fortunate like, Pete Hemmings come along. Him what she married. No, it was always George I liked best. I hoped he'd come forward again. He's bin hangin' back a bit along of her money till now. He's taken a bit of encouraging but I think it's all right now.

They seem to be walkin' out all right now."

It was the longest speech William had ever heard her make, and William shared something of her enthusiasm. William, too, wanted Maggie to marry George. He wanted Mrs. Roundway to be left alone in her cottage again. He didn't like having to sustain long conversations about Sydney whenever he received his cookie boys, and he didn't like his cookie boys having buttons on their boots. It seemed to him new-fangled and unnecessary, and William was very conservative by nature.

But the next time he passed the cottage it was a dolorous face that tried unconvincingly to smile at him through the window. William's heart sank. He was loyal to his friends and always took their troubles as his own. Mrs. Roundway came down slowly to the cottage gate with his cookie boy and disclosed her grief almost tearfully.

"It's that Bert," she said sadly. "He's come back, curls an' all. He's heard of her bein' back home an' an heiress, as you might say, an' he's took rooms at the White Lion an' comin' here every day. His curls is as yellow as ever, an' it was his yellow curls she never could resist. No woman could resist 'em. His curls and his blue eyes. An' he's made up his mind to get Maggie along of her money. He'll spend her money an' drive her to her grave. I know 'im. Never was no good. An' poor George has stopped comin' all along of him. Here's your cookie boy, love. She helped me make it. She put the buttons on its boots. She's that clever."

William walked away thoughtfully, nibbling his cookie boy's head. At the corner of the road he met Mrs. Hemmings. She was smiling and blushing girlishly. Her companion was a tall man who walked bareheaded, displaying a glorious crop of flaxen curls. Mrs. Hemmings smiled at William and he responded with marked coldness.

"Who's the brat?" he heard the flaxen-haired man say as he passed.

*   *   *

For the next few days William was too busy to have much time or thought to spare for Mrs. Hemmings' love affairs. William was a boy of many interests. He had almost forgotten the distress she had shown on their last meeting when next he wandered down the lane past the little house. But it was a face even less cheerful than before that tried to give him its usual smile through the window.

Instead of coming down to him to the gate, she just opened the cottage door and beckoned him. He came slowly up and she held out the cookie boy.

"Here's your cookie boy, love," she said.

William took it absently, and slipped it into his pocket. Then, "Is anything the matter?" he asked.

"It's only—it's only Maggie and Bert," she said gloomily. "I can't keep it off any longer. It's comin' an' it's comin' to-day."

"What?" said William.

"Her takin' him. What I've gone through this last week I couldn't tell you. She's flattered with him tellin' her that he's loved her all his life an' stuff like that. He always had a way with women—him and his yellow curls. It's no use. I've done my best all this week but I can't stop it. There isn't a woman born as can resist yellow curls. The way I've worked this last week—but I've got to the end."

"How have you worked?" said William with interest.

"Goin' about with 'em," she said simply. "Never lettin' 'em have a minute alone. Sittin' with 'em. Goin' for walks with 'em. Fair wore me out, but it were worth it to me if I could stop him askin' her. If he'd got her alone one second all this week he'd have asked her. She's sure to see him as he is in time an' if I can only hold it off till she's seen him as he is. But to-day the end comes. Though I don't know why I'm tellin' all this to a child, I'm sure."

"Me?" said William indignantly. "I'm not a child. Why does the end come to-day?"

She heaved a deep sigh.

"They're goin' for a picnic to-day. On the river. They're walkin' down to the boathouse at Marleigh, an' they're goin' on the river. It's no use. I can't do it. I'm not what you'd call a natural walker an' never have been. This last week's wore me out. I'd do it till I dropped, mind you, but it's the rheumatics. They've come on me sudden. I couldn't walk a yard if I was to die for it."

William was silent for a minute. One of his few friends in the adult world and one who had never failed him was in trouble. William had only the vaguest appreciation of the cause of the trouble, but her voice and expression told him that it was to her a very real trouble. It was not William's custom to leave his friends in the lurch. . . . He stared in front of him, his freckled face drawn into a thoughtful frown. At last he said:

"D'you think—I s'pose—d'you think he'd do it with me there?"

Mrs. Roundway looked at William. There was nothing romantic about William, nothing remotely suggestive of Cupid in William's appearance. There was even something about William's expression that would have chilled sentiment at its very fount.

"No, love," she said simply, "I'm sure that no one would propose to anyone with you about."

William's mind sped over the day in front of him. He had meant to spend it in the woods as a Red Indian, but it was a small enough sacrifice in return for years of cookie boys.

"S'pose I go with them, then," he said, "stick to them all the time but as if I'd just come to help carry things. I bet I'd stick to them all right. I'm good at sticking to people whether they want me or not."

Her face brightened.

"Oh, *could* you?" she said, "*would* you? I'm afraid it would be a very dull day for you."

William was afraid so, too, but he said cheerfully:

"I don't mind," and added thoughtfully, "it might turn out fun in a sort of way, too."

"He's very cunning," said Mrs. Roundway, "very cunning indeed. He'll try to get rid of you, but—it'll be all right if you stick to him. I can't tell you how grateful I am to you, love."

Maggie came downstairs, smiling and blushing.

"This little boy's kindly going with you," said her sister, "to help carry things. There's rather a lot to carry, you know. You'll find him very useful."

Maggie looked for a moment as if she wasn't sure that she would, but she was a simple, good-natured soul, so she smiled at William and said:

"Well, I'm sure it's very kind of you."

And at that moment Bert appeared, bareheaded as usual, his flaxen curls gleaming in the sun.

William's presence was explained to him and there was no doubt at all about his attitude to it. He scowled at William and muttered:

"We don't want no one to carry things. I bet there's nothin' I can't manage. An' a lot of use *he* looks as if he'd be."

But Mrs. Roundway had diplomatically tied up the

provisions in numerous and rather unwieldy parcels, and Bert, after trying unsuccessfully to accommodate them all under his arm, gave up the attempt and presented William with a generous share of them. He would not allow Maggie to carry anything.

"No," he said, fixing languishing blue eyes upon her, "Never. You oughter be waited on hand and foot same as a queen. If I had my way you'd never do a hand's turn."

Then he met William's blank stare and ended irritably:

"Come on you, kid. Look sharp an' mind you don't drop anything."

William's stare became if possible blanker, but those who knew him would have decided to tread warily. Bert, however, did not know him.

The three of them set off together down the road. Bert meant to walk next his beloved. He tried to walk next his beloved. But whenever he thought he'd managed it, the walking mass of parcels that was William was always miraculously between them. Bert finally decided to accept the inevitable and walked without further machinations on the other side of William. The sun still glinted on his flaxen curls as he walked and he cast languishing eyes at Maggie.

"Do you remember, Maggie," he said, "the picnics we useter go when we were young before you broke my heart by marrying Pete?"

She blushed and lowered her eyes.

"I remember goin' a few picnics," she said. "I remember the parish outin' down at Little Marvel."

"Yes. Pete was there. I remember watchin' him and you talkin'. I din't like him, Maggie. I must be honest, I din't like him. I din't think him good enough for you. No one could be that, of course. I remember I watched him and I watched George, too."

"I heard of a man once," said William suddenly, "that had seven fingers on each hand."

Bert threw him a murderous glance, but Maggie, as William had already discovered, was a simple soul with that consuming curiosity about the abnormal that is one of the marks of an essentially normal mind. She turned to William with sudden interest.

"Countin' thumbs or without thumbs?"

"Without thumbs," said William.

Maggie spread out her hands in naïve wonder.

"Fancy!" she said. "You wouldn't think there'd be room for 'em on a person's hand, would you?"

"And I remember lookin' at you that afternoon," went on Bert languishingly, "an' thinkin'——"

"I s'pose he'd have specially large hands, would he?" said Maggie to William.

"An' thinkin'——" said Bert raising his voice.

"Yes, he had *'normous* hands," said William.

"That'd be eight with thumbs, wouldn't it?" said Maggie, and "Eight on a hand! Fancy."

"An' thinkin'," said Bert, "shall I tell you what I was thinkin', Maggie?"

"Yes, Bert," said Maggie absently, and then to William:

"I s'pose he could hold things wonderfully an' play the piano an' such like."

"Yes," said William unblushingly, "and he could play two concertinas at once."

"Lor!" said Maggie and remained in rapt and silent contemplation of the mental picture his words evoked.

"Maggie," said Bert raising his voice, "I'll tell you what I was thinkin'. I was thinkin' that I'd never seen in all my life a prettier picture than what you made sittin' there."

Maggie at last transferred her attention to him.

"Oh, Bert!" she said, blushing and bridling, "was you really?"

"Yes, an'——"

"His hands were so strong," interrupted William, "that he could walk on them same as on his feet. Once he strained his ankle and he walked on his hands for a fortnight till it got well. People got quite used to seeing him going about like that. When it rained he used to carry his umbrella in his teeth."

But either he had overstepped the bounds of credibility in his inventions or Maggie was tiring of the eight-fingered man. She merely said "Lor!" half-heartedly, and returned to Bert.

"Was you reely, Bert?" she said again with a sigh, "an' I'd no idea."

"It was Pete held me off; I thought you was sweet on him."

"I wasn't then," said Maggie, "though I took him later. But I remember that picnic an' me watching you an' Sadie. There was cold chicken an' I couldn't eat any of it. It seemed to choke me."

A determined voice came from the walking pyramid of tea paraphernalia.

"I once heard of a man what ate five chickens one after the other straight off for dinner."

"*What!*" said Maggie. "*Five!*"

"Yes," said William, "five. He ate them straight off one after the other for dinner."

"All the time I was talkin' to Sadie," said Bert in a tone that was languishing but determined, "all the time I was talkin' to Sadie, I was thinkin——"

"Legs an' all?" said Maggie to William with deep interest, "legs an' all—or jus' the breast and wings?"

"I was thinkin'——" put in Bert, raising his voice.

"Legs an' all," said William. "Every bit. Left the bones clean as if they'd been scrubbed."

"*Lor!*" gasped Maggie. "*Five!* It hardly seems possible, do it?"

"I was lookin' at you," said Bert, "an' I was thinkin'——"

"I should think he died after it, didn't he?" said Maggie. "I guess I'd die if I ate five. *Five! Lor!*"

"He din't die," said William, "but he was very ill. He'd got to have five operations before he was well again. And when he got well he din't eat *anythin'* for a month."

"*Lor!*" gasped Maggie.

"I remember sayin' to myself as I walked home that night——" began Bert pathetically.

"I should think that he never wanted to eat chicken again, did he?"

"I remember thinkin'——"

"No. And all the rest of his life," said William in a slow, impressive voice, "he fainted whenever he saw a chicken."

"I walked back home that night thinkin' about you and sayin' to myself——"

"Must 've been awkward faintin' whenever he sor a chicken. I s'pose live ones didn't worry him. I s'pose it was jus' cooked ones."

"Sayin' to myself," said Bert, giving William a look that would have killed anyone else but that slid harmlessly off an aluminium tea kettle, "what a fool I'd been not to try'n cut out Pete and——"

"No, it was live ones, too," said William; "it was all sorts."

"But you see live ones all over the country. He couldn't've fainted whenever he saw a live one."

"He did," said William very firmly; "that's just what

he did. If he went for a country walk he'd be fainting all the time."

"Lor!" gasped Maggie, and after a few minutes' silence again: "*Lor!*"

"Let's have tea here," said Bert shortly.

They had reached a picturesque part of the riverside, where trees overhung a grassy bank. Bert ordered William about rather curtly in the preparation of the tea, but when everything was ready he relaxed and turned his languishing smile again upon Maggie.

"Yes, Maggie," he said, "I've had a very unhappy life. I've never met anyone but you what understood me. Never. All these years I've dreamed of you as a—a sort of—dream. You know what I mean. D'you remember us goin' a walk once an' seein' the sun gleamin' on the church steeple? An' that's what you've always been to me—somethin' high an' bright—like that church steeple what we saw—somethin'——"

William hastily swallowed half a bun and said:

"I once heard of a man——"

Bert groaned, but William repeated firmly:

"I once heard of a man who climbed up a church steeple when he was a boy an' couldn't get down an' had to stay there till he was old."

Maggie's simpering expression vanished like something being wiped off a slate and an expression of amazed interest took its place.

"*What?*" she said. "B-b-but why din't no one fetch him down?"

"Somethin' high an' bright," repeated Bert doggedly, "somethin' that I've always dreamed of as a—a sort of dream."

" 'Cause no one but him could climb so far," said William simply, "an' he couldn't get down."

"As a sort of beautiful dream," said Bert.

"B-but," said Maggie, "how'd he get food an' such like?"

"They had to throw it up," said William. "There was a very good thrower in the village. He'd got prizes for throwing all over the country. He used to throw up loaves an' stuff to this man on the top of the steeple.

"A beautiful dream," said Bert again.

"B-but," said Maggie, "why din't they fetch him off in an aeroplane?"

William hadn't thought of that, but he answered without a second's hesitation:

"Oh, it was a long time ago. There weren't any aeroplanes then. . . . When he grew out of his clothes the thrower used to throw him up a new suit a size larger an' so on."

"*Lor!*" said Maggie again and added compassionately: "What a terrible life the poor man must 've had if he was one that didn't like lookin' down from a height!"

"He did like lookin' down from a height," said William, who did not wish to make his story too heartrending; "he was quite happy up there. He liked it. He could do just what he wanted, you see, an' there was no one to boss him."

"Didn't they never get him down?" said Maggie.

"Oh, yes," said William, "they got him down in the end. He was nearly an old man when they got him down, though. They had to take the tower down to mend the church an' of course it brought him down, too. He fell down right into the middle of the church. They'd put all the hassocks piled up together to make a nice soft place for him to fall on."

"I don't believe a word of it," snapped Bert.

"Don't you?" said William very politely.

"No, I don't," snapped Bert, then turning languishingly

"HE FELL DOWN RIGHT INTO THE MIDDLE OF THE CHURCH,"
SAID WILLIAM. "THEY'D PUT ALL THE HASSOCKS PILED UP
TOGETHER TO MAKE A NICE, SOFT PLACE!"

to Maggie again, "Always dreamin' of you, I was, in those days, Maggie."

But Maggie refused to blush or simper in reply to this compliment. The spell was broken. The man on the steeple had broken it.

"I should think he found it hard to walk after all that time up there," she said to William.

"Oh, no, he din't," said William, "he din't find it a bit hard to walk. You see, his legs had kept strong up there

"I DON'T BELIEVE A WORD OF IT," SNAPPED BERT, ANGRILY.

with him not usin' them. His legs were ever so strong. He could run faster'n anyone with him having saved up his legs all those years."

"Lor!" said Maggie again.

Bert had been fixing upon William a glance that would have made a more sensitive spirit quail. William, not being a sensitive spirit, was hardly aware of it. But suddenly the darkness of the glance lightened.

"Now you'd like to go'n' wash the cups up, wouldn't you?" he said to William in quite a friendly voice. "The best place is jus' down beyond that bend there. The bank slopes easy right down to the water there. You came to help, didn't you? You jus' step off with the things an' get 'em washed."

William, who had made quite a good tea despite the steeple-dweller's demands upon his inventive powers, arose slowly and began to collect the remnants of the feast. He was not in the least deceived by Bert's new manner of friendliness. He knew exactly what was in Bert's mind. Once William was out of sight and hearing round the bend of the bank, Bert could exert all his fascination, recover his influence, and, uninterrupted by William, press his suit upon the heiress.

"All right," said William obligingly, "I'll go'n' wash them. You two stay here'n' rest till I get back. I'll wash the cups an' spoons an' teapot. . . ."

He collected the things, made as if to depart, then turned suddenly.

"You mean that place jus' round the corner by the willow-tree?" he said.

"Yes. You can get right down to the water there."

And the gallant Bert turned to his beloved with a smile that isolated the two of them from the world in general and the departing William in particular.

But William still hadn't quite departed.

"Yes, I know the place," he said conversationally; "I should just think I *do* know the place."

He spoke in a mysterious tone. Maggie, who had just been surrendering herself to the isolating effect of Bert's smile, was intrigued by it. A mysterious tone was to Maggie as the scent of the fox is to a hound. She knew no peace till she had run it to earth.

"Why do you say it like that?" she said.

William laughed shortly.

"Why, don't you *know*?" he said. "It's the place where a witch was s'posed to have drowned herself in the days when there *was* witches, an' if you wish for anythin' there the partic'lar day she drowned herself it comes true.

"What day did she drown herself?" said Maggie eagerly.

"S'posed to 've been June the sixth," said William carelessly.

"It's June the sixth to-day," said Maggie.

"Why, so it is!" said William in a tone of intense surprise. "Fancy!"

"I s'pose it's all a make-up?" said Maggie doubtfully, but in a tone that pleaded to be told it wasn't.

"*Course* it is," snapped Bert, whose isolating smile had changed to a ferocious frown.

"I 'spect it is," said William; "I 'spect it's jus' a sort of chance when it does happen."

"Have you ever wished?" said Maggie.

"Yes," admitted William as if guiltily—"often."

"Does it come true?"

"Yes," said William. "It's funny, but it generally does. Jus' a sort of chance, of course."

"An' you have to wish just there—just by the willow-tree?"

"Yes, jus' where I was goin' to wash the things."

She rose.

"I'll come along and help you with the things," she said. "Come on, Bert. Seems a shame to leave him to do 'em all himself."

Bert followed morosely, making no further effort to reassert his influence till they had washed up and were sitting again on the grass by the river bank. Then gradually and very determinedly he led the subject back to himself again.

"Did you—did you care for me at all in the old days, Maggie?" he said.

Maggie heaved a sentimental sigh.

"It was your hair, Bert," she said; "I used to dream of it at nights. I've often thought of it these years. But I little thought to find it the same. Not a grey hair nor nothin'."

He passed his hand over the gleaming curls.

"Oh, my hair!" he said carelessly. "It's always been a nuisance to me. The times a day I wet it tryin' to take the curl out. I'd give anythin' to have ordin'ry hair. I keep hopin' it'll start comin' out or gettin' grey, but it doesn't."

"Oh *Bert!* I think it *beautiful*," said Maggie softly.

"I heard of a man once," said William, "whose hair started growing so quick he couldn't keep it cut fast enough. If he only went to the barber's once a week it'd grown down to his waist. He had to go every day, an' even then it'd sometimes got nearly as far as his waist."

"*Lor!*" said Maggie, turning her whole attention to the contemplation of this phenomenon.

"Yes," said William, warming to his subject, "it got so as if he went to church with it cut quite short it'd be over his shoulders by the second lesson an' down to his waist by the last hymn. People used to go to church to sit behind him to watch it grow."

"*Lor!*" said Maggie again.

"In the end it got so as he'd gotter have a barber to go about with him to keep it cut short. If you had him to tea you'd gotter ask his barber too, an' the barber 'd start cuttin' his hair every few minutes. If he didn't it'd get all over the place."

"*Lor!*" said Maggie again, gazing at him with wide-open mouth and eyes.

Bert uttered a snort that expressed anger, contempt

and ridicule. But it was plain that he had ceased to compete with this young Baron Munchausen for the interest of the beloved. He lit a pipe and smoked in silence for a time, during which William developed at leisure several themes similar to the theme of the man with quickly-growing hair. Maggie gazed at him still open-mouthed and ejaculated "Lor!" at intervals. At last Bert took his pipe out of his mouth, and, fixing William with a cold eye, said:

"What time d'you go to bed?"

"About eight," said William guardedly.

Bert transferred his gaze to Maggie.

"Maggie," he said, "I'll be callin' for you at nine to-night an' I hope you'll come for a little walk with me."

Maggie switched her mind from the region of the abnormal to the region of the romantic.

"Yes, Bert," she said, blushing.

Bert fixed meaning eyes upon her and said:

"I've a question to ask you, Maggie, an' I think you'll know what it is."

Her eyes dropped, her blush deepened.

"Yes, Bert," she said.

William's heart sank. He'd have no chance at all of accompanying them on a walk at nine o'clock at night. And, anyway, he couldn't hang round them all day and every day. No, things would have to take their course. Yet—he was sorry. He'd wanted to help his friend. . . .

"Now," said Bert with rising cheerfulness, "let's go'n' get a boat an' have a little row."

They walked down the river to the boat-house. As they went, William told Maggie about a man who was bitten by a dog and ever after barked instead of talking and spent most of his time chasing cats, but there wasn't any zest in the telling of it. Bert, secure in the knowledge that his turn would come later, did not attempt to compete with him and the whole thing fell flat.

Then he helped Bert and the boatman to get the boat out.

It might have been noticed that, while Bert was leaning down over it, William examined closely the mop of flaxen curls and that something of his despondency dropped from him as he did so.

Bert got in first in order to help Maggie into it. William got in next to hold the boat closely to the landing stage. And then, before Maggie had entered, the boat swung out suddenly into mid-stream.

"What'd you let go for?" exploded Bert.

"Sorry," said William succinctly, "I can work it back all right."

But he didn't. No one quite saw what he did, but in a few seconds the boat was overturned and William and Bert were floundering in the water.

Maggie screamed and wrung her hands on the bank.

" 'S all right," called William from the water, "I'll save him."

And he seized hold of Bert's head and pulled. In a few seconds William was holding on to one side of the overturned boat and Bert the other. But it wasn't the Bert they knew. It was an elderly man with a bald head except for a thin wisp of grey hair on the top of his head. And on the water just by the boat floated a bedraggled flaxen wig.

Maggie moaned and covered her eyes with her hand.

Her sister's wish was fulfilled. She saw Bert as he really was.

*   *   *

William walked slowly down the road past the cottage.

Mrs. Roundway smiled and nodded from the window,

"THERE YOU ARE, LOVE," SAID MRS. ROUNDWAY. "IT WAS
SUCH A PRETTY WEDDING!"

then came hurrying down with a cookie boy in her hand.

"There you are, love," she said. "It was such a pretty wedding. She and George have gone to Brighton for the honeymoon. It's—rather nice to be alone again. I'm one that likes quiet. That Bert never turned up again after your picnic, you know."

"Di'n't he?" said William carelessly.

It was nice to think that Maggie wasn't there any more. She was fascinatingly credulous but she talked too much. He was aware that after this one speech of general explanation Mrs. Roundway would resume the smiling silence of years. One other explanation she had to give.

"I hope you don't mind, love. I've made it the old way. I'm not quite sure how she used to do them boot buttons."

"I like them best without boot buttons," said William.

Then he walked on, happily munching his cookie boy.

Chapter 10

William and the Prize Pig

William was aware when his father promised to take him to the pantomime for a Christmas treat that he would have to tread very carefully between the promise and its fulfilment if he wished the fulfilment to materialise. He realised that the promise had been rashly made and that his father would rather play golf than take him to the pantomime any day, and would secretly welcome any excuse for abandoning the project.

The other Outlaws were almost as anxious for William to go to the theatre as was William himself. For it wasn't only the theatre. After the theatre William's father was going to take William to tea to an old aunt of his who lived in London. She was an old lady who neither liked nor understood boys, but she was very correct and had prided herself from earliest youth on doing the right thing. And the right thing in the case of a boy was a tip. She never sent Christmas presents to William, but whenever William's father took him to see her—which wasn't often—she gave him five shillings.

It had always been the custom of the Outlaws to pool their tips. Hence the anxious interest with which the Outlaws viewed William's approaching and precarious treat. The five shillings was badly needed for a new toboggan.

"If I was you," said Douglas earnestly, "I'd jus' do nothin' between now and then—'cept eat at meal times an' go to bed at night. Then he can't have any 'scuse for not takin' you."

"An' wash an' brush your hair a lot an' that sort of thing," supplemented Ginger.

William surveyed the prospect of this existence without enthusiasm.

"You *can't* do nothin' but that," he protested. "There's twenty-four hours in a day. You *can't* wash an' brush your hair for twenty-four hours. You'd prob'ly get some disease, if you did."

"You can sit quiet an' read a book," said Ginger.

William threw him a glance of dark suspicion, but Ginger's face was a face of shining innocence devoid of mockery.

"I've read all the books I want to read," said William tersely. "No, I'll just go for quiet walks between washin' my face an' brushin' my hair an' such-like. I'll jus' go for quiet walks with you. He can't mind that, can he?"

The Outlaws agreed that he couldn't and were relieved by William's decision. For the prospect of taking their walks abroad without William had been a depressing one and they preferred even a lawful expedition with William to a lawless expedition without him. Moreover, there would be all the attraction of novelty about a William bent upon lawful purposes only, a William taking a quiet walking between washing his face and brushing his hair.

"Yes, that'll be all right," said William, his spirits rising. "I'll jus' do that—jus' take a quiet walk in between keepin' myself tidy. I'd better do that 'cause of gettin' a little fresh air. They say people die what don't get any fresh air an' I shun't like to die before I've been to the pantomime. Wun't be fair on *him*, either," he added virtuously, "now he's bought the tickets."

So the Outlaws met as usual at the corner of the road the next morning and set off for the quiet walk whose object was to provide William with the fresh air and exercise necessary to his existence till the Saturday of the treat.

It was, of course, William who suggested going round through Mr. Ballater's back garden to look at his pig. Mr. Ballater had a pig of gigantic proportions that had won prizes at every local show for miles around. Mr. Ballater took an inordinate pride in his pig. He fed it and tended it with his own hands. He allowed it no rivals. It was said that he had surreptitiously photographed every pig in the neighbourhood who might possibly pose as a rival to it, and kept copies of the photographs in an album next to photographs of his Eglantine. He worshipped Eglantine as a savage might worship the totem of his tribe. Eglantine had a great fascination for the Outlaws, too. They loved to gaze at the enormous bulk of her, at her tiny eyes sunk so revoltingly in her mountain-like cheeks, to watch the unwieldy mass of her as she moved lumberingly across to her trough from her sleeping quarters or to her sleeping quarters from her trough.

They entered the back garden cautiously. They were not welcome visitors at Eglantine's shrine. One of their favourite amusements some months ago had been to bring curious and, as one would have thought, inedible substances for Eglantine to eat, and watch the enjoyment with which she consumed them. Mr. Ballater had been much mystified and distressed at that time by the gradual failure of Eglantine's appetite. When he brought to her the nourishing viands he prepared with his own hands she merely turned away her mountainous head distastefully. It was only by hiding in a neighbouring tree in an attitude of acute discomfort for several hours that he caught the Outlaws red-handed in the act of feeding her with large quantities of the cinders and sawdust for which Eglantine had acquired a perverted taste. He had fallen upon the Outlaws with such fury and put them to flight with such terrible threats (for Eglantine had been losing nearly a pound a day) that he had defeated his own ends by investing his back garden with that glamour of danger that the Outlaws found so irresistible.

"Let's jus' go'n' look how she is," said William. "Well, we won't give her cinders or sawdust to eat or do anythin' wrong like that. But there can't be any harm in jus' goin' to look at her."

The Outlaws, who had been finding the quiet walk rather dull, did not need much encouragement.

They entered Mr. Ballater's back garden cautiously and hung over the side of the sty, gazing wonderingly at Eglantine, who turned a half-hidden eye in their direction.

"She's fatter than ever," said Ginger in a voice of awe. "I bet if you pricked her with a pin she'd go off pop."

"I bet she doesn't like his stuff half as much as the stuff we used to give her," said Douglas.

"It was fun watchin' her crunch cinders," said Henry wistfully.

"Seems to me," said Ginger, "as if she was turnin' into an elephant. I bet you could ride on her back now jus' the same as if she was an elephant."

"I bet you couldn't," said William pugnaciously. The life of quiet virtue that he had led for nearly a day was getting on William's nerves.

"I bet you could," repeated Ginger.

No one ever knew who undid the latch, but they found themselves suddenly inside the sty.

"Try, then," challenged Ginger. William seated himself tentatively upon the enormous back. Eglantine cast a fatuous glance up at him, but remained otherwise unmoved.

"There!" said Ginger triumphantly.

"That's not ridin'," protested William, "that's sittin'."

"It's what I call ridin'," said Ginger firmly.

"You can't call it ridin' when it's not *movin'*," said William indignantly.

The other Outlaws supported William's view. Riding, they considered, implied motion.

"All right," said Ginger, accepting the challenge; "one of you show her some sawdust an' if she'll get up an' go to it with William on her back then *that'll* be ridin' all right."

This was agreed to, and Henry went out to the carpenter's shop down the road to borrow some sawdust. Fortunately the carpenter, unlike the rest of the adult population of the village, was a friend of the Outlaws, and allowed them to watch him at work and to carry off his sawdust for their own purpose. (William had lately carried on extensive experiments with a view to making wood out of sawdust and glue.)

Henry returned with a good supply of sawdust, opened the sty door and held out a handful enticingly. The Outlaws had by now completely forgotten everything but the burning question of whether you could ride on Eglantine or whether you couldn't.

"Come on," said Henry, "come on. Puss! Puss! Puss! Pig! Pig! Pig!"

Eglantine looked up. She saw sawdust. She smelt

sawdust. Her small eyes gleamed. Lumberingly she arose and, disregarding William's weight on her back (perhaps hardly noticing it, for it was a mere feather compared with her own) ambled across to the door where Henry stood with his handful of sawdust. There she ate the delicious morsel greedily. Ginger cheered.

"Well, that's ridin' all right," he said. "I guess you can't call *that* not ridin'!"

"I bet you couldn't get her to run," said William; "see if you could get her to run."

"I bet I could," said Henry and Ginger simultaneously. Henry held out another handful of sawdust and began to retreat before the slowly-advancing bulk of Eglantine. Eglantine's appetite was whetted by that one luscious mouthful. She literally adored sawdust. She saw another handful in front of her and hastened to reach it before it should disappear. She ambled, she lumbered forward. She broke into a trot. She was aware subconsciously of an unaccustomed weight upon her back; but she was a pig of one idea, and at present that one idea was sawdust. Moreover, the new sense of freedom stimulated her. She had discovered suddenly the use of her legs. She could trot. She could run. The discovery was exhilarating. She trotted. She ran. And before her, ever retreating, was that luscious handful of sawdust. Henry, his whole mind taken up with the thrill of making Eglantine run, backed slowly round the house to the front garden and crossed the lawn and disappeared into the bushes. Eglantine, seeing the ambrosial feast disappearing, forgot years of indolence and scampered across the lawn as fast as her legs would take her, William riding triumphantly upon her back. It was at this moment that Mr. Ballater chanced to look out of his dining-room window. His face blanched, his mouth and eyes opened to their fullest extent. There was his Eglantine, his cherished Eglantine, who never stirred from her repose—except to stagger the few inches from her trough to her sleeping quarters—scampering—*scampering* across the lawn with a common human boy upon her sacred back. Eglantine, who had a show next week, losing pounds of precious fat by this unseemly gambol. Beside himself with fury, he rushed out and seized Eglantine by her inadequate tail. Eglantine, William and Mr. Ballater rolled together on to the lawn. Henry, Ginger and Douglas, realising that discretion is the better part of valour, took to their heels. Mr. Ballater, still beside himself with fury, seized William's ears and shook him violently till Eglantine, excited by all this unusual commotion, charged him in the stomach and all three rolled over on the grass again. Mr. Ballater recovered first. He sat up, removed one of Eglantine's hind feet from his mouth, and, fixing William with a ferocious glare, said severely:

"I know you, my boy, and I know where you live. I shall call to see your father this very evening."

Then he arose with great dignity and led the recalcitrant Eglantine as best he could back to her sty. Eglantine was, considering her previous lack of exercise, almost incredibly recalcitrant. Her taste of liberty had gone to her head and her failure to win that second handful of sawdust had embittered her spirit. She butted her master in all directions, and, when he finally secured her, lay on the floor of her sty with an expression of ill-humour on her face that was almost human. Her master stood leaning over the gate and gazing at her tragically.

"*Pounds* she must have lost to-day," he said, "literally *pounds!*"

Meanwhile William, much shaken and battered by Eglantine and her master, was meeting the other

Outlaws on the road where all of them had taken refuge. The full meaning of the situation was only just dawning on them.

"He'll tell your father an' you won't be able to go to the pantomine," said Douglas dolefully.

"An' we were going to buy a toboggan with that money," said Henry.

"Yes," said William gloomily, "an' *he* nearly pulled my ears off an' *she* kicked me so's I'm all bruises."

"P'raps he'll forget to tell your father," said Henry without much hope.

"No, he won't," said William. "I could tell he wouldn't by the way he pulled at my ears. It's extraordinary to me how fast my ears seem to be stuck on to my head. I bet he'd have had 'em right off if they'd been anyone else's. Then he'd 've been put in prison." The thought of this seemed to afford him a certain gloomy pleasure. "Put in prison," he repeated, "where he couldn't keep pigs or pull people's ears off."

"Yes, but he's not in prison," said Ginger, "an' he's goin' to go'n' tell your father to-night."

"P'raps if you tell your father about your ears he'll let you go to the pantomine to make up," said Henry, vaguely consoling.

"No, he won't," said William; "you don't know my father. And he's not fond of pantomines."

"What'll we do then?" said Henry.

"We've jus' gotter stop him goin' to my father," said William.

"How?" said Henry.

"We've gotter *think* of a way," said William irritably. "You seem to 'spect me to think of a thing the minute I've said it same as if I was a sort of conj'rer. I'm not magic. I'm only yuman same as everyone else. I've s'ggested that we stop him goin' to my father. There mus' be ever so many ways. *You* might try to think of one."

They had reached the old barn now and sat on the floor in frowning concentration.

"Poison him," suggested Douglas at last, his face brightening.

This idea, though attractive, was considered impractical.

"Lock him up in his house till after William's been to the pantomine an' got the five shillings," suggested Henry.

"He'd break a window an' get out," said William, "an' then there'd be far worse for all of us than jus' not goin' to a pantomine. No, we've gotter think of somethin' more *cunnin'* than that."

"All right," said Henry, offended. "If you c'n think of a more cunnin' way than lockin' him up in his house, think of it."

"I bet I will, too," said William. "I bet I c'n find one all right, if I think long enough. People in books always find ways of stoppin' other people doin' things they don't want them to, an' I bet I'm as good as a person in a book any day."

"*How* do they stop people doin' things they don't want them to?" said Douglas.

"Sometimes——" began William, then suddenly his face shone. "*Yes!*" he said, "that's how *we'll* do it."

"How?" said the Outlaws eagerly.

"We'll find out somethin' he's done wrong in his past an' hold it over him that if he goes an' tells about the pig we'll set the police on him."

The faces of the Outlaws shone eagerly at this, then clouded over as its one weak spot dawned on them.

"S'pose he hasn't done anythin' wrong in his past," said Douglas.

"He doesn't *look* as if he'd ever done anythin' wrong in his past," said Henry sadly; "he's got a—a *good* sort of face."

"Yes," said William eagerly, "but that's why he's never got found out. With him havin' a good sort of face people took for granted that he hadn't done it. If he'd had a bad sort of face they'd have known he did it."

"Did what?" said Henry the literal.

"Did whatever he did," said William.

"Well, what did he do?"

"That's what we've gotter find out," said William, and added feelingly, "I bet he murdered someone pullin' their ears out."

"But we haven't any proof he's done anythin' wrong at all," persisted Henry.

"If he hasn't done anythin' wrong," said William, "why's he livin' in the country keepin' pigs?"

This question seemed unanswerable to everyone but Henry, who ventured mildly:

"P'raps he likes livin' in the country keepin' pigs."

"*Course* he doesn't," said William. "He may like livin' in the country, but he doesn't like keepin' pigs."

"How d'you know?"

"Cause no one *could* like keepin' pigs," said William firmly. "There's nothin' *about* pigs. I mean, if he kept wild animals or snakes or even butterflies or birds-—somethin' *int'restin'*, anyway—you might think he was keepin' 'em because he wanted to keep 'em. But *pigs* . . . he mus' be keepin' 'em so's to stop people suspectin' that he was a crim'nal. I bet he's a crim'nal same as that man at Beechcroft. Prob'ly he wears a wig, too, like that man called Bert. I bet his real hair's black."

Such was the magnetism of William's personality that his band was now firmly convinced that Mr. Ballater was a world-famous criminal in hiding.

"How 're we goin' to find out?" said Ginger eagerly.

"Jus' watch him an' listen to him," said William. "Prob'ly he's got some confederation comin' to see him sometimes. They gen'rally do. Come to that I don't s'pose he's stopped. You don't often find 'em stoppin'. I mean, once you've got into the way of stealin', you sort of can't stop all at once. I bet it's stealin' that he did. Where'd he get his money if he's not a thief? He doesn't go up to London to an office same as our fathers do. He doesn't earn it. He *mus'* have stole it. I bet he's stealin' now from all the people about here. I bet that pig's jus' to put people off."

"But—but it doesn't give us much time to find out he's a thief an' tell him before your father comes home to-night," said Ginger.

It turned out, however, that William's father was not coming home that night. He was staying with friends in town, so that gave the Outlaws one extra day.

"We oughter be able to do it in *that* time," said William with his unfailing optimism. "We'd better start at once. We'll go back now an' start watchin' his house an' listenin'. We'll keep a good look out so's the minute he sees us we'll start runnin' away. An' I advise anyone he catches hold of to take care of their ears," he ended with deep feeling.

"Oh, do shut up about your ears," said Ginger wearily. "We're riskin' our lives jus' so that you can go to the pantomine, an' you will keep on an' on an' on about your ears."

"You'd keep on an' on an' on about your ears, too, if he'd got hold of them same as he got hold of mine," said William spiritedly.

"I'd have shut up about them by now, anyway," asserted Ginger, and continued hastily before William

could contradict him, "anyway, let's go back now an'
watch his house to see if we can get any clues to the
wrong he did in his past."

They went back to Mr. Ballater's house and William
posted them at various points. Ginger was to guard the
front gate, Henry was to guard the back gate, and
Douglas was to hide in the shrubbery that commanded
the kitchen door. William, as leader, chose the most
exciting part for himself. He was to hide outside the
open drawing-room window to overhear any conversation that might be going on.

It happened that Mr. Ballater had had an aunt and
cousin to lunch. The aunt had retired to rest after the
meal, and the cousin was talking to her host in the
drawing-room. She was a nice cousin, the sort of cousin
you confide in, so Mr. Ballater was confiding in her. He
was telling her about Eglantine. He had already told her
about the dastardly boy who had let her out of her sty
and ridden—*ridden*—her across the lawn.

"Must have lost *pounds*," he moaned, "and upset her
so much that she wouldn't touch her dinner—and the
show next week."

The nice cousin smothered a yawn and uttered a
sympathetic murmur. Mr. Ballater was encouraged to
deeper confidences.

"Of course," he said, "I have a good deal of jealousy
to contend with. You know how little minded people are
where pigs are concerned. I once grew marrows, and it
was just the same with those. Cucumbers, too. There's
something about pigs and marrows and cucumbers that
seems to bring out the worst in people, seems to paralyse
their sense of truth. You'd be surprised if you knew the
people that have told me that Eglantine is nothing to pigs
they've had. Just the same as people did with marrows.
Fortunately I've got a check on most of the people that

have kept pigs about here, because I managed to get snapshots of most of them, and when they begin to talk about it I just bring them out and show them the photograph of their pig beside the snapshot I've got of Eglantine taken at just the same distance. Even the Vicar—he's not kept them for a few years now—but even the Vicar started the other day saying that his prize pig was quite as big as Eglantine. I took out the photograph to show him. He didn't like it at all. Ordinarily he's a perfectly truthful man, of course. It's amazing to me——" He crossed over to a bureau and took out a snapshot album and pointed at it at the first page. "That's the Vicar's," he said; "I took it about two years ago."

William had just crept with elaborate secrecy to the drawing-room window and was crouching beneath it to listen to whatever was going on inside. This was the first and only sentence he heard. No sooner had he heard it than Mr. Ballater accidentally knocked over an occasional table and William, startled by the noise, fled. But he did not regret his departure. He had heard enough to settle all his doubts. He reached the road and uttered the low, clear whistle with which he summoned his hand. They assembled with eager haste.

"He *is* one," said William triumphantly. "When I got there he'd got someone in with him and he was showing whoever it was the things he'd stole. He was just showing something he's stole from the Vicar. He was jus' sayin' 'This was the Vicar's. I took it two years ago.' Tellin' 'em straight out like that."

"What was he showin' 'em?" said Ginger excitedly.

"I cun't see," said William, "but I could jus' see that there was a lot of silver stuff in the room. I 'spect he was showin' him some of that. I heard him movin' then so I came away, because I espect he's a pretty ruthless sort of man if he finds anyone's found out about his secret career of crime. Well, I *know* he is, from my ears."

"How 're we goin' to let him know we know?" said Henry. "I mean about his career of crime?"

"I votes we write to him," said Douglas, who never liked to run unnecessary risks. "I don't think it'd be quite safe to *tell* him. He might set on us."

So they wrote a note and put it through his letterbox. It was short, terse, and in the best traditions of melodrama. It read quite simply:

"All is nown fle."

It was very beautifully written in William's best writing, but it didn't have much effect, because it fluttered beneath the hall mat and wasn't found till a week later.

"But it won't be much use to me—him fleein'," said William, "if he wrote to my father first."

"*Tell* you what," said Ginger with a burst of inspiration, "we'll find out what he stole from the Vicar an' take it back. Well—even if he's wrote to your father—if we take back something that was stole from the Vicar, that'll make it all right, won't it? They'll sort of cross each other off, I should think—lettin' the pig out an' takin' back somethin' that's been stole."

The others thought so, too, but there were obvious disadvantages to the plan.

"How 're we goin' to find out what he stole?" said Henry.

"We'll jus' go along to the Vicarage an' see," said William vaguely.

They trudged along the road to the Vicarage whistling cheerfully. It was turning out an adventure after their own hearts.

At the Vicarage they slowed down and looked at William. The Outlaws were not *personæ gratæ* at the

Vicarage. Many little scores paid and unpaid lay between them and the Vicar's wife. She was just coming out of the front gate as they reached it. She wore her Sunday clothes and was obviously in a good temper.

She was going away for the night to speak at a Mothers' Meeting Conference, and there was nothing in the world that the Vicar's wife enjoyed more than speaking at Mothers' Meeting Conferences—or, indeed, anywhere at all. So she beamed through her pince-nez at the Outlaws, quite forgetting that only a few weeks ago they had put years on to the life of the Vicarage wheelbarrow and that entirely owing to them the church pillars had had to be wreathed at Christmas with laurel instead of holly.

"Well, dear boys," she said brightly, "and what are you about this fine day? Not spending it *quite* uselessly, I hope? Trying to give pleasure to others besides yourselves, I hope?"

"Please," said William earnestly, "did you have anything stole about two years ago?"

"Stolen, dear boy, stolen. Past participle, stolen. I steal, he stole, the teapot has been stolen."

"A teapot, was it?" said William eagerly.

"Well, as a matter of fact we *did* have a teapot stolen about two years ago," she said. "A beautiful silver teapot. It was a great grief to us. The only thing we've ever had stolen. Stolen, note, dear boy, not stole. Past participle, stolen. I steal, he stole, the teapot has been stolen."

"About two years ago?" said William.

"Yes, my dear boy. Why?"

"I jus' wondered," said William non-committally.

"Ah, but you shouldn't, you know," said the Vicar's wife reproachfully. "You shouldn't wonder. Curiosity, you know. Idle curiosity. You remember what the

"WELL, BOYS, WHAT ARE YOU ABOUT THIS FINE DAY? NOT
SPENDING IT QUITE USELESSLY, I HOPE?"

"PLEASE," SAID WILLIAM EARNESTLY, "DID YOU HAVE
ANYTHING STOLE ABOUT TWO YEARS AGO?"

Vicar said about idle curiosity in his last sermon, don't you?"

Ginger made an inarticulate sound that might have meant that he did, and she sailed on down the road towards the station, smiling vaguely, her lips moving silently. Already in imagination she was addressing her Mothers' Meeting.

"A teapot," said William in a brisk, businesslike tone of voice. "That's what he mus' have been showin' his confederation. Come on. Let's go back an' get it. Well, even if he's wrote about the pig, it'll make up for it—gettin' back somethin' stole out of a thief's den."

"It might be a bit diff'cult," said Douglas doubtfully, "if he's one of these desp'rate criminals what you read about in books. I'd almost as soon miss that five shillings as get gagged an' left in cellars same as people get in books."

"I bet he won't be there at all," said William. "I bet he'll have got that note and be fleein' abroad for all he's worth."

"Takin' the teapot with him," said Douglas gloomily, "an' writin' to your father before he goes."

They entered the gate and looked about cautiously. The aunt and cousin had gone home and Mr. Ballater was hanging over Eglantine's sty, gazing at her sadly and adoringly. *Pounds* she must have lost to-day running across the lawn like that and missing her dinner. She'd forgotten the sawdust now and was eating her meal with every appearance of enjoyment, but still she must have lost *pounds*. And the show next week. . . .

The Outlaws crept up the empty front garden in the shelter of the bushes to the drawing-room window. Cautiously they peered in. And the first thing they saw was a cabinet full of old silver pieces among which was a silver teapot.

"*There* it is!" gasped the Outlaws.

Almost before he had said it William was over the window-sill and across the room.

"Be careful," hissed Douglas, "he'll be comin' back with his gags and things!" But the cabinet door happened to be unlocked, and William was back with the silver teapot in a few seconds.

"Quick," he said in a melodramatic whisper as he whipped it under his coat. "Quick, before he comes back!" They fled precipitately to the gate, then down the road, not pausing to draw breath till they were near the gate of the Vicarage. Then William took the teapot from under his coat and they examined it.

"I don't see how it can *help* bein' the Vicar's," said William, as if trying to quiet some small doubt in his mind. "He had it stole about two years ago an' I heard this man sayin' he stole it from the Vicar about two years ago, so I don't see how it can *help* bein' the one."

They approached the back door of the Vicarage. The Vicar's wife, who had a great respect for her front doorstep, had trained the juvenile population of the village to approach the Vicarage by the back door.

Still holding the teapot under his coat and with his Outlaws ranged behind him, William knocked tentatively at the Vicarage back door. An untidy housemaid opened it. She looked at the Outlaws as if she didn't see them. She *didn't* see them. She saw only the milkman. She and the milkman had plighted their troth the night before, and to-day the housemaid, in the fashion of maidens who had just plighted their troth, saw the image of the beloved wherever she looked. She even gave William a fatuous smile. William, who wasn't used to smiles, fatuous or otherwise, from housemaids, was so startled that for a minute or two he quite forgot what he'd come to say. Then the housemaid realised their presence and assumed the forbidding scowl with which he felt more at his ease.

"We want to speak to the Vicar," said William.

"Well, you can't," said the housemaid ungraciously; "he's busy."

"It's very important," said William.

"I don't care what it is," said the housemaid, "he wasn't to be disturbed except for sudden illness or death. Are you sudden illness or death?"

William admitted reluctantly that he wasn't either.

"Well, then, he can't be disturbed for you," said the housemaid tartly; "he's writing his sermon, so go away."

"What about *her?*" said William; "when will *she* be back?"

The housemaid had no need to ask who "she" was.

"She's stayin' away till to-morrow," she said, and added piously, "Glory be!"

"Well," said William, drawing the teapot from under his coat with a dramatic gesture, "we've got this back. It was stole—stolen, stole two years ago."

The housemaid gave it a fatuous smile. To her it wasn't a teapot. It was the milkman. William was disappointed by her receipt of his news.

"You make the tea in it for tea," he went on. "Don't tell him. Just see what he says when he sees it. It'll be a nice surprise."

The housemaid emerged partially from her day-dream and gazed at William's face with the distaste that she now felt for every face that was not the milkman's.

"What did you say?" she demanded curtly.

"I said make tea in it an' take it in to him."

The housemaid had returned to her dream again. She received the order with automatic resignation as though it had been given her by the Vicar's wife herself.

"A' right," she said dreamily, taking the teapot from his hands and gazing through him with the fatuous smile. "A' right."

William and his band hastily departed.

"She's balmy," said Ginger.

"Let's go back and see if we c'n see him doin' anythin' else," said William.

They returned to Mr. Ballater's house and met him issuing from his front gate in hat and overcoat.

"He's fleein'," exclaimed Ginger. "He's found the letter an' he's fleein'."

"Well, as long as he's not written to my father first," said William.

Then they went home to tea.

*   *   *

Mr. Ballater was having tea with the Vicar. Mr. Ballater generally went to have tea with the Vicar when the Vicar's wife was away. They discussed on these occasions pigs and cucumbers and marrows. The Vicar's wife never allowed the Vicar to ask him to tea while she was at home, because she said that he wasn't a spiritual man. She said that no man who thought so much about the size of pigs and cucumbers and marrows could possibly be a spiritual man. But in her absence they always forgathered and enjoyed a chat. The Vicar had just finished "tenthly and lastly" as Mr. Ballater was announced, and so he could give a free mind to the proportions of Eglantine. Mr. Ballater was as usual waxing lyrical over the proportions of Eglantine. He was feeling much happier about her because she'd had a nice little nap in the afternoon, and he felt that with a lot of food and rest she'd soon make up that pound or so she'd lost that day. Still, he told the Vicar the whole story.

"Fortunately," he ended, "I know the boy, so I can

complain of his conduct to his father, and I hope he will take active measures. A valuable animal like that . . . *pounds* it must have lost."

"I remember," put in the Vicar, "in the case of that pig I had one or two years ago—a really *gigantic* creature——"

And just then tea was brought in. The housemaid was still living in a glamorous dream in which the only clear thing was the milkman's face. There had appeared in the kitchen a strange teapot and she had hazy recollections of having received instructions from someone or other to make the tea in it. So she'd made the tea in it. She placed it upon the tea-table. The Vicar poured out tea, and Mr. Ballater seized the opportunity to get in again with Eglantine, and all went merry as a marriage-bell till suddenly Mr. Ballater's eyes fell upon the teapot. He stared. His eyes bulged. He faltered in the middle of a description of Eglantine's weekly menu. His teapot, his Georgian teapot . . . he could have sworn that it was his Georgian teapot, the one his godmother had given him last year. The Vicar was wielding it quite unconcernedly. The Vicar was an absent-minded man without an eye for details. He could not have described the teapot in which his tea was generally brought to him. He could not have recognised it had it been shown to him in company with a dozen strange teapots. To the Vicar a teapot was just a teapot, a thing containing tea with a handle and a spout. He asked no more of it. He poured the tea from Mr. Ballater's Georgian teapot before Mr. Ballater's gaping eyes with no thought in his mind but a determination to convince Mr. Ballater that Judith had been every bit as big as Eglantine and that that snapshot that Mr. Ballater had of her was out of focus and made her look about half her real size. He found it unusually easy to stem the flood of Mr. Ballater's rhapsodies. Mr. Ballater sud-

SUDDENLY MR. BALLATER'S EYES FELL UPON THE TEAPOT. HIS
TEAPOT!

denly seemed unable to do anything but gape helplessly
at the teapot. As a visitor the Vicar found him rather
disappointing. There wasn't much satisfaction in saying
that Judith was as large as Eglantine if Eglantine's
master didn't contradict him. The whole thing lacked
zest. The Vicar, in fact, wasn't sorry when Mr. Ballater,
still gazing at the teapot as if it were a ghost, rose to take
his leave quite an hour earlier than he usually took it. He
walked down the drive like a man in a dream. The Vicar
watched him from the window. A sudden explanation of
his strange behaviour occurred to him.

"He's beginning to realise it at last," he said with a smile. "She *was* as big—every bit as big."

Mr. Ballater almost ran up his front drive, flung open his front door and hurried into his drawing-room. And there his worst fears were realised. His silver cabinet was shorn of the brightest jewel in its crown. His teapot had gone. His Georgian teapot. And his godmother was coming to tea to-morrow. He must act at once. Perhaps the Vicar had a dual personality—a sort of Jekyll and Hyde personality—part of him a Vicar and the other a thief. He must get it back at any cost. Pale with horror, he set off again down the road towards the Vicarage. On the road he met four boys. One of them was the boy who had treated Eglantine so outrageously that morning. That reminded him. He mustn't forget to go and see his father to-morrow. The Outlaws stood and watched his figure till it was out of sight. Then William said sternly:

"Well, he's takin' a jolly long time to get off. I thought he was fleein' the last time we saw him."

"He's gettin' his loot together," said Henry. "Pity we didn't take a few more of those silver things he'd stole an' stop him gettin' off abroad with 'em. That cupboard was full of 'em."

"Let's get some of 'em now," said William. "If I've got back a lot of stole things it'll sort of make it all right case anyone's told my father about that pig. I remember now there was a sort of silver cream jug and sugar basin that went with the teapot. I bet they mus' be the Vicar's, too. He prob'ly took 'em at the same time. I bet he'd be jolly grateful to me if I got 'em back, too. He'd prob'ly be so grateful that he'd ask my father to take me to the pantomine anyway, even if someone 'd told him about that pig."

The Outlaws looked rather doubtful.

"I don't know that I would," said Douglas. "He

might come back and he'd be desperate, of course, with bein' found out."

"Well, I'll jus' have a try," said William; "the rest of you keep a look-out down the road and jus' give the danger whistle if you see him comin'."

The Outlaws had an elaborate code of whistles which they practised regularly, but many of which had never been required and probably never would be required. They included special whistles for help in such contingencies as attacks by lions, pursuit by Red Indians and meeting with sharks when bathing.

The rest of them stood at the corner of the road, and William entered Mr. Ballater's house again cautiously by the drawing-room window. He went to the cabinet and to his amazement found it empty. He listened. Sounds came from upstairs. He crept upstairs. The sounds came from a bedroom. He peeped in. An unsavoury-looking individual stood at a dressing-table opening drawers. There was a half-filled sack on the floor. William had no doubt at all as to the identity of the unsavoury-looking individual. It was Mr. Ballater's confederate who was collecting the "loot" to take with them in their flight from justice. William felt righteously enraged at this plot, and determined to foil it. A bold plan came to him. He tiptoed into the room, slammed the door, locked it, and slipped the key into his pocket. It was the work of a second, but in that second the unsavoury-looking individual had turned round, revealing a face as unsavoury as the rest of him, and hit out fiercely at William. William dodged the blow, flashed across the room to the open window and slid down the water-pipe. The unsavoury individual was too large to slide down pipes, so he contented himself with battering against the locked door and uttering horrible threats.

*   *   *

The Vicar and Mr. Ballater came down the road together. They carried the teapot tenderly between them. They were still discussing the mystery of its curious disappearance from Mr. Ballater's house and its still more curious appearance at the Vicar's.

"From what the maid says," said Mr. Ballater, "it sounds like the same boy. I mean the boy who made Eglantine run—*run*," his voice trembled, "across the lawn this morning. I've rung up his father. He's away till to-morrow evening. I'm going to see him then."

They entered the gate of Mr. Ballater's garden and walked up the drive. They came round the side of the house. A boy was sitting in the middle of the rose bed beneath a bedroom window.

"That's the boy," said Mr. Ballater excitedly.

The boy addressed the Vicar calmly.

"Good!" he said, "you've got *him*. I hoped someone 'd catch *him* before he'd fled right off. I've got the one that stayed to c'lect the things. I've got him up there. He's got all the rest of the things in a sack. You can hear him shoutin' if you listen."

*   *   *

William's father had arrived home.

"I suppose, my dear," he said wistfully to William's mother, "that nothing has happened to prevent my taking William to the pantomime to-morrow? I mean no complaint from neighbours or anything like that?"

"Oh, no dear," said Mrs. Brown. "Just the opposite. Mr. Ballater says he caught a thief for him. He's most grateful to him. There was something about a pig and a teapot, too, but it was such a complicated story that I couldn't follow it. Anyway, the upshot of it all is that he caught a thief for Mr. Ballater, and Mr. Ballater's so grateful to him that he's going to take them *all* to the Zoo next week, for a little treat."

"Heaven help him!" said William's father feelingly.